The Monks of Arden

Ethard Wendel Van Stee

iUniverse, Inc.
New York   Bloomington

The Monks of Arden

iUniverse books may be ordered through booksellers or by contacting:

iUniverse
1663 Liberty Drive
Bloomington, IN 47403
www.iuniverse.com
1-800-Authors (1-800-288-4677)

ISBN: 978-1-4401-7998-3 (sc)
ISBN: 978-1-4401-7999-0 (ebk)

Printed in the United States of America

iUniverse rev. date: 10/8/2009

Other books by Ethard Wendel Van Stee

Moira's Scythe (2001)
I Didn't Come From Nowhere (2001)
The Remarkable Life of Frances Emily Steele (2001)
Three Plays (2001)
A Woman of No Means (2003)
This I Need To Know (2004)
The Bloodstone (2005)
The Hangman (2005)
Madimi (2008)

Contents

Acknowledgements

I wish to thank Cheryl Lopanik and Nathan Harris for their expert editing and thoughtful suggestions for improving this manuscript.

(*) Asterisks in the text denote entries in the glossary at the end of the text.

Prologue

Llewellyn of Gwynedd was of noble descent, a prince whose story began with the fall of Troy after the gnarled Priam in impotent rage hurled his spear at charging Pyrrhus. The avenger, casting a disdainful eye at the puny threat, brushed aside the shaft as it glanced off his shield. Rushing upon the aged king, Pyrrhus seized him by the hair and dragged him to the altar through his own son's blood. There, he buried his sword to the hilt in the old man's flank. With Troy in flames, Priam died.

Aeneas, of another branch of the Trojan House, begged his father to make haste. "Hurry," he implored, as the lumbering Anchises climbed upon the young man's back. On to Sicily they fled, leaving behind Troy's smoldering ashes, thence to Carthage and Pallanteum, there to found that noble race of Romans whose empire embraced the entire world.

Brutus, grandson of Aeneas, put his stamp on Albion and his son Prince Camber ruled the place called Cambria named for his noble self. His descendant was Queen Gwalaes, child of King Ebrancus called Cambria Wallia or Wales.

Wales matured to become a land of three kingdoms, Gwynedd, Powys, and Deheubarth, but among these the greatest was Gwynedd, ruled in time by Llewellyn through the reign of King John known as Lackland.

Chapter One

In the Beginning

The midwife and two attendants hovered over the queen as the squalling newborn made its appearance. The mother's moans subsided. Putting their heads together to form a shield from the prying eyes of the ladies of the chamber, the women muttered among themselves.

"What do you think?" whispered one.

"Whooee," exclaimed another. "The work of the devil."

"Quiet," said the midwife. "Think nothing of it, my lady. She is touched, given to fits. In her village she is revered, but she makes trouble sometimes. She is here as a medium to convey God's blessing. . . . The king demands that his queen give him a son," the midwife whispered. "Girls, girls; too many girls; that's all she gives me, he says."

"Do we give him a boy?" whispered an attendant. They busied themselves washing the tiny body and soothing the exhausted queen. Other ladies prepared the crib. The midwife examined the distinguishing parts for several minutes until the infant's objections ended the delay, whereupon she declared in loud voice, "It is a boy!" and handed him to the wet nurse.

~~~

"Show me my son," demanded the king.

A nursemaid removed the swaddling cloth and presented the infant to the short-sighted Llewellyn ap Gwynedd. "Scrawny thing, isn't he? Hmm. Not much of a boy either. Oh, well, I suppose I'll have to make do." The baby started to cry. "He doesn't seem to care much for his father, does he? Here, take him." The maid passed the child on to a waiting wet nurse and all grew quiet.

~~~

A few days later, the wise old midwife summoned a noted surgeon from Conwy. The queen's chief attendant escorted him to the nursery where the infant lay.

"Look at this child," she said. "When it was born, superstitious women thought it was the work of the devil. I seen parts not quite right, but never like this."

She uncovered the infant and spread its legs. A prominent swelling the size of a grape protruded from where a penis might be. The surgeon took one look and dented it with the tip of his index finger. "Cyst," he said. He withdrew a roll of instruments from a pocket in his robe and picked out a small sharp lance. "Hold her down" he instructed the midwife. With a single quick motion he slit open the cyst and placed a towel over the site. The infant barely whimpered. The surgeon patted the area with the towel and when he removed it, the cyst was gone.

~~~

"This way, your grace." The captain of the palace guard led Queen Eleanor from her chamber down the stone steps leading to the river gate, where he escorted her aboard the royal galley. Oarsmen struggled to move the boat upstream, but they had not gone half a mile before city rabble had crowded London Bridge and began to pelt her with stones and garbage, forcing her to seek refuge at St. Paul's Cathedral.

"Where is my son?" she demanded to know.

"He has returned from the campaign in Wales," said the captain of the Tower garrison. "He is at Windsor Castle as we speak. You must lie low, my lady, while I return to the fight to drive Montfort's men from the Tower. The king will be rescued and you and the king and Prince Edward will be reunited."

Having earned the eternal enmity of Henry III, Simon de Montfort was chased down and thrown to the anti-baronial rabble who took great sport in tormenting him to death. As the last scream during his dismemberment reverberated upward through the Tower keep, another sounded to take its place. This time, it was that of a squalling infant, blindly seeking his wet nurse's breast.

"My god, Edward," said the king, "no sooner is Montfort silenced than the shrieks of some stray urchin assault my ears."

"Booty, father. Booty. Llewellyn's firstborn. You think this bairn howls; you should have heard his father when we made off with him."

"The princess has started giving you children. Why do you need to bring in an outsider? You should have taken his falcons instead."

"You know perfectly well, Father, that Alphonso is dead. The rest are girls, the same as old Llewellyn's brood. Besides, I have enough falcons, just not enough sons."

"So, you intend to pass him off as your real son?"

"That I do, Father. His father is Llewellyn ap Gwynedd. He comes from good stock. He'll grow up and never know."

"What about the succession? Suppose the princess gives you a son of your own."

"I'll manage that if the time comes."

~ ~ ~

"Am I not fulfilling my duty to give you sturdy offspring?"

"Yes, but I cannot risk losing you," said Edward, somewhat disingenuously. His wife was barely out of her teens. "I do not want to tax your health unnecessarily."

The prince and Princess Eleanor debated what to do about the Welsh infant Edward had snatched from Llewellyn at Gwynedd Is Conwy.

"What is he called?" said the princess.

"I heard them call out the name Penfelyn . . . for that yellow hair, I suppose . . . I have it," said the prince. "You shall go on a tour to Irnham. You will stay with the Luttrell family."

"To what purpose, Edward?"

"The child will be part of your entourage, and in a few months you will return home with a new baby boy. How does that sound?"

"Perhaps after we come back," said Eleanor, "if he remains cloistered here for a few years, when he finally does come out, busybodies will have lost interest in counting on their fingers and toes trying to figure out why they ever scratched their heads over this. It will no longer be an issue."

"I am afraid it will always be an issue. One day I will be king and you will be queen. Busybodies never stop prying and speculating."

"I can go to Irnham, of course, but why? Why do you insist on sheltering this kidnapped bairn? Because he's another boy? I'm not so sure. He frightens his nursemaids."

"You are talking gibberish, Eleanor. How on earth could a boy only a few weeks old frighten anybody?"

"They are the ones who feed him and clean his bum. They know things you do not. The Welsh wet nurse who came with him said some at Conwy believed he had the devil in him."

"The devil? By my baldric and sword, I do not know what you are talking about. "

"Your son Alphonso came into this world a sound lad without ambiguity. Not so this hapless little chap."

"He is what I say he is, Eleanor. I insist on it."

"As you will, Edward. As you will, but be forewarned that to force him down a path other than what is ordained by God may very well destroy him and imperil your soul."

~~~

"To the White Tower and move smartly," the captain ordered. A large tilted carriage rumbled behind five horses harnessed in single file. The armorial of Plantagenet identified it as a royal conveyance. The body was further decorated with the silhouettes of eagles against a background of forest green. The cartwright had painted the undercarriage and iron-clad wheels red. Woodcarvers fashioned ornate gargoyles that were mounted at the corners fore and aft.

The carriage was covered with a tightly woven golden tapestry twenty feet long supported on arches of tough and flexible ash. Two windows on each side could be closed during inclement weather. It was in this fine carriage that the ladies and gentlemen of the privy chamber installed fur rugs and satin cushions for the royal family and their attendants. The children's governess arranged a box of dolls and other toys in one corner.

Wagons carried tents and a portable pavilion; others, food, water, and kitchen essentials. Two grooms attended a string of a half dozen palfreys that trailed behind the wagons.

The palace guard provided ten archers and ten crossbowmen, plus twenty more men-at-arms for protection. Armored knights on powerful destriers stationed themselves at the four corners of the wagon.

On the day of their departure, the princess gathered her staff to bid them farewell and leave instructions about their conduct while she was away, as well as her expectations upon her return. Since the king and the prince would be busy with the residue of Montfort's forces at the Isle of Ely, the lord chamberlain would function as representative in their absence.

Grooms mounted the lead and fifth horses harnessed to the carriage. The household staff formed two lines facing each other at the tower entrance. Footmen stationed themselves on either side of the steps to the rear entrance of the carriage as the princess exited the tower. She was followed by two ladies-in-waiting, her young daughters Eleanor and Joan, and a nurse carrying a covered basket. With everyone aboard, the bishop gave his blessing and the procession left the Tower of London and proceeded to Ermine Street, which would take them north to Irnham.

~~~

King Henry's military forces were stretched to the limit. He had committed his navy to an expedition into the Holy Land. His final land offensive to subdue what remained of the Montfort barons who had fled to Ely, therefore, had to be supported by mercenaries. Both sides of the dispute had been reduced to chest-thumping and shouting at each other, except that the king still had access to funds and the barons did not. What the king lacked was a sufficient number of men-at-arms. Since the companies sold their services to the highest bidder, and the barons had exhausted their resources, the king won the auction. But the king had had to pay a heavy price. In order to secure the funds, he was forced to sign the Treaty of Abbeville with Louis IX, in which he agreed to give up a claim on Normandy, Maine, Anjou, and Poitou already lost by King John. Louis agreed to let him keep Gascony and parts of Aquitaine. In effect, he sold a territorial claim to the French king in exchange for Louis' friendship and the funds necessary to subdue the remnants of the barons' revolt.

Ely had long been a refuge for dissidents. Surrounded by impassable swamps, it was an island in the fens easily defended by a small force. This relative isolation was, however, a double-edged sword. Difficulty of access was offset by the difficulty of escape. If entrapment were effected, escape was nearly impossible.

This accident of geography was not lost on Captain Erich von Hofstein, commander of the Prussian military company hired by Henry to rout the bloodied remnants of the barons' revolt.

The Wolf Company, as their captain had named them, was a mercenary army of three thousand men-at-arms, among them archers, crossbowmen, cavalry, and infantry. This was not some ragtag collection of military adventurers, but, rather, a disciplined military organization with the captain at its head and a handful of knights serving as his direct subordinates. They had a paymaster, smiths, carpenters, cart- and wheelwrights, cooks and bakers, a surgeon, trumpeters and pipers, and even a legal staff to negotiate their mercenary contracts.

The captain divided his mission into two parts: gaining access to the Isle of Ely and subduing the enemy. He sent two spies ahead, who reported back to him that the barons' forces were depleted and weak. The captain judged that their conquest would be less of a challenge than actually getting his troops to Ely Cathedral where the barons were holed up.

He sent six men to scout the perimeter of the isle. The news was not good. Two of the men had drowned in the soupy mire of the fen. The isle was isolated except for a single causeway built by the Romans centuries before, but still passable on foot. The captain concluded that to send his troops in single-file would be to invite disaster, even in the face of the reduced force that camped in the cathedral. The answer was to widen and strengthen the causeway in order to get his cavalry and wagons from the high ground, across the fen, and onto the isle quickly in massive numbers.

The Wolf Company disembarked from its barges on the River Nene at the old Roman town of Durobrivae. From there they decamped to a rise four miles to the northwest of Ely. For three months, they felled trees and widened the causeway to accommodate their war machine, whereupon they moved in force to surround Ely Cathedral. The company took the barons' men prisoner without resistance and turned them over to the king's men. In return, the captain of the king's guard handed the Wolf Company's treasurer two large sacks of gold florins.

~~~

As Princess Eleanor's entourage approached their destination, St. Andrew's church emerged above the landscape atop a small hill. Clustered around the base of the hill were cottages made of wood, a few more substantial houses, and fish ponds. As they drew near the south side, Irnham Hall came into view.

Sir Geoffrey Luttrell and Lady Agnes welcomed Princess Eleanor and her children to the manor as honored guests. Of the four Luttrell estates, Irnham was the grandest. Irnham Hall, the ancient seat of the Paynells passed on to Geoffrey Luttrell. Lady Agnes had prepared a special guest house for her visitors. One room was assigned to the princess for private use by her and her attendants. The remainder of the indoor space was furnished with a large bed, a narrow trestle table for the use of the nursemaid when attending the infant Penfelyn, a bench, and a crib. The other children, the nurses, and the children's governess shared the big bed.

The grooms slept with the horses in the stable. The footmen and men-at-arms were housed in village inns, with the soldiers performing guard duty in shifts.

The arrival of the royal guests was marked by a lavish banquet held in the great hall. Representatives of the neighboring noble families came from as far away as Lincoln, Derby, Leicester, and Peterborough to honor the princess who would be the next queen of England, and her son the infant Penfelyn, designated the Earl of Snowdonia.

The boy was just learning to walk and soon became the darling of the Luttrell daughters. They vied for turns at tending to him, giving him toys and tidbits, and leading him around hand-in-hand.

Under the ever-watchful eyes of his nurses and attendants, the little earl was allowed to be the center of the children's games. He was always surrounded by a bevy of girls: his sisters Eleanor and Joan, and the Luttrell daughters Margery, Lucy and Elizabeth. The Luttrell brothers Andrew and Aubrey thought it great sport to try to upset the girls' play, but they were so outnumbered they were rarely successful. Besides, they were old enough to understand the noble status of the little earl, and restrained themselves when attempting to get his attention.

One of the estate's cabinet builders was an adept woodcarver who had fashioned an exquisite doll's head from a choice piece of lime wood. He passed it on to Lady Agnes's dressmaker who created several tiny gowns with drawstrings at the neck that could be changed at will. For hair, she had snipped several locks from the head of a blond housemaid, which she stuck on the head to create a little girl's dream doll.

"Like you. Like you," the little girls squealed as they thrust the doll in the little boy's face.

The Luttrell sisters were so enchanted with the doll that they wanted more of them, which the obliging household staff supplied. The imperious little girls demanded that the same blond housemaid donate her hair for every one of them. The woman had to keep her head covered for some time after that until her hair regrew.

The five young girls were fond of sitting in a circle with young Penfelyn in the center. They cradled their dolls and passed them around among themselves. The infant propped up in the middle showed great interest in this activity, welcoming any opportunity to hold a doll offered to him. The boys continued to circle the little party astride their hobby horses, charging between the seated girls at every opportunity in their attempt to attract young Penfelyn's attention and offer him a ride, but the only toy they could all agree on was a large ball filled with moss that they passed from one to another. The boys, unlike the girls, quite naturally hurled the ball with all the force they could muster and were pleased when they succeeded in knocking one the girls off balance. They would laugh and she would threaten tears. At this point their chaperones invariably stepped in to stop the mayhem, much to the delight of the young earl who laughed at all the fun the entire time.

~~~

A year passed during which the infant Penfelyn grew rapidly. By the time he and his mother were preparing to return home, he was racing around on his hands and knees ready to learn to walk. He began using words one and two at a time and asserting his independence.

During their stay in Irnham, the men of Princess Eleanor's entourage had become the darlings of the local demimonde, living the easy life in town of well-placed young men with much time on their hands. Among them the young knight Richard of Leicester had grown smitten with a certain merchant's daughter. Toward the end of the year, her physical proportions showed certain changes, suggesting that in order to maintain public order, Richard would either have to marry her and take her back to London, or he would have to remain in Irnham.

The princess and Sir Geoffrey concluded that to take a country girl back to London under the royal umbrella was out of the question. She and now he would have to make their way in the village and the princess would have to return to London short one equestrian guard. Richard, it seems, had had either the good luck or the bad luck, depending on your point of view, of being required to abandon his potentially upward trajectory as a knight of the royal court to become a yeoman merchant with a wife and child in the village of Irnham. On the plus side, he had just earned a predictable, if pedestrian, future.

~~~

Contrary to the custom of baptizing babies at or shortly after birth, the ceremony celebrating the prince's new son took place when he was a year old. Boniface of Savoy, Archbishop of Canterbury, presided at the christening on Whitsunday in the year 1270. The spectacle commenced with a gathering on the porch of St. Michael's cathedral. Present were the designated godsibs* Lord Thomas and Lady Elizabeth of Aylsworth and Lord Gilbert of Monmouth. The prince and princess accompanied their son who was in the arms of his nurse. Here, the child would be instructed before he could be christened. He was forbidden entry into the church before instruction because he was not yet a Christian.

The archbishop began the required exorcism by making the sign of the cross on the baby's forehead. Placing his hand on the whole head he said, "What is the child's name?"

"Penfelyn of Snowdonia," the prince replied.

The archbishop then spat into his left hand and used his right thumb to smear saliva on the infant's nostrils and ears. He then made the sign of the cross on the baby's right hand saying, "So that you may sign yourself and remain in the Catholic faith forever. Go, Penfelyn, into the temple of God."

The christening party entered the cathedral and gathered around the baptismal font. Dozens of invited guests followed them in and took their places in the sanctuary.

The archbishop added drops of chrism, a mixture of oil and balm, into the font. The nurse removed the boy's christening gown and passed him into the arms of the archbishop, who glanced at him once, but then could not help but take a second look. "What is the child's name?"

"Penfelyn of Snowdonia." The prince repeated.

The archbishop addressed the infant in Latin. "Do you renounce Satan?"

The godsibs replied on his behalf. "I renounce him."

"And all his works?"

"I renounce them."

"What do you seek?"

"Baptism."

"Do you wish to be baptized?"

"I do."

The archbishop immersed the infant in the baptismal font three times. "I baptize thee in the name of the Father . . ."

Penfelyn resurfaced with a howl that could be heard out in the street. The priest struggled with the wet and slippery one-year-old and immersed him another time. ". . . and of the Son . . .," and finally in an orgy of flailing and holy words, ". . . and of the Holy Spirit. Amen."

The shrieking Penfelyn was welcomed into the Church in a spray of holy water that left the archbishop and the prince, princess, and nurse maid drenched. The priest quickly handed the child back to the maid who dressed him, as the clergyman and onlookers dried themselves.

~~~

The prince sent a secret dispatch to Grand Master Guillaume de Villaret on the Isle of Rhodes, in which he invited the Knights Hospitaller, who successfully conquered the isle, to join the prince's force on its way to Cyprus.

Mounting Crusade to regain Acre. You must join me in this effort to regain control of the Holy Land. The Templars and Louis IX are with us. We will launch our attack from Cyprus. Your nobles and knights will establish a beachhead to the north of the city, the Templars to the south. The French will join the Wolf Company in a frontal assault. We depart on Ascension Day. God and the winds willing, we should reach your shores by the holy day of the Assumption of Mary.

Signed: Edward Plantagenet, Duke of Aquitaine

Upon receiving the dispatch, Villaret and his men departed for Cyprus, where they immediately began the construction of floating siege towers to be towed to Acre by Edward's war galleys.

~~~

"God and my king have ordained that I should join his Crusade to drive the infidels from the holy land," the prince declared. "Wife, you must accompany me on this holy adventure."

"But what of the children?" she protested.

"We shall send them to Cippenham Moat along with their tutors."

"I do not want to leave my children for such a long time," she continued. "They will scarcely remember their parents by the time we return."

"It is a price we must pay. It is our sacred duty."

"How long will we be away?"

"Preparations have begun. I have already ordered the fleet to assemble. We shall go by sea. It will take a month for us to reach Cyprus where we will launch our invasion. We should return in two years, if not sooner. Time will pass quickly and your sacrifice will be to the glory of God."

~~~

The mamluks, former slave soldiers highly trained as riders, archers, lancers, and swordsmen, had assembled a large defensive force in Acre behind the formidable stone works constructed ironically by their enemy Louis IX during an earlier, failed occupation. A thousand men-at-arms gathered around a large force of artillery arrayed immediately behind the sea wall. The principal defensive weapon against a seaborne invasion was the trebuchet, a catapult capable of hurling missiles four hundred yards. Loaded with balls of Greek fire, they constituted a fearsome defense capability.

The English fleet headed toward Gibraltar and included twenty siege galleys of a hundred-twenty oars each. The professional oarsmen were assisted by sails on the open sea. They divided themselves into two teams who worked in shifts in battle, one shift maneuvering the galley and the other shift fighting.

The prince had ordered built thirty-six taridas at the Smallhythe shipyards. Specially designed to transport horses, they had flat bottoms, were oared, and could be beached where the horses would be unloaded through a ramp in the stern. Each transport carried forty horses and their grooms plus the oarsmen. The remainder of the fleet consisted of twenty war galleys, ten supply ships, and the prince's royal galley.

The ninety-foot long, eight-hundred ton war galleys with crews of eighty could transport five hundred men-at-arms with their squires and equipment. Edward's fighting force on its way to Cyprus totaled fifteen hundred horses and ten thousand men, three thousand of whom were fighters from the Wolf Company.

The Knights Templar prided themselves in their small, elite force and were already on Cyprus. They also controlled a large banking network the Crusaders had access to. King Louis IX of France, with the help of the Templar bank, commissioned Italian merchant ships and sailed south to the northern coast of Africa where he caught the easterly current. Four hundred Knights Hospitaller sailed from Rhodes to Cyprus where they joined Louis's hired fleet at the port of Paphos Ktima.

Prince Edward's mighty fleet remained becalmed at sea for the three days required for the royal galley to reach Rhodes, where the princess would be installed in the Hospitaller's castle for the duration of the siege. Bidding her farewell, the prince left the royal galley at the port and joined his captains for the remainder of the voyage to Cyprus. They arrived on the holy day of the Assumption of Mary, as predicted. The prince took this as an augury of great things to come. The next month's activities included military training exercises, a tournament, and the construction of castles on the siege galleys.

Louis's forces took the southern current aboard the Italian merchant ships they had commissioned for the voyage. They arrived in Cyprus in time to complete Edward's plan. Louis's infantry included serfs, whose skills ranged from carpentry and shipbuilding to farming and agriculture. They would fight when they must, work when they could. Louis's men divided themselves between the warriors who strutted among themselves and the locals, and the agrarians who sought to establish an agricultural base from which the army could launch itself. In the end, the martial spirit prevailed.

~~~

"The mamluks have destroyed Haifa to deter the Christian Crusaders," said Edward, "but the joke is on them. That undefended rubble shall be the launching pad for the Templar's surge from the south."

The Hospitallers deployed to the north and the Templars to the south. The siege began. But the Templar captain did not reckon with the parched desert heat; his small number of troops surged ahead without sufficient water. Their energies flagged as their thirst soared. Their horses collapsed, and they were vanquished by the smug mamluks. The southern force of Edward's advance crumbled.

Edward summoned the Templar commander Jacques de Molay to demand an explanation.

"What in the name of our savior Jesus Christ were you thinking?"

"My knights are the greatest tactical force ever brought to bear on these oriental heathens."

"Your tactical force ran out of water, for God's sake. How do you account for that?"

Edward would have sacked him on the spot if he could, but that was not possible.

~~~

Edward's assault force was sea bound from Cyprus. The mamluk commander sultan Aybak monitored the prince's approach from his redoubt. About a quarter mile offshore, beyond the range of the mamluk archers and artillery, six of the prince's war galleys lined up in a row, port to starboard. They separated into units of two ships that maneuvered to within a hundred feet of each other. In addition to constructing castles fore and aft on four of the war galleys, the Cypriot carpenters had constructed three siege towers and placed them on their sides aboard three small barges. Oared pilot boats towed the barges into the spaces between the parallel galleys. Seamen quickly lashed the galleys together and pulled the ships close enough to allow them to erect the towers and lift them off the barges which, freed of their cargo, slipped out of the way. When the operation was complete, the machines consisted of three large platforms of two galleys each, supporting siege towers that could be driven up to the sea wall.

"What fools these Christians are," the sultan laughed. "I have five hundred crossbowmen, a thousand archers, and three hundred cavalry staring at their puny fleet."

At a range of four hundred yards, Aybak launched a barrage of stone missiles. The ship's captains ordered the vessels forward as many of the projectiles splashed into the sea. A few landed on deck causing little or no damage. Heartened, the siege galleys' captains pressed forward toward the sea wall.

"Their defenses are useless," the Englishmen cried out. The rain of boulders ceased, but moments later to the horror of the men on deck, the sky lit up with orange balls of flame hurtling toward them like fiery comets. "Greek fire*," they screamed.

~~~

The Hospitallers established a beachhead at the poorly protected port of Achziv seven miles north of Acre. Two thousand knights, archers, and infantrymen disembarked and began their southward advance to engage the mamluks as they attempted to repel the prince's war machine. Their commanders did not know that the mamluks had stopped the Templars, and that there was no south flank in their planned pincer maneuver. As they approached Acre, the sultan ordered reinforcements from the south, who circled east of the city and met the Hospitallers head on. After two days of intense fighting, the Crusaders were forced to retreat to their ships, where the mamluks bade them farewell with a shower of bolts and arrows.

~~~

The rain of fire on the fleet continued. Men on deck were doused in flaming pitch. The panicked victims jumped into the sea only to have the fire burn even hotter. They did not even have time to drown. The prince was taking heavy casualties, but the force, inspired by God, pressed on. The siege platforms crashed against the sea wall inside the minimal range of the trebuchets. Wicker ramps dropped down from the towers onto the top of the wall. Archers and crossbowmen on both sides exchanged fire, mamluks from the wall and stone towers, and the Crusaders from the castles fore and aft on the war galleys. Infantrymen with swords poured across the ramps to meet their opponents. The carnage continued for several days. Seamen attempting to suppress the fires set aboard their war ships by the Greek fireballs fell in great numbers to the crossbowmen's bolts. Eventually, the onward rush of Crusader swordsmen began to slow as they depleted their resources.

Soon the situation grew desperate, and the galley captains ordered the lines securing the siege platforms cut. The burning towers fell into the sea and the oarsmen began their retreat. Edward was ashen. Five of his original ten galleys survived in a condition that allowed them to move beyond range of the defender's artillery. A mile offshore he met with his commanders and captains.

"You have performed heroically and have nothing to be ashamed of. I accept responsibility for this defeat. I am not sure that all of Christendom would have been able to mount a force sufficient to unseat these heathens. They own our Holy Land."

Edward was correct in one respect, for this, the ninth Crusade, would be the last.

The survivors of the fleet limped back to Cyprus where the prince received the news that his father was dead. King Henry III died on the sixteenth of November in 1272. He was sixty-five years old. On the nineteenth of August in 1274, Prince Edward, known as Longshanks for his height of over six feet, was crowned King Edward I. In time Queen Eleanor presented him with a healthy son, Edward Prince of Wales.

Chapter Two

Revelation

The death of Henry III and accession to the throne by her husband Edward conferred on Queen Eleanor duties and obligations not her responsibility when she was only a princess. Formerly, she had taken a passing interest in her children, though the messy day-to-day matters of keeping them clean and clothed were in the hands of various nurses and attendants. As queen, she grew so distracted by court matters that her children were no more than a swarm of little people she entertained briefly each day when she could fit them into her busy schedule. The king was always visiting one of his many estates. He was rarely present, and so the responsibility of managing Windsor castle fell to her. Not only was she responsible for directing the chamberlain's duties, but she also had to be intimately familiar with those of the seneschal.*

At least twice a year, good King Edward visited Windsor to gather his wife and children around him for an hour or two of family time. Upon his departure, he often left the queen pregnant. He was genuinely fond of them all, if only in a somewhat detached way. On special occasions, he would present them with gifts: silver buckles for the boys and ivory brooches for the girls. Longshanks, as he was known, would uncoil his six foot two inch frame and invite his daughters to sit on his lap. Young Edward and Penfelyn, or Pen as he was known inside the family circle, vied for their father's attention. Among toys, tops were the boys' favorite. They would wrap the strings and send the tops twirling across the floor, Edward always trying to outdo Pen in order to secure their father's favor. Pen did his best, but Edward usually outperformed him. Pen would casually cast his top on its wobbly way and then go to his mother's knee as it spun across the room. Edward would immediately claim victory and strut around the room with a look of disdain for his brother.

When Pen and Edward reached nine and seven years of age, the era of play ended and the era of rigorous education began. The scholar Nicholas of Wessex was summoned from Oxford to become the court tutor and master grammarian. His principal assignment was the education of Pen and Edward, but he also instructed boys of the lesser nobility and those of higher-ranking court officers.

Academic lessons were finished by eleven each morning. The boys ate some bread and cold boiled beef at midday to prepare for a long afternoon of physical training. They began by running a lap around the inside of the castle wall under the supervision of Master Peter of Wyndom, a renowned athlete and foot race champion. This was followed by various exercises designed to build strength. As hard as he tried, Pen, heir-apparent to the throne, had difficulty keeping up with his younger brother who never missed an opportunity to gloat over his superior physical prowess.

Following a brief rest, Master Peter turned the boys over to Sir Geoffrey of Gaunt, the equestrian coach and master of martial arts. Here they received the same training as squires before graduating to knighthood. Their instruction began with animal husbandry, where they learned about the basic anatomy of horses and their care and feeding. This was followed after a few weeks by riding lessons. As their skills developed, they moved on to practice basic skills that would lead to perfecting combat and jousting techniques.

The boys were nearly exhausted by days so full of activities, but they would have preferred to do more laps around the castle wall than to be finished off every other afternoon by the court terpsichorean who, because of certain ecclesiastical proscriptions, disguised himself as a jester. The king dismissed Edward's complaints, although Pen seemed to rather enjoy it, informing him that this was an instruction required to hone the social skills necessary to their becoming well-rounded and proper royal gentlemen, and that some day the Church would lower its eyebrows toward the practice.

Late afternoons on the other days, Andre de Valois, assigned by the king to Windsor from the court of his friend Louis IX, gave lessons in two-handed swordplay. Young Edward found this to his liking in preference to the estampie.* Swords crafted for grown men were too heavy for the young trainees, and so Valois ordered several of lighter weight for his pupils. This suited Pen, because he felt with some chagrin he had not developed the upper body strength to match that of the other boys.

Pen at thirteen was taller than Edward at eleven. Because Edward was the more aggressive of the two, the fighting master viewed them at first as reasonably matched sparring partners. Where Edward was impetuous, Pen was calculating. But in two years time, Pen came to dominate his younger brother through his swiftness and cunning. Valois saw a genuine talent with the sword in the heir-apparent, and so informed his father.

As the boys' strength and equestrian prowess grew, they graduated to the paddock outside the castle walls. There they would combine fighting and riding skills into the chivalric emblem of manliness, jousting in preparation for war. Generations of jousting instructors, older knights at the end of their careers, had devised a fiendish training machine known as the quintain, a spinning crossbar mounted atop a post. A small target was attached to one end and a lightly padded ball covered in leather to the other. The target and ball were at the chest height of a mounted rider. After a few preliminary passes on foot, Pen and Edward took turns, astride the palfreys that served as stand-ins for war horses, charging the target with wooden lances scaled to match their small stature.

When they succeeded in striking the target, the arm went spinning, with the padded ball whipping around from behind to hit them in the middle of the back if they did not move quickly enough. Had the boys considered the possibility they might escape the quintain's punishment by deliberately missing the target, they would have been disappointed, because the instructor was ready to spin it around by hand when they missed. After being whacked or even unseated a few times, their reflexes sharpened. Though Pen was Edward's superior at swordplay, he was bested by Edward in the paddock, often rising from a tumble off his horse with tears in his eyes.

Although he was accustomed to the rough and tumble of the joust, the old knight began to feel sorry for Pen. Informed by dispatch that Pen was not his most apt pupil, the king grew irate and demanded that the old knight work the boy harder to toughen him up. In time, Pen was able to negotiate the quintain with success. As they grew older, larger, and stronger, the royal sons continued training and maintained their readiness to move up to armor and lance astride a warmblood charger.*

~~~

Though the manfully-wielded lance, sword, maul, battleaxe, and mace were hallmarks of the successful knight in battle man to man, the bow in the hands of a trained archer was the premier weapon of the infantry in war. Every serf, peasant, and farmer was skilled in its use, as were specialized men-at-arms. Arrows pierced the armor of enemies and the hides of game.

A seasoned large and powerful adult bowman would wield a six-foot-long bow with as much as a hundred-pound pull. His father would have begun his training at about age seven, training that never stopped, that continued into adulthood. Men so trained developed tremendous upper body strength, making the English infantry a fearsome land fighting force.

The king's master bowyer supervised teams of journeymen and apprentice bowyers and arrowsmiths to meet the garrison's need for a continuing supply of bows and arrows. Staves of mountain-grown yew brought in from the Scottish Highlands were the wood of choice. For the purpose of training, the craftsmen made bows of different sizes and strength tailored to the individual boys.

Pen, Edward, and the others were required to stand still with their left arms extended and hold them there until the pain forced them down. This went on for weeks until they built the endurance to hold a stave of yew for fifteen minutes in preparation for the day Sir Geoffrey would replace the staves with bows. Only then were they ready to learn the fine art of archery.

They began with bows four and one-half feet long, with a pull of twenty-five pounds. Monday through Saturday, they held their bows in position and repeatedly drew back the linen string. Back and forth, back and forth they continued until they could do no more, but each week they found they were able to perform an increasing number of repetitions. When they were strong enough, Sir Geoffrey moved them up to bows five feet long with thirty-five pounds pull. And so it went. When their upper body strength was sufficient, training with arrows began. To Pen's dismay and Edward's delight, Pen was never able to graduate to a six-foot-long bow with a forty-five-pound pull. But Edward's triumph was premature. Soon after the target training began, both he and Sir Geoffrey were in for a surprise.

Following Sir Geoffrey's instructions, Pen and Edward each stuck eight light arrows from their leather sheaths into the earth in front of them. Edward took aim at the target, a wooden mock-up of a warrior's shield. Proudly, he drilled the center of the shield with his first arrow. Sir Geoffrey nodded toward Pen, who withdrew an arrow from the ground, nocked it, drew back and released. Within ten seconds he repeated the maneuver and released two more arrows lacing a tattoo on the shield with his brother's arrow in the exact center of a small triangle.

Edward was awestruck. Never would he have considered the possibility that his brother would be capable of such a feat. Sir Geoffrey had seen such a performance before, but not by one so young and so early in his training.

Word of Pen's prowess with the bow spread quickly. When competing teams of boys chose up sides for competitions, each side wanted Pen. Snickers behind the prince's back ceased.

At the end of the first phase of archery training, Sir Geoffrey presented Pen with a custom-made bow. It was five and one-half feet long with a pull of forty pounds. The bowyer fashioned it from a choice yew stave and inlaid it with ivory at the grip. Pen was five feet six inches tall and weighed eight stone. The bow matched his stature, though reduced in size from what might have been expected for another boy at his stage of development.

~~~

"You may present them," said the king on one of his rare visits to Windsor.

The chamberlain bowed and left the royal presence, returning moments later with two young boys in tow. The boys bowed and stuttered, "Your majesty."

The chamberlain immediately cuffed them along side of the head and whispered, "You speak only at his majesty's order."

"Yes, sir," said one, and the chamberlain cuffed him again.

Pen and Edward observed the proceedings with detachment.

"Which one is Eldric and which one is William?" said the king.

The boys looked to the chamberlain for guidance. He nodded and gestured toward the king.

"I am Eldric the Lesser, your majesty."

"I am William of Pembroke, your majesty."

"How old are you Eldric?" said the king.

"Twelve years, your majesty."

"Tell me of your mother, the countess."

"She is well, your majesty. She hopes that you are also, and sends her best wishes."

"And you, William?"

"Twelve years, your majesty."

"And your mother, Lady Pembroke? I received word that she has been ill."

"Yes, my lord. She instructed me to assure you she is on the mend, should you inquire as to her health."

"All well and good. These are my sons, Penfelyn, Earl of Snowdonia, and Edward, Prince of Wales. You boys are here to serve as pages. You will also receive training to become squires to them on the day they earn their knighthood."

"I want that one," said the fair-haired Pen, pointing to Eldric. Edward shrugged and accepted the assignment of William as his page.

~~~

Pen and Edward, attended by their pages, took command of their new society. In the eyes of the two new young people, their power and prestige soared to hitherto unimaginable heights. Though sons of nobles, back in their own castles they had no special status and were subordinate to everyone but the lowliest staff. Here, they answered only to the young princes and their teachers.

A dozen more noble sons had been farmed out to Windsor for a substantial fee. They were expected to become literate and learn the arts and graces that would lead them into service as sewers, henchmen, and perhaps even squires who one day might be elevated to the knighthood.

The princes' rooms were located in the royal apartments at the east end of the Upper Ward. The other boys were relegated to a room on the third floor above the state apartments. A labyrinthine passageway, at first known only to the princes, wound around inside the castle wall, giving them access to the state apartments without going outside.

The sixteen twelve-to-fourteen-year-olds quickly formed two factions: the *Monarchs*, as Edward designated his quartet, and the *Baston Boys*, symbolized by the swagger sticks they carved for themselves. The boys, pitted against each other in the paddock, were known for confrontations in the labyrinth after dark, to do some chest-thumping and mock saber-rattling, but never did the Baston Boys overstep the bar that separated the nobles from the royals. Not so, the other way around.

~~~

Pen felt he had no one to talk to. He did not fit well into the boys' club. His brother was not interested in talk. Pen had Eldric, of course, but there were barriers to intimacy that should not be breached. His closest companion was the journal he kept.

I do not understand why the boys even younger than I grow muscular as their voices coarsen. It is a mystery. My face is smooth, and I blush to write that for some reason my hips seem to widen. The boys are always in a state of agitation. If I never hear another story about the Baston boys and the housemaids, it will be too soon. They have little use for books and music, preferring to fornicate and roughhouse among themselves. I am forced to join in their games, but find them repellent. Yesterday, my brother and the others were pushing and shoving in the courtyard and generally behaving in their customary unruly manner. Andreas pushed Charles from behind, and Charles fell into me. I tumbled backwards onto the ground with Charles on top of me. He put his hands on my chest to push himself up and was suddenly overtaken by a look of astonishment. He said nothing, but rose as quickly as he could and got as far away from me as space would allow. His expression was one of great puzzlement. I found it rather pleasant.

~~~

At the king's insistence, Master Peter and Sir Geoffrey have demanded that we work our bodies to the extreme in order to toughen up for future combat. My chest has expanded, especially in front, which I attribute to the vigorous exercise I have endured for so many years. Edward has not even noticed. He prefers wrestling matches with Piers Gaveston, his favorite Baston Boy. I am certain that my page Eldric has noticed, but he has said nothing. Could it be that Charles did also?

~~~

I have befriended Lady Ariel Shore, one of my mother the queen's ladies-in-waiting. I had no one else to talk to about something quite embarrassing that happened to me recently. One day after lessons in the paddock, I discovered blood on my braies.* Lady Ariel informed me that spending so much time in the saddle, I was bound to develop piles and they would go away and it was nothing to worry about. I was greatly relieved to learn of this. I do not understand why Sir Geoffrey said nothing of it.

~~~

Day after day I was plagued with those bloody piles. I began to fear I might bleed to death if something was not done. Having already consulted with Lady Ariel, I decided to confide in my page Eldric to find out if he had any ideas. He is such a sweet boy.

"Eldric, I have something very personal to discuss with you . . . man to man."

"Yes, my lord."

"Have you ever found blood in your breeches?"

"I beg your pardon, sir."

"Well, Eldric, I have. Lady Ariel told me it was nothing to worry about. I must have you examine me quickly. I am afraid I may be dying."

"Dying, my lord? I hardly think that. You are the very picture of robust good health."

With that Pen lowered his breeches and braies. He had never seen such a strange look on anyone's face as the one on his page when the boy looked down at him. He grew alarmed. "What is the matter, Eldric?"

"Sir," he said. "I have sisters. I think I know the source of your concern."

With that, Eldric stood facing his master and dropped his own breeches right there before Pen's eyes. Now, the prince was sure he was the one with the puzzled look on his face. "Look at me," he said. "Now look at yourself. What do you see?"

Pen began to cry. He had heard that boys and girls were different, but until now never knew or even cared about how.

"What is that?" Pen said with sudden alarm in his voice.

"You mean my penis, sir?"

"Yes. That thing. Are you some kind of freak, or am I supposed to have one?"

"I am not a freak, sir. Just a normal boy."

"O Lord, why have you done this to me? I am a man without a penis."

"Begging my lord's pardon for saying so, but you are not a man without a penis. You are a woman. Women do not have penises. I have many sisters. I know of such things."

They both pulled up their breeches as fast as they could. They stared wordlessly at each other until Eldric said, "What shall I call you, my lord? My lady?"

"You will call me, 'my lord,' Eldric. This must remain a secret between us. Grave matters of state are at stake here."

"Yes, my lord."

"But what about the blood, Eldric?"

"If you take care of it the way my sisters do, no one will be the wiser."

"Yes, of course. What you told me to do. Yes. I will do that. Nothing must change as far as the other boys are concerned, Eldric. I can hold my own against them most of the time. They must not know of this calamity."

Pen felt it necessary to pay another visit to Lady Ariel. He had never thought about men and women, boys and girls in that certain way until recently. The boys in the yard seemed to know everything.

They bragged about their conquests of the servant girls. Pen laughed right along with them but had no idea what they were talking about, so he concocted an excuse for seeking an audience with Lady Ariel.

"What is it you wish to know, your majesty?" she said.

"I am now fourteen years old and soon the king will choose a bride for me. One day she will be queen. What am I supposed to do?

Lady Ariel suppressed a smile. "How much do you know?"

"Not very much, I am afraid. I have never been around girls. I think that we boys have something, uh, down there that they do not."

"That is correct, my lord. Think of yourself as a planter and your bride as a newly-ploughed field."

"I have plenty of peasants to do that work."

"Not this work," she said. "You will have discovered by now that from time to time in the dark of night your royal member has grown quite stout and even, perhaps, given forth an unusual substance."

Her expression demanded an affirmative answer. "Of course," Pen lied. "And what of it?"

"That substance is the seed that when placed in fertile ground produces a child."

"No, no, no, no," he said. "That cannot be all there is to it."

"Indeed, there is more. Have you ever watched a stallion mount a mare?"

"O God, no . . . I mean yes, I have seen that."

"Weeks after the stallion finishes, the mare's belly begins to swell, and ten months later she foals. That's the same as a woman having a baby."

"O God. How awful. I never imagined . . . I will have to mount my wife?"

"It has been done, my lord, but usually it is accomplished face to face. By this time your royal member should have come to full attention and will be prepared for entry."

"Entry?" he bawled.

"Do not be shocked," she said. "God in his infinite wisdom has seen fit to make it a pleasurable experience for you."

"What about my wife?"

"Well, that's another matter. It is our duty, you see."

~~~

Pen did the best he could to maintain his accustomed identity in the presence of the other boys. More than once when the boys were playing rough, Eldric, lately more protective of his master, would step in between Pen and his assailant to deflect the attack. No one took special notice of Eldric's close attention to his master, since it was his duty as a page.

In the paddock, the pupils lined up on horseback in two rows facing each other. A page could hold his master's horse until the charge began, but once loosed, the riders were on their own. They were expected to approach their opponents on the practice field with their lances lowered, but the preferred mode of final combat in real life was face to face, on foot with swords and maces.

The training exercise required the two rows of horsemen facing each other to advance at a trot, reign to a halt, drop their lances, and jump out of the saddle to the ground, hitting it with a rolling motion. They were supposed to end up on their feet and brandish their swords while dressed in full armor, hauberk,* helmet, and shield. Pen surprised himself at his strength and agility. In a few months he had mastered the maneuver with great celerity.

One of the boys facing the royal line had let it be known he considered himself superior to what he called the sissified prince and he set about to prove it. Having charged and successfully completed their dismount, Pen and the boy stood facing each other with wooden practice swords drawn. The foolish lad attempted a straight thrust toward his opponent's chest at which point Pen deftly parried without moving his body and whipped him sharply across the ribs. The boy tumbled to the ground with a yelp, losing his helmet in the process. To his great embarrassment, the rest of the boys broke into peals of laughter.

Stepping in, Sir Geoffrey said, "There is an important lesson here for all of you to learn. Never underestimate your opponent, especially if he is French."

~~~

"What a stroke of good fortune! The day has come," said Edward. "That Scottish lout King Alexander has fallen from his horse and killed himself. He has no immediate heir. That means the little Maid of Norway will claim the throne."

"Congratulations, Father," said Pen. "Perhaps now England and Scotland will be joined. . . but why is this especially good news?"

"I have observed your performance in the practice yard and am impressed by how you have progressed in recent years. One day, you will surely become my worthy successor. So, you are now of an age to perform your first ritual of allegiance to the Plantagenet dynasty. You shall be betrothed to the little maid Queen Margaret. The day you and she are pledged, Scotland will be ours."

"But. . . I am just a boy," said Pen.

"You are sixteen years old by my reckoning," said the king.

Pen's brain was reeling. He saw the day of his unraveling rushing toward him. His first impulse was to run as far away as he could go, maybe France, maybe change his name, maybe hide in a monastery.

"How soon will this take place?" he ventured to ask timidly.

"I should think as soon as possible. I have already sent emissaries to meet with the regent to make the arrangements for a state ceremony."

"The regent? If she is queen, why does she need a regent?"

"She needs a regent, son, because she is only two years old. I am not sure she even talks much yet."

~~~

"I am to be engaged, Eldric. Can you imagine that?"

"It was bound to happen, my lord. Who is the lucky girl?"

"This is not a time for jokes. The king scared me half to death when he told me, but I do have some breathing space. She is the Queen of Scotland and only two years old. The betrothal will be purely ceremonial."

"What happens ten years from now?"

"We will have time to figure out something, Eldric. In six years I will enter the knighthood. God grant that the king does not die in the meantime."

~~~

"Sometimes I feel like a prisoner trapped in this castle," Pen lamented.

"I wish there was something I could do," said Eldric.

"If I were a commoner, I could mingle with friends of my own choosing instead of those wretched ruffians whose only nobility is in their lineage."

"You have the tourneys," said Eldric meekly.

"Yes, and I have the bruises to show for it."

~~~

"The king has ordered a feast in celebration of my betrothal. This will be my first public appearance in a very long time," said Pen.

"You have been able to conceal your true identity up to now, but I am afraid, my lord, your day of reckoning may be fast approaching."

"We must figure out a way to postpone that as long as possible, Eldric. The ideal knight is tall, blond, and bearded. Two out of three is not enough."

"My lord, I may have a solution, if you will permit me."

"Yes, yes, by all means," said Pen. "Tell me."

"I have certain connections on the outside, but I do not wish to imperil those who might be living on the edge of respectability. About the beard, my lord. I know someone who knows someone who knows a master of disguises. He could make you look like the ideal knight."

Pen's eyes widened. "It might work, Eldric," he said as he hugged the boy with enthusiasm. "If this is successful, your friend of a friend of a friend will be handsomely rewarded." He pressed Eldric's body to him and felt a slight stir. On a whim, Pen thrust his hand inside the front of the lad's breeches. "Have you ever thought about this?"

"Well . . . no, my lord . . . yes, my lord."

Pen's hand lingered for a minute or so. *Lady Ariel, was right*, he thought.

~~~

Sir Arnaud of Gascony, who oversaw the castle garrison, was puzzled the day he was summoned to the presence of the young prince, whom he had never seen up close.

"There is a band of actors known as the Greenwood Men that plies its trade in London," said Pen. "I have need of the services of one of their troupe. He is called Kallias. Find him and bring him to me."

"Yes, my lord. I will dispatch two men immediately."

Two soldiers dressed in civilian clothes took to the road and arrived in the city at sundown. They made a few inquiries and discovered that the actors could usually be found in Southwark, a haven for criminals and free traders where they were beyond the reach of the London authorities. They went straight to the Tabard Inn and identified themselves to the innkeeper, who was visibly shaken at being questioned by agents of the king. The leader of the Greenwood Men, he informed them, was a man called Arkwright. He and some of his company would come in for ale after a performance.

"They go round and put on Robyn Hode entertainments wherever they can collect a few shillings. They're across the river inside the wall somewhere tonight. They'll be here late."

"Thank you, my good man," said the soldier. "We will wait. You do understand your lips are sealed, do you not?"

"Yes, sir. I do sir."

The soldiers passed the hours playing dice and drinking. They were in a good mood when Arkwright arrived. The innkeeper nodded in their direction and went on about his business. The soldiers rose from their bench and confronted the actor. He attempted to bolt but they seized him by the arms, one on each side.

"Don't kill me," pleaded the terrified man.

"We are not here to kill you, Arkwright. We are the king's men, and we need to have a word with one of your troupe."

"And who would that be, sir?"

"He is called Kallias."

Upon hearing his name, a wiry fellow with his hat pulled low tried to get out the door. The soldiers released Arkwright and blocked the man's escape.

"You are Kallias?"

"Yes, sir. I done nothing to you. What do you want?"

"Sir Arnaud, castellan* at Windsor has requested your presence at the castle. You will come with us to the Tabard. We leave for Windsor at dawn."

~~~

"You are to be my second assistant," said Pen to the awestruck little man. "Eldric will fit you out in your livery."

"Y-yes, sir," Kallias replied, not knowing what else to say. The prince was not in the least threatening, which emboldened him to ask, "Why am I here, my lord?"

"Before I tell you, you must understand the rules. Your mission is secret and so you will not discuss it with anyone other than Eldric and me. I will pay you well for your services, more than you could every hope to earn as an actor. Betray this trust and you will never be heard from again. Is that understood?"

"Yes, my lord, but why me?"

"You are known to have a special talent, to be a master of deception. You will put that talent to work here. I have heard you can turn one man into another. Have I been misinformed?"

"You have not, my lord. That is my profession."

"Your cleverness will be put to the test, Kallias. Not only will you create a transformation in the moment, but you will also create a progression of changes that will keep you in our presence for some years."

"I have sworn fealty to you and, given my charge, I will serve you best when there are no secrets between us. You must reveal yourself to me for me to do my magic. I cannot operate in the dark."

"Very well," said Pen as he stared into the man's eyes and began to disrobe.

Pen slipped the cowl from his head to reveal a cascade of wavy fair hair. He opened his robe and let it fall to the floor. His shirt was loose but failed to conceal the outline of his breasts. Kallias shifted uneasily as the revelation proceeded. Although his suspicions were aroused, he was still not prepared for the image that was revealed when Pen took off his shirt and lowered his breeches. The prince was not a boy, but a beautiful young woman.

"This is the secret," said Pen. "We three and an old nursemaid or two are its only keepers. Your charge, Kallias, is to make sure that in the eyes of the public I remain a prince and not a princess for the foreseeable future. Matters of state are at issue here. If the truth were to be revealed prematurely, England could find herself in great peril. You are a very important man."

Kallias was totally confused by a surge of pride mingled with a degree of sexual curiosity, but prurience faded with the passage of time, for he was never to see Pen displayed in that fashion again.

~~~

Kallias was permitted one final performance with the Greenwood Men. As usual they were to perform one of their many stories of Robyn Hode.

"I wish to go with you *in cognito*. You will assist me and my page in dressing us as monks so we may move undetected through the crowd."

To venture out from Windsor to London was a covert act of defiance of the king who was battling local authorities for control of the city. Edward was appalled by its lawlessness and violence and was determined to control the unruly elements that had made the city ungovernable for two decades. Edward pushed Henry de Waleys, his choice for mayor, into office and installed a royal warden, Ralph of Sandwich to crack down on criminality.

Theatrical productions were the least of their worries. The Church would rail, but the king had more important problems to contend with. The word was out that to be on the safe side, Arkwright had stopped venturing inside the city walls and instead established a makeshift outdoor theater in an open field east of the Tabard Inn. Settled as it was beyond London's jurisdiction, Southwark was allowed to go about its business largely unmolested, and located at the southern foot of London Bridge, city people found it easy to reach.

The journey from Windsor to London was not without its perils. The road was frequented by wealthy travelers, a route favored by bandits. Dense forests along the way provided them with ample cover. At Kallias's suggestion and upon the order of the prince, the castellan had assigned two bodyguards to accompany the royal entourage. They, like the prince and his assistants, were disguised as monks, although they were well armed beneath their cowls.

Arkwright advised them to travel on foot in order to complete the ruse. They were young and fit and the sojourn would not be difficult for them. They left Windsor mid-morning on a pleasant day in August.

"You must tell me of this play of yours," said Pen. "I have read the classics, but know nothing of popular entertainments. We will have some time. Add to my education."

"Yes. . . ahem. . . my lord. I come from a humble background. My mother and father were actors and so it was natural that I should become one as well. My father's brother is a trickster. He taught me about the disguises I have applied to my trade, but I learned the stories working with the Greenwood Men."

"What of this Robyn Hode of whom you speak?"

"We entertain the masses with tales of Robyn, Adam Bell, Clym of the Cloughe, Wyllyam of Cloudeslee, yeoman heroes to the common people."

"Were they real persons?" said Pen.

"That I do not know, my lord. All I know are the stories passed on. The old folks speak of them, but I think it is only of what they have heard. There is but one tale, twice told, then thrice. They are knights of the people pledging allegiance to God and king. They are kind to women and children. They are ferocious fighters against those who would prey on the weak. They rob the rich and give to the poor. Oppressed as they are by the powers that be, begging your pardon, my lord, they hunger for such stories. I suppose that to some it gives a small measure of hope."

Pen listened with fascination, turning over and over in his head, the single moral to the stories. He was lost in contemplation until his reverie was interrupted by the sound of hoof beats. Looking up he watched as two armed men galloped toward the little band. They were followed by two more on foot. One of them, obviously the leader, jumped down from his horse, confronted them, and bowed deeply from the waist.

"I am William d'Orsay," he said. The four men wore mail and cuirasses and brandished swords. "I can see that you are but poor monks, but nonetheless, I am obliged to inform you that you are on my toll road. I cannot let you pass without obtaining the contents of your purses."

Pen and the two bodyguards formed a circle with their backs to Kallias and Eldric, who were in the middle. The dismounted rider and the two men on foot walked slowly toward the three king's men. By way of a signal, one of the bodyguards threw back his hood. Pen and the other bodyguard did likewise. The prince's eyes, nose, and perfect mouth, framed by his golden locks, but for the lack of a beard, presented a royal portrait of the ideal knight. Simultaneously they threw open their robes and drew their swords in a coordinated movement.

Pen had never been in live combat before, but remained cool and to the surprise of d'Orsay, in a single motion, ran his sword through the man's throat. The bodyguards quickly dispatched their immediate adversaries and watched the one on horseback try to get away. He got about ten feet before one of the bodyguards produced a spiked mace on the end of leather strap and hurled it into the back of the man's head. The whole operation was over in minutes.

"You performed very well, my lord, if I may say so," said a bodyguard. "I would be willing to serve under you anytime."

~~~

Arkwright greeted Kallias upon his return to the troupe, asking where he had been. Kallias dissembled, mumbling something about illness, before moving on to his duties. Pen, Eldric, and the guards wandered about the fringes of the gathering audience. People took them for monks and they drew a few stares.

Kallias worked with his actors, adjusting their costumes, and readied them for the performance. The audience formed a semicircle and the show began. The lead actor covered in a hauberk, wore a baldric and wooden sword and carried a longbow. He walked to the center, followed by a dozen men in forest green tunics who also carried longbows.

"The noble robber does not commit crime," he began. "I, Robin of Loxley, right wrongs."

The crowd murmured their assent.

"I take from the rich and give to the poor. I never kill, but in self-defense or in defense of the defenseless."

"Yes, yes, good Robin."

"I know that you admire and support my principles, that you will offer me succor when I am on a mission on your behalf. I pledge to you that I shall not die and abandon your cause but by treason. I honor God and king and fair maidens."

The crowd cheered.

Chapter Three

Liberation

"For a farthing, she let me snip her hair," said Kallias. "I think it matches yours quite well, my lord. Since you are to be a developing lad, I shall have to work a special magic. Get comfortable. This will take a little time."

"The boys in the paddock," said the prince, "the Monarchs, they call themselves, are showing a slight darkening of the upper lip and a few straggling hairs on the chin. I should not want to get too far out ahead of them. Better to blend me in to the best of your ability."

"Only with the aid of a burning glass could you be betrayed, my lord."

"No one will get that close, I can assure you."

"This is how it is done," said Kallias. "I have here a yellow resin called lac that is soluble in the distilled spirits of wine. It is a rare substance from India that when applied to the skin is invisible and easily removed, hence its utility in adhering false hair. I have prepared a few short strands of the girl's hair and will dip their ends in the resin and apply them one by one. Only through such care will you be able to appreciate the perfection of my craft."

Kallias's practiced hand worked swiftly. Within the hour, the prince's facial transformation was complete. "Eldric," he said, "fetch a binder. We must flatten that chest. My lord, I would advise you to wear the binder at all times and avoid clothing that fits too snugly about the bosom. I see evidence that one day you may be quite amply endowed, in which case continuing a successful ruse may limit your costume to that of a monk's habit."

~~~

Bishop Dolgfinnr left St. Magnus Cathedral in Orkney and traveled to London to formalize the betrothal of Queen Margaret to Prince Penfelyn. He was greeted by Bishop of London Richard Gravesend. Longshanks towered above the assembly gathered on the porch of St. Paul's Cathedral. With the queen and Pen at his side, they entered the church and marched solemnly to the altar. Herald trumpeters lined the nave and sounded a fanfare announcing the arrival of the royal family. Papal legate Cardinal di Forenzi sent by Pope Gregory X and Archbishop of London Charles Benedict flanked the bishops.

"Are you ready for this, son?" said the king inspecting the newly emerging peach fuzz on the prince's face.

Pen watched the king's face carefully to see if he detected anything odd in his expression. "I am ready, Father."

The London bishop offered an invocation seeking God's blessing on the promised union. He then led Pen in the *verba de futuro*, the spoken vow to marry sometime in the future.

"Here today," Pen intoned, "I pledge my troth to Queen Margaret, the Maid of Norway. I further pledge that since she has passed but two summers, I shall remain faithful to her . . . *some snot-nosed Viking bairn* . . . until she reaches the age of fourteen years, at which time we shall be joined in holy matrimony. . . *God forbid that this should ever come to pass*. To symbolize this pledge I present you, Bishop Dolgfinnr, with this iron ring as a token of my fidelity to your queen."

The subsequent prayers were long and dull. Longshanks was getting restless. "The dowry, bishop. You have the contract?"

"Yes, your majesty," said Dolgfinnr. "As regent, on behalf of her majesty, I convey to you the earldom of Orkney and Caithness in exchange for this promise of marriage."

"It is done, then," the king beamed. Pen remained expressionless, tallying in his head the number of years likely to be left to him to plan his future. *Do not die, your majesty,* he thought.

~~~

The assembly left St. Paul's and proceeded to Westminster for the betrothal feast. The royal family and the clergymen rode richly caparisoned palfreys. They were surrounded by guardsmen from the castle garrison, knights armored in cuirasses, archers, and infantrymen armed with halberd and sword. Grooms and other servants walked before and behind the entourage.

Upon their arrival, the banquet was laid out and ready in the great hall. The king and queen rode into the hall on horseback. They dismounted and they and the royal offspring took their places on the dais. The ranking clergymen sat at trestle tables near the front. Behind them were the various nobles and their wives from neighboring estates.

Served over a half dozen courses was a sumptuous meal that included roast quail, doves and partridge, goose, venison, roasted boar and other wild game, gilded and slivered calves' heads, fish, roasted peacock, mutton, cheeses, nuts, fresh fruits, oysters steamed in almond milk, ale-flavored bread, stewed cabbage, fresh fruit preserves, tarts, and custards. The diners ate with their fingers from bake-hardened trenchers and washed down everything with great drafts of wine and ale. Red-eyed nobles toasted the queen and the prince and his betrothed. Toasts followed other toasts as the crowd grew louder. All but Pen and the queen were swept up in the growing revelry.

"I really must retire," the queen whispered to her husband. Edward was well lubricated but had the dignity to remain upright, even as many in the audience stumbled and fell. Pen drank only a little watered wine, and though he was not amused by the unconstrained celebration of his betrothal, he knew he had to remain to the end as befit his royal station.

~~~

The visiting nobles left various baubles and gifts for the prince, but the best was saved for last.

"Pen," said Edward. "You are a good son and have done great service on behalf of your king and country. The king owns many estates. They shall be part of your inheritance when you ascend the throne. In the meantime, I shall give you as a down payment on your legacy, an estate of your own. In addition to being Earl of Snowdonia, I now declare you Duke of Warwick,"

Problem solved, said Pen to himself.

The Duke of Warwick's new home would be Kenilworth Castle in Warwickshire. The news flashed through the court like wildfire. Kenilworth had its own staff, but below stairs betting was on who would be chosen to leave Windsor with him. His page Eldric and the recently employed Kallias were a sure thing. No one bet on any of the ladies of the chamber, assuming that it would be an all-male retinue. Punters lost a chance to make a killing in the betting pool when they failed to appreciate the close relationship between Pen and the widow Lady Ariel Shore. When Pen selected her, the queen acquiesced in deference to her son. Lady Ariel seemed pleased.

Andre de Valois pleaded that his task in the English court was finished, and, although he was honored by the offer, he would prefer to return to his family in France. Sir Geoffrey of Gaunt declined an invitation because of his age, but had been training his successor, a young knight named Sir Llewellyn ap Rhudd whom he offered to send in his place. Sir Llewellyn was well qualified to be the prince's new Master at Arms.

~~~

A hundred variously liveried staff bowed to the royal presence as they crossed the wooden drawbridge, passed the barbican, and proceeded through the gate in the curtain wall enclosing Kenilworth castle. They formed a respectful corridor that stretched from the gate to the main entrance of the residential keep. As the prince approached, the chamberlain Lord Philip Ardsley and seneschal Sir Malcolm Edmonds, flanked by Robert de Hockele, young abbot of the nearby Cistercian Stonele Monastery, and two White Monks emerged from the main entrance.

Grooms took the reins as the royal retinue dismounted and proceeded inside. Five hundred mounted men-at-arms rode behind the keep and delivered their horses to the stables along the far north wall. Dozens of staff unloaded forty-five wagons laden with the prince's personal belongings and supplies for the castle.

The chamberlain conducted Pen, Eldric, Kallias, and Lady Ariel up a flight of stone steps to the prince's privy chambers. Two rooms were connected to a central reception area, a lavishly appointed larger room for Pen and Lady Ariel, and a smaller room for the Yeomen of the Chamber Eldric and Kallias.

"Lady Ariel," said the lad. "You may be thinking the boy prince needs a mother to share his room, but not all is as it seems. You will be my lady-in-waiting. I leave it to you to bring in the requisite, but limited, number of chambermaids who can be trusted, as you are, with what amounts to a state secret."

"Yes, my lord," said Lady Ariel nonplussed. "This all quite extraordinary, if I may be permitted to say so."

"Within these confines you free to speak your mind when we are alone. Indeed, I command you to do so."

"May I know the secret, my lord?"

"You may, nay, you must." Pen doffed his cap and tossing it aside shook free a head of blond curls. He peeled off the false beard and rubbed his face on his sleeve. Removing his blue silk surcoat exposed the white linen shirt he wore underneath. As he leaned over and slipped off his pointed shoes and hose, the truth began to dawn on Lady Ariel. Although it was cold inside the stone keep, Pen pulled off his shirt and braies, removed the binder that was wrapped around his chest and stood facing Lady Ariel so she could take a good look at his naked body.

"This is the secret. My father needed a son and so the midwife gave him one, me. Even now he thinks I am a young man and eventual heir to the throne. Eldric and Kallias have been keepers of the secret for months. And so now must you be also. Fetch me a robe, Lady Ariel. It is quite cold in here."

"What about your mother?"

"That is very murky. You would think she would have known from the beginning. Somewhere a surviving midwife or wet nurse, dugs long grown dry, knows the truth. I suspect that I was born of another and taken from her when I was an infant to be raised by Prince Edward and Lady Eleanor while Henry III was still on the throne. The women would know. But even that explanation does not answer the question fully. Perhaps one day I shall discover the truth."

"It will be my pleasure to serve you, my lady," said Lady Ariel.

"*My lady* among ourselves. *My lord* elsewhere," said Pen. "The boys got used to it. So shall you."

"The prince, the duke, and the earl," she mused. "A woman."

~~~

Kenilworth Castle was one of the most easily defended castles in central England. Earlier in the century, King John extensively upgraded the castle by ringing it with strengthened towers set in a curtain wall and constructing a fortified dam to create a lake that surrounded the castle on three sides. Entrance required crossing a drawbridge over a water-filled moat. Kenilworth's only architectural rival was Warwick Castle, located five miles away on a bend in the River Avon, and occupied by William de Beauchamp, ninth Earl of Warwick.

"If he was not king and not my friend," said Beauchamp, "I would raise hell with Edward for giving his effeminate son the title of duke and planting him next door. As it is I must bow before him and say yes, your grace."

"Yes, your lordship," said the chamberlain.

"We might as well get this over with," said the earl. "We shall have a reception and feast."

"Yes, your lordship."

~~~

"The Earl of Warwick has sent an emissary, your grace," Lord Philip announced. "He requests the pleasure of your company at the castle for a feast and celebration of your recent elevation to Duke of Warwick."

Pen sent his acceptance thanking the earl before retiring to his privy chamber. "The earl can't be too happy about this," he said to Lady Ariel, "but if he can keep the lid on his passion I am sure that time will straighten out the matter."

Pen summoned Lord Philip and Prince Edward, whom the king had sent to Kenilworth, ostensibly to serve as a political advisor to his older brother. As a result of his pleading, the king sent Edward's special friend Piers Gaveston with the prince in the titular role of assistant advisor.

"Let us dispense with some of the formalities," said Pen. "I shall be attending a reception at Warwick. I feel like something of an outsider right now given the friendship that exists between the earl, the king, and you, Edward. It is no secret that the earl is chafed by both my elevation to the rank of duke, and by my presence here in his precinct."

"Perhaps you overstate the importance of our mutual esteem, your grace," said Edward. "You are to be king one day. Rather than three against one, I propose that it be four against the world."

"What a lofty sentiment, my friend," said Gaveston. "Perhaps we should just hug each other and proclaim this the best of all possible worlds."

Edward and Lord Philip were unable to stifle smiles. Pen was unmoved. "Gaveston," he said. "What are the chances of an outbreak of violence?"

"Out of the question," he replied.

"Warwick perceives me as a threat," said Pen. "You are his friend. You have consulted with him. We do a delicate dance. How are we to resolve the tension?"

"Diplomacy, your grace," said Edward.

"You have been silent, Lord Philip. What do you say?"

"What Warwick fears most is a loss of sovereignty, a loss of power. He may even believe you aim to seize his lands and usurp his authority."

"The diplomatic route then," said Pen, "would seem to require my disabusing him of that notion as quickly as possible. He is the king's vassal, not mine. I am the king's representative, nothing more. I touch only tangentially on the earl's relationship with his sovereign."

"But what is your agenda?" said Edward. "What is your role in the grand scheme? Do you merely hunt and joust until the king's demise?"

"You do not know me, Brother. Neither do any of you. The shortest distance between two points is a straight line. The fact was known to the ancients. According to that formulation I sit here today at point A. Point B is the throne. So, how do I traverse the intervening route? The answer lies not in further acquisition, but in preservation. Warwick, whether he likes it or not, is minder of a piece of the king's vast estate. Today the king is our father. Tomorrow I am the king. In the meantime, Warwick is a mere custodian. What serves the king's interest, serves my interest. It serves the king's interest for me to keep him happy."

~~~

Pen had to make a show of force to Warwick, and so he arrived at the castle with no fewer than three hundred horsemen and one hundred personal attendants, who dispersed to the stables and shops that lined the inner curtain wall. The earl's men greeted them as equals with no trace of animus. They enjoyed themselves at the earl's expense while the royal entourage braced itself for the rigors of a state encounter they would have preferred not to be part of.

The atmosphere was electric as the duke entered the great hall. Rich tapestries hung from the walls. A wide, red woolen runner for the duke to walk on led to the foot of the dais. The earl stepped down, bowed and greeted Pen with a show of warm affection. Pen reciprocated and signaled for the presentation of the gift. Two courtiers moved forward in lockstep bearing a finely crafted hinged wooden case about five feet long and a foot and a half in depth. The earl's sour expression softened.

"A gift for you, my friend," said Pen to the earl, "Erober, the sword of Guthram, Viking warrior and king, taken by Alfred at the Battle of Edington. I offer this is a symbol of our friendship and continued cooperation on behalf of our king, Edward."

"What is he up to?" the earl whispered to his aide.

"I cannot say, my lord, but I think it best to accept graciously until we figure it out."

"You are probably right," said the earl as he humbly accepted the duke's gift. "It certainly is a fine relic."

~~~

Weeks later at Kenilworth, the gamekeeper was heard galloping across the drawbridge shouting, "Your grace, my lords." Reigning up, he leapt down and leading his horse on foot, raced toward the keep.

"What is all the commotion?" said the chief steward, who met him at the main entrance.

"Bandits, poachers, my lord," he said breathlessly.

"Well, which is it, my man?"

"They are butchering stags and boars and loading them onto wagons. I barely got away with my life."

"How many are there?"

"Ten or fifteen, my lord, at least. Them's what I could see. I patrolled the area two days back. Weren't there then."

"Where are they now?"

"Can't say for sure. I left them four hours ago. They were on the move heading north toward Atherstone. If we hurry, we can catch up with them before they reach Watling Street."

Sir Malcolm struck a bronze gong with a hammer three times to summon the garrison commander Sir Guy de Lacy. "There is a major poaching operation underway in the Arden. Ten or fifteen men, maybe more, involved. Get your men together. Take the gamekeeper. He knows where they are. I will inform the duke."

Pen was intrigued by the notion of rogues in his forest and informed the castellan* that he would be leading the armed force.

"Eldric, my little man, today we ride into the wood."

"Yes, your grace, and what shall you be wearing?"

"Light battle gear, Eldric. We will be chasing down poachers. Where is Kallias?"

"Here, your grace."

"How does my beard look?"

"I will tidy it up a bit after you put on your hauberk. You are quite the handsome young man, your grace."

Eldric helped Pen with the binder and then slipped a linen shirt over his head. Pen sat back as Eldric pulled black woolen hose up to a point where he could fasten them to a belt worn over his braies. "Are you ready, your grace?"

"Ready," said Pen.

Eldric placed a woolen cap on Pen's head and helped him on with a plain, close-fitting leather jerkin for protection against chafing. He and Kallias then took hold of the heavy mail shirt made especially from silver hardened with copper. They lifted it over Pen's head as he raised his arms to work them into the sleeves. The yeomen lowered the hauberk until the hood rested on the woolen cap. The bottom of the garment reached to mid-thigh.

"The green surcoat," said Pen.

Kallias fetched the surcoat as Eldric pulled Pen's boots over his hose.

Kallias opened his toolkit, removed a few strands of hair and a comb and proceeded to polish his transformation of *her grace* into *his grace.*

"Your sword and dagger, your grace," said Eldric.

"Come with me, Eldric." Pen slung the baldric over his shoulder and they strode from the privy chamber, filing down the stone steps and out the front entrance.

The head groomsman stood waiting with a richly caparisoned charger for the duke and a palfrey for Eldric. Sir Guy signaled for his twenty-five mounted men-at-arms to fall in behind him. With Pen in the lead, the armed force left the castle precinct and followed a well-worn path into the dark heart of the Arden Forest.

~~~

The wood was so dense that it had defied the best road-building engineers since the Romans. There were trails, however. Ever since the Celts crossed the Strait of Dover from the European mainland a thousand years earlier, trails had been etched into the English landscape, crisscrossing the countryside in a web of avenues passable only on foot.

Pen's band continued its way eastward through the forest dense with thickets and brambles. The fern-lined path wound its way beneath a canopy of ancient oaks. From time to time, they would pass an open area covered with bluebells and cow parsley.

"Over here, Sir Guy" said Pen. "Someone's been camped here."

"Probably our quarry," he said.

The remains of a campfire, still warm, were surrounded by bones etched with gnaw-marks left by the teeth of the poachers' dogs. At the edge of the clearing, rooks, rising and returning in annoyance at the intruders, feasted on piles of offal left by the poachers after dressing their take.

"They are not too far ahead of us, your grace. If we move smartly we should catch up with them in one or two hours."

Pen reined his horse back onto the trail and spurred him up to a canter. The rest of the troop followed.

~~~

The campfire was not the only trace the marauders had left in their retreat. The trail could have been followed by children on a scavenger hunt.

"This is who they are, Sir Guy," said Pen, using his sword to pick up and hold aloft an abandoned pennon: The Templar Cross.

The failure of the last Crusade was followed by the disintegration of the Knights Templar. Ragtag remnants came into conflict with King Edward. They broke apart into roving bands of dissidents whose interest lay more in poaching and thievery than in Jesus Christ.

Johannes Michaelensis, in a report to Bernard of Clairvaux, observed that the Templars *despised the love of justice that constitutes its duties and did not do what it should, that is defend the poor, widows, orphans and churches, but strove to plunder, despoil and kill. As St. Bernard put it, they have descended into knavery.*

~~~

A broken wagon, a broken man left to die on the side of the path; such was the detritus shed by a once proud order now reduced to theft and banditry. Sir Guy spurred his horse ahead of the prince and poked at the man with the tip of his halberd. The man groaned and looked up from deep inside his tattered cowl.

"Have mercy, sir," he said weakly. "I have broken my leg. My master left me here to die."

"How are you called?" Sir Guy demanded to know.

"I am Gwyn de Lacy, my lord, squire to Sir Laurent de Molay."

"De Lacy, you say," said Sir Guy with a nod to the prince. "Who is your father?"

"Thomas de Lacy, sir. He was a noble Crusader who died in the battle of Acre."

"Thomas de Lacy was my uncle, squire. I am Guy de Lacy. You are my cousin."

"God be praised," said the squire with tears in his eyes. "What will you do with me, Sir Guy?"

"With your permission, your grace, I will send him back to the castle."

Pen nodded his approval. "But I need to ask him a few questions before he goes. Squire, how many men are in your band?"

"Twenty men, sir, along with their wives and children. There are a few slaves we picked up along the way, servants to Sir Laurent."

"How are they armed?"

"Five long bowmen and five men with cross-bows. Beware of the crossbowmen. The rest of the men are cooks, a wheelwright, a blacksmith, squires and menservants."

"Take him to the castle," said the prince.

"God bless you, your grace. God bless you."

~~~

They wound their way slowly through the forest, noting evidence of human activity. Ten miles east of Kenilworth, on the south side of the River Leam, was a small settlement of free peasants known as Leamington. The odor of roasting meat permeated the air.

"The prince is coming. The prince is coming," shouted a small man clothed in drab brown linen as he ran toward the handful of cottages. He disappeared inside one of them and quickly re-emerged wearing a shabby red sash and followed by a pretty young girl with dark matted hair and a bruise on her face. Ever watchful, Sir Guy, followed by the gamekeeper, took the lead and walked their horses slowly.

Leamington was a settlement without walls that had sprung up in a clearing in the forest. A dozen small cottages formed a cluster around the main path. The peasants had built a watermill on the river to grind their grain for bread. There was a smithy, and a common pig lot. Chickens and geese wandered about and squawked in competition for kernels of grain dropped on the ground.

"Do you speak for your people?" said Sir Guy.

"Yes, my lord," said the frightened little man. "I am Robert Giveney."

"The Duke of Warwick wishes to know if a band of marauding knights has passed through here recently."

"Yes, my lord. Yesterday they did," he said as his eyes darted from one armed horseman to the next. "But they moved on. They needed water and they took two of our pigs when they left."

Smoke rose from behind the cottage.

Sir Guy sent a sergeant to check it out. When he returned, he reported that was where the smell of cooking meat came from, and it was not from a pig.

"What are you roasting back there?" Sir Guy demanded to know.

"We are honest people, my lord. We have done nothing wrong."

"What are you roasting back there?" Sir Guy repeated.

"Mercy, my lord. Mercy. Before they left, they had their way with my daughter and paid with a haunch of venison, but they also took the little bit of money we were saving to build a church."

"That is property stolen from the king," said Sir Guy. "Seize him."

Pen stepped forward and raised his hand to the commander. "It is my gift," he said.

"Blessings upon you, your grace."

Upon hearing the exchange, the formerly empty street suddenly teemed with villagers, men, women, and children, all bowing low in the presence of the duke and his entourage. Pen dismounted and walked among them. He held out his hand to the children who shyly took it in smiling approval.

"What is your name?"

"Margaret, your grace."

"And yours?"

"Edward, your grace."

"Edward is a wonderful name. That is the name of my father the king."

Two wide-eyed girls standing nearby swooned.

"Who were the men who took your daughter?" said Pen.

"I heard'm call each other *Wolf* and *Bear*."

~~~

Sir Guy sent a sergeant ahead to scout the trail out of Leamington. He returned an hour later to report that Templars were camped in a clearing two miles away. Their archers and crossbowmen ringed the encampment. The sounds of squealing pigs being butchered alerted the scout to their presence.

Pen's troop moved silently out of the village. They found the Templar encampment on the banks of a stream running through a shallow gulley. Sir Guy signaled his archers to take the high ground and surround the encampment. Sir Guy loosed the first arrow, felling the crossbowman guarding the path. Within seconds, Sir Guy's bowmen had eliminated all the Templar archers and crossbowmen.

Pen rode into the middle of the encampment with his bow at the ready. "Sir Laurent de Molay? Come forward."

Stepping out was a tall man with dark wavy hair wearing a dirty white surcoat with a red cross in the center of his chest. "I am Sir Laurent. Who wants to know?"

"I am Prince Penfelyn, Duke of Warwick. You, sir, have been poaching in my forest."

"That I have. And what do you propose to do about it? I was known to pay the king's levy at one time. What I have taken is bought and paid for."

Sir Guy's men formed a circle around the slightly built Pen and the massive Sir Laurent, keeping the Templar fighting men at bay. Pen dismounted and handed his bow to Eldric. Sir Laurent drew his sword and Sir Guy's men took aim just as Pen raised his hand to stay their action. Pen drew his sword. It had a thin gleaming blade that stood out in contrast to the Templar's two-handed broadsword.

"There's no way out of this for you, Sir Laurent. Live or die, it is your choice."

"Live now only to die later, is it, your grace? Suppose you and I fight it out one on one. The winner and his men go free."

"Think carefully, Sir Laurent."

"Give me your royal assurance that your men will honor this bargain after you have fallen."

"You have my assurance," said Pen.

Like a charging bull, the Templar lunged forward, holding his sword vertically in front of him. As he moved into range, he raised the bronze Zweihänder aloft to start his swing. Pen elevated the point of his arming sword to shoulder height and took two steps to the side of the Templar, who brought his heavy blade down with a force that would have felled an ox. The blade cut through the air inches from Pen's arm and embedded itself in the earth. Pen laid the point of his weapon against his adversary's exposed neck, and seizing the middle of the blade in his left hand, gave it a forceful thrust. Sir Laurent's spinal cord was severed, and with no control over his limbs, he slipped to the ground in a twitching lifeless heap.

"I will take that belt purse," said Sir Guy. "Now bury your leader. The men called *Wolf* and *Bear* step forward."

Giving themselves away, two men looked around nervously and tried to bolt into the wood. Soldiers stopped them. Other soldiers rounded up the other men, bound their hands behind them, and shackled them in line on a long rope.

"Put the children in the wagons," said Sir Guy.

A sergeant led the tethered men up the path toward Leamington. The women followed behind trailed by the wagons. Three of Sir Guy's guards brought up the rear.

~~~

As they reached the edge of the village, children, seeing who they were, rushed from the cottages to greet them. Their mothers tried to restrain them, but to little avail. Ever mindful of the dangers of the forest, Sir Guy led the procession, but the only danger was the possibility of being mobbed by happy villagers. The noisy welcome grew subdued when the Templar prisoners and their group came into view. Sir Guy and Pen dismounted.

"Mayor Robert," said Pen. Giveney's chest swelled at the appellation. "Please fetch your daughter."

The girl emerged from the cottage, went to Pen and bowed. "Stand up, child," he said. He put his hands on her cheeks and tipped her head to get a better look at the bruise on her face. "It looks a little better today. A tree did not run into you, did it?"

The girl could not suppress a smile. "No, your grace."

"Bring the men called *Wolf* and *Bear*," he ordered. With guards at their elbows, the two men were made to face the girl. "Are these the men?"

The girl looked down with fear in her eyes. "Yes, your grace."

"What would you have us do with them?"

At that point, Giveney stepped forward and said, "Please forgive me, your grace, but we can take these two off your hands. No need for the crown to concern itself with them further. You have done us a great service in bringing them to us. Our smith serves as our constable when we need one. He will take care of them."

"I can agree to that," said the prince. "I am sure they will receive their just deserts at your hands."

"That they will, your grace."

A big man with large forearms stepped forward and seized the two prisoners, who let out groans as his powerful hands clamped down on their wrists. He led them away in the company of two deputies.

Pen spoke in a low voice to Sir Guy, who handed him Sir Laurent's belt purse. It bore the Templar Cross. He handed it to Giveney. "For your church," said Pen, "for service to the king."

Chapter Four

The Men of Arden Forest

"William," said Alan Wallace, "as your father I order you back to the abbey. Your time will come."

William Wallace was a strapping teenager with a prodigious mind. Bowing to his father's wishes, he resumed his studies, but deep inside his resentment of the English, especially King Edward seethed. The death of the libidinous Alexander III endangered the delicate political balance between Scotland and England. The elevation of Margaret, the two-year old Little Maid of Norway to the throne threatened the already fragile barrier to the complete takeover of Scotland by the English.

I shall put an end to this, he thought.

Alan Wallace determined that his son should one day rise to knighthood. In addition to his academic studies with scholars at Paisley Abbey, young William had the benefit of receiving training from Scotland's finest equestrian masters and martial arts instructors. He rapidly turned into an aggressive young warrior.

~~~

King Edward ramped up his campaign against the Scots. He had received word that a young upstart from Paisley was engaging in border raids. Believing them to be more of a nuisance than a serious threat, he summoned his sons from Kenilworth to make sure the annoyance did not develop into open rebellion. Believing his two sons to be superior to the Scots in every way, he reasoned that the operation should be a good training exercise for them.

Pen Plantagenet, Duke of Warwick, led northward a contingent of two hundred men-at-arms commanded by Sir Guy de Lacy. Gwyn de Lacy served as Sir Guy's squire. Edward was accompanied by his close companion Piers Gaveston. Eldric and Kallias, Yeomen of the Chamber served the prince.

The distance separating the two teenaged antagonists was two hundred miles and closing. Ten days after their departure from Kenilworth the prince arrived at Solway ford at the River Esk.

A campaign that would last nearly four years began with a single shot from a hidden Scottish archer. Aimed at the prince, the arrow went wide of its mark and glanced harmlessly off the shield of a mounted outrider. Sir Guy ordered everyone to take cover. The prince and his entourage melted into the forest.

Two young warriors, seventeen-year-old Pen and sixteen-year-old William Wallace tested their mettle against each other. Had they ever met on the ground, standing face to face brandishing their swords, they would have been an even match. However, Pen was a product of the tradition of the feared English bowman, and like his fellows possessed a sagittary prowess that gave him an advantage over potential adversaries. On a larger canvas, each had been instructed in the art of war, but neither had any first-hand experience in organized conflict. On the English side, that weakness would be buttressed by the military leadership of Sir Guy.

"Your grace," said Sir Guy, "my scouts tell me that William Wallace leads a group of young Scots rebelling against the king. Daily they attract new sympathizers and recruits to their roving bands. Their numbers are growing."

"Where is their greatest concentration?"

"Between here and Glasgow."

Thus began a protracted game of hide and seek. Wallace's men would not have stood a chance in a direct confrontation with the English force, and Wallace understood the fact. He readily came to prefer ambush and hit-and-run tactics as he gradually consolidated his forces. He was a fox pursued by a relentless pack of hounds.

~~~

Casualties on both sides were remarkably few. While the enterprise failed to highlight Pen's potential virtues as a warrior, it did sharpen his wits and teach him how to survive in the forest with a band of armed men. In truth, Wallace was a source of greater vexation to Pen's father than to him, but the king was occupied with the Welsh to the south, and had little time and no resources to bolster his son's campaign.

Pen played "Where's Wallace?" from Solway to Glasgow to Edinburgh. They reached Newcastle-Upon-Tyne in the year 1290. There he received a dispatch from the king: *Return to London immediately. Your mother Eleanor and your betrothed Queen Margaret are both dead.* Margaret had died on November 28, 1290, followed by Eleanor of Castile three weeks later. Eleanor's funeral took place in Westminster Abbey on December 17, 1290, where she was subsequently buried. Margaret was interred next to her mother in Christ's Kirk in Bergen.

The death of Queen Eleanor was of such moment that Pen's memories of the Maid of Norway were all but forgotten. Pen grieved briefly at the death of his rather remote mother, but overcame that feeling when he realized the Norwegian bairn also had died, thus liberating him from the tyranny of what could have become a sticky situation. Patience, leavened with a little good luck, seemed to have won out.

~~~

Though Pen and his men had been away for nearly four years, little had changed at Kenilworth. The Earl of Warwick, William de Beauchamp, returned from Queen Eleanor's funeral in London and once again offered his condolences. Terms remained cordial.

~~~

"The duke gave you a fine gift in the sword, Erober," said the earl's chief counselor Philip Langley. "He has avoided raising tensions. Of course, he has been away for a while, but now may be an opportune time to reinforce a strategic alliance."

"What do you propose?"

"Alice, your lordship, your ward Lady Alice de Toeni. She is ripe for the plucking, if I may say so."

"That is putting it rudely, counselor. She is a lovely child."

"A betrothal would secure your position. He was betrothed to Queen Margaret some years ago when she was only two years old. I am told she was only nine when she died, thus freeing the duke for another attachment. That attachment could make you godfather to the future queen. The prince is now twenty years old and soon to be knighted. What a magnificent couple they would make."

~~~

The villagers of Leamington put to good use the pouch of gold coins the prince had taken from the Templar renegades and given to them. When Pen, Eldric, Kallias, and Sir Llewellyn, rode into town they were greeted by an explosion of townsfolk emerging from their cottages. They all bowed respectfully, barely able to contain their enthusiasm, until Pen signaled for them to rise.

Towering above the heads of the crowd was the new Church of St. Peter. Abbot Robert de Hockele sent Dean Gordon Hillebrand from Stonele Monastery to hear their confessions and to say mass.

Robert Giveney, now the duly elected mayor, emerged from his tavern as the royal riders dismounted. The ever-watchful Sir Llewellyn stayed close to Pen, and, with his hand on the hilt of his sword, scrutinized the crowd from which emerged a man in clerical garb.

"Your grace," he said. "I am Dean Gordon Hillebrand. You have given true meaning to the word nobility. The Church, and speaking for the town, thanks you for your generosity."

"Your grace," came the greeting from the bowed head of a young woman. Pen could not see her face.

"Rise," he said.

She looked at the prince and said, "The bruises have completely disappeared."

"Mayor Giveney's daughter," he said with a smile of recognition.

"That I am."

"How are you called, Mistress Giveney?"

"Charlotte, your grace."

The mayor stepped forward. "You must be in need of refreshment, your grace. Please honor me by letting me serve you in my tavern."

The crowd parted to create a clear path for their four guests.

"Will you join us, dean?" said Pen.

"Your grace," he responded with a slight bow of his head.

Two men were asleep inside, one on the floor, and one with his head on the table. Giveney whispered something to one of the men who had followed them to the door.

"Begging your pardon, your grace," he said, as he and another man hurried inside and dragged the two bodies out the back door.

The mayor signaled to two barmaids, who hastily produced a pair of trestles from the back of the room. They set them side by side in the middle of the floor and placed planks lengthwise to make a table. One of the women rushed to a trunk in the corner and produced a red linen cloth trimmed in gold fringe. The mayor set the only chair in the room at the end of the table. It was a crude affair, but it did have armrests.

"You are a fine host to unannounced guests, Mayor Robert." Pen sat down in the chair, and Eldric, Kallias, and the dean sat on benches. Sir Llewellyn chose to remain standing by the door. "Sit with us, Mayor Robert. Charlotte. Charlotte, where are you?"

"I am here, your grace."

"Come over, Charlotte. Come stand next to me."

Charlotte was young brunette of a stature similar to Pen's. She wore simple peasant's attire that was neat, clean, and mended.

"I can tell by how you articulate your speech, Charlotte, that you are possessed of a good intelligence. Have you received some education?"

"I have, your grace. Your church brought us Dean Gordon, and Dean Gordon brought us learning – one blessing leads to another."

"She has been a fine pupil, your grace. Had it not been for your generosity she would have remained an ignorant village lass."

Mayor Robert produced a haunch of beef that had been roasting for hours on a spit over the fire. One barmaid distributed trenchers all around while the other brought tankards of beer.

The mayor apologized to the prince for not having a good wine to serve. "I could send someone over to the church for a skin of sacramental wine," said Dean Gordon with a wink.

"That will not be necessary, Dean. Beer suits me just fine," said Pen with a smile as he turned his attention to the mayor's daughter.

"Charlotte has studied books and the Bible," her father announced proudly. "She is a fine storyteller."

"That is wonderful," said Pen. "I love stories. Charlotte, would you honor us with one of yours?"

"Yes, but it is I who in the telling would be honored," said Charlotte. "I call this one The Queen's Tale."

~~~

Long ago, almost before the beginning of time, were two island kingdoms in the North Sea: Zetland and Faroe. They were ruled by the Viking King Harald I. The Pictish people of Zetland hated the Vikings of Faroe. But for the fact they were separated by one hundred seventy miles of violent North Sea, King Galan of Zetland would have been in a constant state of active rebellion against Harald.

King Harald rose before his court and announced, "Today the festival begins. I have conquered Norway. Norway is mine."

The members of the court bowed and cheered their monarch.

"Join me, my comrades in the great hall. Let the celebration begin."

The men packed the hall where tables were laden with pitchers of beer and mead dispensed from tap-bowls by the most beautiful women in the kingdom of Faroe. Other servants distributed polished and beautifully adorned drinking horns.

"Drink, my subjects," cried the king. "Drink until you are overfilled, then drink some more."

The men grew louder and louder as more and more drink passed their lips. They laughed and shouted. They all yelled and told stories at the same time. No one listened to anyone else until a shattering blast of trumpets sounded from the dais.

The king stood and raised his horn. "I have the most beautiful wife and concubines in the kingdom. You shall be treated to this vision of feminine perfection. I will stage a beauty contest for all of you to look at but none to touch. Let your imagination soar. Send for Queen Botheior."

~~~

It so happened that Queen Botheior had chosen to hold her annual banquet for women at the same time the king chose for his beauty contest. The queen granted the king's emissary an audience and instructed him to tell the king that she would be unable to participate in his spectacle.

"Let him parade his lovely young mistresses before the drunken lechers. I have more important things to do."

The king was furious, more at a blatant act of insubordination than at her refusal to join the parade of women.

"I cannot let this challenge to my authority go unpunished," he bellowed to his counselors. "Make known far and wide my decree that Queen Botheior is no longer queen. I banish her. I shall find a new wife."

~~~

Equal in beauty to Botheior was the lovely Pictish maid Pritani. Though a product of that detested race of Zetlanders, she had found a place at the periphery of the court. In addition to her beauty, she possessed something Botheior did not: cunning intelligence. She did not escape the wandering eye of the monarch who commanded her to join the seraglio in his beauty pageant.

Pritani had her eye on the future and readily acceded to the king's wishes. Day after day the king's bacchanal continued. On the seventh day, full of beer and with brains turned to mush, the revelers assembled themselves as best they could in the great hall.

One by one the king's concubines paraded across the dais, embracing the cheers of the bleary-eyed spectators. But the king saved the best for last. Pritani, wearing nothing but a translucent purple veil, glided like a swan across the stage. The crowd fell silent, dumbfounded by her staggering beauty. After a moment of silence, the king rose and once again raised his horn with a toast. "To Queen Pritani," he declared.

~~~

Pritani's lady's maid escorted her to a separate palace for her year of purification. "We are here to serve you, my lady. Whatever you desire, except your freedom, is yours."

"You may return the jewelry and extravagant clothes to the safekeeping of the wardrobe mistress," said Pritani. "I will have no need of them."

Each night, Pritani retired to the comfort of down-filled satin bedclothes. Her attendants slept on the floor beside her bed should she have need of them during the night. Armed eunuchs wearing black facemasks were stationed at the doors and all entrances to the palace. No man was permitted entry.

When she arose in the morning, she would eat a crust of bread soaked in wildberry tea. Two dressers then helped her don her day robes, light for the summer and heavy for the winter. If it was not raining or snowing, they would leave the palace proper and stroll the grounds for half an hour. Upon their return she would go to the place of bath and massage, where hot water boiled up from geothermal springs to heat the pools of water and the stones upon which she would lie for her massage.

The blind eunuch Torvald was chosen to give her a massage every morning, for no man, not even a eunuch, was allowed to look upon her body during the purification. Artists who applied her makeup and hairdressers plied their trade daily in order to perfect her appearance for the night she would share the king's bed.

The king demanded regular reports on her progress. Her attendants assured him she was growing ever more beautiful by the day, and that her patience and sweet disposition could not fail to please him. As the months wore on, the king's fantasy robbed him of interest in the women of his harem. They were left in the company of each other, and he in the company of his fervid imagination.

~~~

The long-awaited night finally arrived, and Pritani was presented to the king. He was overjoyed at the appearance of his new queen. He held a magnificent banquet in her honor before they retired to his bedchamber.

History does not record details of the king's success or failure in his midnight adventure, although we do know that Pritani remained childless. Regardless of the king's performance, Pritani's must have been a success, because her reputation soared in the eyes of both king and court.

~~~

Pritani's uncle Drostan was a deputy churl* whose duties consisted of keeping beggars away from the palace gate. With free access, he was able to maintain indirect contact with his niece. As part of his duties, Drostan pompously patrolled the palace grounds, flaunting the authority of the king as he eavesdropped on harem gossip and kept up with reports on how his niece fared in her new role as queen. It was through such idle chatter that he learned about a plot to assassinate the king. Uncle Drostan got word of the plot to Pritani who passed it on to the king in the name of her uncle.

~~~

Prime Minister Hakon was informed of the plot and immediately grew suspicious. The news had come to the court by way of a member of that inferior race of Zetlanders, which made it suspect from the very beginning. Hakon reasoned that the intelligence might have been planted in order to divert the king while the conspirators spun some nefarious plot to attack him from another direction.

Hakon made his suspicions known to the king without daring to cast an aspersion on his queen. The king praised him for his loyalty and promoted him from prime minster to personal counselor.

Hakon made a special point of confronting Drostan with the news of his new status and demanded his immediate obeisance.

"I would never bow to a stupid sycophant, Hakon. I have always believed that for the king to take your advice would be to imperil his royal existence. You are a liability to the king. He would do well to bind your hands and feet and toss you into the sea."

"You have not heard the last of me, Drostan," Hakon fumed. "Enjoy what mean pleasures are left to you. Before the year ends you shall be enshrined in the annals of infamy. Your ashes will mingle with the royal middens."

~~~

"Your majesty," said Hakon. "Place your generals under my command and I shall eliminate this threat. I am your loyal subject and I commit myself to supporting your continued reign over the kingdom. We cannot allow usurpers to gain control. I know who they are, a nest of vipers whose leaders cower in Zetland."

Taking Hakon's advice, the king decreed that the Zetlanders should be wiped out. Armed with the decree, Hakon organized a genocide that would forever eliminate the Zetlander threat. Hearing of this, Pritani appealed to the king, but she had fallen out of favor. The king of appetites had grown weary of her and actively sought yet another beauty to adorn his bedchamber. To be rid of her, the king offered her anything she wanted, up to half his kingdom, to go away and leave him to his follies. Pritani's newly sharpened instincts informed her that she could bargain for a greater prize.

"But, my dear," the king pleaded, "I have decreed that my warriors shall eradicate your people. What is decreed cannot be revoked."

"I bow to you, my king, but as your wife I demand that you attend a special banquet in your honor prepared in advance at the queens' residence. Since you offered me anything, up to half your kingdom, you must attend on the provision that you agree to certain demands I shall levy on you at that time."

~~~

The banquet came and went, but Pritani did not present her demands.

"I shall prepare a second banquet in your honor, my liege," she said afterward. "I shall not prepare it in advance this time, but only after you agree to accept my terms beforehand."

The king's honor required him to accept the arrangement, and so the second banquet was prepared.

~~~

Hakon raged like a baited bear at the crushing of his dignity at the hands of the Zetlander Drostan. "I shall have his head," he declared.

Hakon's friends convinced him that Drostan was part of the plot against the king by his countrymen, so he would be well-advised not only to wipe out the Zetlanders, but also to raise Drostan's head on a pole before the palace as a notice to all who would dare to cross him. He would gain favor in the eyes of the king for quelling the assassination plot and eliminate his bitter enemy in a single campaign.

~~~

Drostan's revelation of the plot to assassinate the king met with royal accolades. The king wanted to reward him and consulted with his personal adviser Hakon on how best to bestow such an honor.

"What is the matter, Hakon?" said the king. "Why is your face turning red?"

Hakon had expected to get the king's approval for Drostan's execution, but instead he was put in charge of an awards ceremony in his honor. Soon, Drostan's stature eclipsed that of Hakon, and Drostan became the king's favorite.

~~~

Pritani prepared to play her final cards. Hakon believed that she was his last hope for redemption in the eyes of the king. In one last, desperate move, he entered the palace garden where Pritani sat admiring the flowers. He rushed fervently to her side and knelt. The king, still seeking a solution to his problem of how to get rid of his wife and yet keep his honor, happened on the scene in the garden. The first thought that crossed his mind was that Hakon was assaulting, or even trying to rape his wife.

The king confronted them, and Hakon protested that his majesty had misunderstood. Pritani saw opportunity in the event and said nothing to disabuse the king of his belief.

The king summoned his guards and they took Hakon away. The next day his body could be viewed outside the palace gate, impaled on the very pole he had erected for Drostan.

~~~

The king appointed Drostan as his new prime minister. Pritani believed that she was now in a position get the king to call off the massacre of the Zetlanders, but she was wrong. She pleaded and even begged the king with tears in her eyes, all to no avail. Once decreed, there was no turning back.

"I implore you, your majesty," said Pritani. "Give us permission to respond to the decree in whatever way we can devise."

The king readily agreed to the demand, breathing a sigh of relief that he might be successful this time in ridding himself of this annoying woman. "Write what you like," he said, "so long as it does not conflict with other edicts and laws."

In his role as prime minister, Drostan has possession of the king's signet ring. Any edict so sealed was the law of the land and irreversible.

Let it be known, the decree began, that the king has granted permission to the people of Zetland to defend themselves against anyone who tries to carry out the provisions of the first decree.

The people of Faroe were confronted with two opposing decrees from the same king: one ordering the annihilation of the Zetlanders and one ordering their defense. The Zetlanders greeted this outcome with such enthusiasm that they declared themselves victors over the Faroese.

"The final outcome of the conflict," said Charlotte "is in some dispute. Descendants of Zetland believe their forebears massacred the Faroese. Descendants of the Faroese believed their forebears wiped out the Zetlanders. If one day someone discovers the location of these island kingdoms, we may learn the truth."

~~~

By the time Charlotte had finished her story, everyone in the tavern was smiling. She had captivated her audience, not least among them, the prince himself.

"You have a very special daughter, Mayor Giveney," said Pen. "Father Dean, you are to be congratulated on your tutelage. Mayor, I see much promise in Charlotte and ask your permission, if she is in agreement, for her to accompany me to Kenilworth where I shall provide her with further instruction."

Both Charlotte and her father burst with pride. To be given special attention by the heir to the English throne was beyond all expectation. They both readily agreed.

Chapter Five

Recruitment Continues

The Earl of Warwick decided not to let the prince's new availability in the marriage market go unattended. He arranged for a lavish banquet to be held, ostensibly to celebrate his ward Lady Alice's sixteenth birthday.

Beauchamp summoned the famous London dressmaker Madam Belle to Warwick to create for Lady Alice the most fashionable and appealing attire for the occasion. She arrived at the castle with a retinue of patternmakers and needlewomen who brought a supply of fine cotton lawn and colorful oriental silks.

"I am very excited, madam," said Lady Alice. "I am to be the center of attention. I saw the prince once before. He is a beautiful man, and I must be beautiful also."

Madame Belle selected a bolt of soft cotton lawn. "Run your hand over this, young miss," she said. "This goes next to your skin."

Madame took Lady Alice's measurements and created a tailored, but loose-fitting, shift that reached her ankles. "What is your favorite color, Lady Alice?"

"O madam, I don't know. I like the colors of flowers and of the sky."

"I think your guardian has something special in mind for you. The prince will notice you above all others present if you choose red, red with gold trim. What do you think of that?"

"Red? That sounds so perfect, madam. Yes, I like red."

The team quickly measured, cut, and stitched to create a shimmering red satin robe, close at the neck, that dropped to the floor. Around her waist was a yellow satin sash, the end of which fell to her knee. It was fastened with a gold buckle. The court hairdresser brushed out Alice's auburn curls, letting them fall loosely down her back. Lady Alice was ready for her very special evening.

The invitations included advice regarding decorum in the presence of the prince and the young people. Wine was to be drunk only in moderation. Food scraps and bones were to be fed to the dogs under the tables discreetly and were not to be thrown at them from a distance. Temperance and restraint were the order of the day.

For the occasion, the great hall was divided into three stages of descending height, the dais in the front for the royals and nobles, the platform of intermediate height in the middle for the honored guests, and the main floor for the lesser courtiers.

At the appointed time, the nobles, barons, and landed gentry arrived and took their places in the hall. They were greeted by the soft sounds of a musical ensemble consisting of harp, lute, vielle, and psaltery, accompanied by the double-reed shawm, recorders and flutes, tabor, drum, and tambourine.

The Earl of Warwick, his counselor William Langley, and Lady Alice de Toeni entered the hall through the main entrance. The crowd split to the left and to the right to give them open passage to the dais. They were followed by Lord Philip Marmion and his daughter Elizabeth from Tamworth Castle, who took their places at the intermediate level. When all of the invited guests had found their places in the hall, trumpets announced the arrival of Prince Penfelyn, Duke of Warwick and Earl of Snowdonia and his entourage. Lady Alice had beamed at the adoring crowd as she made her initial appearance, but her expression went blank as she watched Charlotte Giveney enter at the side of the prince. Her eyes darted across the crowd, and she spotted Elizabeth Marmion, two girls her own age, both dressed as elegantly as she, and every bit as beautiful.

The prince and Charlotte joined the Beauchamps on the dais. The earl rose to make a toast. The crowd grew silent and attentive. "To the king," he declared.

"To the king," they responded in unison.

"To the prince," he toasted once more.

"To the prince," they responded.

"Today," he announced, "I introduce to the world on the occasion of her sixteenth birthday, my ward Lady Alice de Toeni."

Alice bowed her head demurely in acknowledgement, failing to conceal a quick glance at the prince. Pen nodded to her in response.

The prince sat, followed by Warwick, and then by the guests in the hall. The music continued as a steady stream of servitors delivered pitchers of wine, plates of meats of all kinds, wild game, peacocks stuffed with oysters and chestnuts, apples, breads, and several varieties of fish.

In the eyes of the earl, the banquet and Lady Alice's introduction had been a great success. Alice had her doubts.

~~~

At the conclusion of the festivities, the earl invited the prince and Charlotte, Lord and Lady Marmion and Elizabeth, and Lady Alice de Toeni to his private residence, where they gathered around a blazing fire to encourage intimate conversation. Attendants offered wine, tea, and biscuits to the guests.

"Charlotte," said the earl. "Permit me to introduce you personally to my ward Lady Alice de Toeni. You appear to be about the same age; and this is Elizabeth Marmion who resides with her parents Lord and Lady Marmion at Tamworth Castle."

The three girls looked at each other with a trace of suspicion. They smiled weakly and nodded.

"Charlotte comes to us from the village of Leamington," said Pen. "She has been tutored by a dean from Stonele Monastery. I have taken her as my ward to further her education."

Charlotte was quite beautiful and richly attired. Alice was crestfallen. Elizabeth sized up the situation and decided to stand out of the way as Alice, feeling herself on the defensive, sought to gain the prince's favor.

"Charlotte is a gifted storyteller," said Pen in an effort to crack the ice. "Alice, do you have a story to tell?"

Alice looked at her benefactor who beamed, in response to the question. "She can tell a story as well as anyone, better than most," he said.

"Do you have one for us?" said the prince.

"Let me tell you the scholar's tale?"

~~~

Once upon a time in the city of Pompeii lived a law clerk known as Brutus Abstemius. Brutus earned a small salary in service to the courts located in the Basilica, which rose majestically at the far end of the Forum.

Each morning he left his bed at dawn and dashed cold water onto his face. He carefully folded his blankets, donned a dark blue tunic over the underclothes in which he slept, and tied on his sandals for the short walk to the tribune's office where he worked. On his way, for breakfast, he purchased two slices of bread and a cup of wine from a street vendor in the Forum.

Beautiful Flavia Fabulus was the granddaughter of the notorious Sallust and husband of the handsome Richli Deservidus. They lived in the great Sallust house to which were attached six shops, including a bar.

Each morning at dawn they arose from their beds in their respective rooms. Richli dashed cold water on his face, tied on his sandals, and summoned his valet to help him into his white toga. For breakfast Richli ate a crust of bread washed down with a cup of wine, whereupon he set out to make his morning calls, which began with collecting the rents from his wife's tenants.

Beautiful Flavia's toilette took longer. She too had slept in her underclothes, a nighttime tunic, loincloth, and brassiere. She summoned her lady's maid who helped her into her outer wear, a red tunic called a stola with orange trim. All fashionable ladies wore their hair high on their heads in rising tiers of curls. For this preparation she summoned the ornatrix. Having finished her hair, the ornatrix applied chalk to the lady's brow, ashes for eye shadow, and red lead for rouge and lipstick. For breakfast she ate a crust of bread and drank a little wine before donning her cloak for a stroll in the Forum.

The legionary Vesuvius Eruptus lived in the barracks at the far end of town. Each day he would carry dispatches between his commander and the office of the proconsul in the Basilica. Many times he observed Beautiful

Flavia on her stroll in the Forum. His interest in her grew and he began to follow her at a discreet distance as she wove her way through the business district visiting jewelry and clothing shops.

One day, when the legionary could no longer bear to just observe her from afar, he decided to accost her politely in the hope of receiving a favorable response. In preparation for the occasion, he went to unusual lengths to assure that his helmet, shield, and sword shone brightly, that his short tunic was spotless, and his well-muscled body glistened with oil. On his way to his hoped-for rendezvous, he stopped at the Sallust bar and gulped down three cups of wine.

Armed with an empty dispatch case and filled with the courage of the grape, he strode down the middle of the Forum toward the Basilica and contrived to intercept Beautiful Flavia and her maidservant.

"Good morning, my lady," he said.

Beautiful Flavia was taken aback. "Who are you?" she asked.

"I am Vesuvius Eruptus," he said with an unsteady bow.

"Is that supposed to mean something to me?" she replied. "I can see that you are a legionary, a bit of a ruffian, even if you are a rather good looking one."

"Praise from one as beautiful as yourself is undeserved by this humble creature. Please, I beg of you, tell me your name."

"I am Flavia Fabulus of the house of Sallust, and you are out of line."

"It is my love for the beautiful woman who stands before me that drives me to such madness."

Flavia's maidservant suppressed a smile.

"Come, Hebe," said Beautiful Flavia to the young woman. We must be on our way. His rough stonemason's hands have built roads and aqueducts. They are too unrefined to build a bridge of love between us."

The two women abruptly abandoned the lovesick Vesuvius, but not before young Hebe tossed him a sly smile.

Vesuvius was disappointed that his first attempt to promote a liaison with his fantasy lover came to naught, but it would not be his last. The following day he had actual dispatches to deliver, and while in the Basilica spotted a pale young man inscribing documents. A man of learning, he thought.

"Sir," he said. "I see you are a man of letters. I am in need of your assistance. I will pay you two sesterces for your services."

Brutus Abstemius listened to the man's story, how he fumbled for words in his quest for the favor of a noble lady.

"I will write the words," said Brutus, "and take your money. Study the words carefully and recite them as your own."

Having completed his morning rounds, Flavia's husband Richli Deservidus took himself to the Stabian baths where he exercised in the central sports field. After working up a sweat he plunged into the warm pool. He adjusted himself to the temperature and moved to the very hot pool. From there he plunged into the icy cold pool. In the next to last step in this ritual, he exited to cover himself in oil and pour sand over his body. Using a strigil he scraped himself clean and repaired to the barber's chair for a shave.

The public baths in Pompeii were available for the use of all citizens. It was not unusual for Richli Deservidus to wile away another hour at a nearby brothel at the same time Vesuvius Eruptus was taking his place in the baths. They must have passed each other going in and out, not knowing their paths would cross again in an unexpected way.

Brutus rolled his eyes as he wrote out a speech for the legionary lout who believed in his heart he might actually have a chance to take Beautiful Flavia as his lover. Vesuvius eagerly gave Brutus the money and took his precious script to the countryside for study. Brutus was not an unkind man and so he tried to keep the language as simple as possible without condescending. After a week, Brutus felt he was ready for his second encounter with Beautiful Flavia.

"Oh, it is you again," said Flavia, when the legionary accosted her in the Forum. "I hope you have a more polished speech to deliver this time."

Vesuvius was emboldened by this obvious invitation to make his case to her once again. "You have chosen not to close off my heart with a glance of dismissal or word of reproof. It is with gladness that I allow the spurs of desire to drive me forward in my quest for your approval. If you will be patient and not dismiss me as a knave or a fool, I shall attempt to rise above my inadequacies in search of your favor.

"Love rises above social distinctions. It is not the sole property of either high born or the low. Love is like the attraction between two lodestones that are draw to each other by an invisible force. Love is nature and so I may select as the object of my love any woman I choose, as long as I have no depravities or defects of character."

"I could not agree more," said the man in the white toga, who had just joined the conversation. "Legionary, I am Richli Deservidus, husband of the beautiful woman you are addressing."

Taken aback, Vesuvius interrupted his speech. He was a trained warrior and unafraid of any potential physical conflict, but the thought of verbal combat with this man terrified him.

"S-sir," he stuttered. "You wife is a beautiful woman."

"She is, isn't she?"

"Yes, she is, a beautiful woman, I mean."

"Have I not seen you at the Stabian baths?" said Richli.

"You have, sir."

"I say, when you have finished here, why not join me there for a sporting match? When we are finished, I will buy you a drink at my bar up the street, the Sallust place. That is where we live. I will see you there, then, say in one hour. Now, I must be off. I have one more business errand to run."

"Do not say another word," said Beautiful Flavia to the legionary. "Your noble attempt to upset the order of things compels me to inform you that you are engaging in an exercise in futility. Love, of course, does not make distinctions among class, but love's arrow cannot bridge the class divide. Love's arrows may fly hither and yon, but they are able to reach only a certain height. I can assure you, legionary, that I am beyond your reach. Now tell me, who wrote those lovely words for you?"

Vesuvius made the best out of a losing situation by turning his attention to Beautiful Flavia's maidservant Hebe.

"His name is Brutus Abstemius, my lady," he said as they parted. "You can find him in an office over in the Basilica."

~~~

Flavia Fabulus rifled through her files and pulled out an old contract for wine deliveries to her bar. "Hmm, I think this provision can be struck out, and I will change the delivery schedule, not enough to make any difference, of course."

She tucked the document into the pocket of her cloak and she and Hebe headed for the Basilica. The legionary watched them from across the Forum as they climbed the steps to the entrance.

"I will only be an hour or so," she said to Hebe. "I am sure I saw that bold legionary staring at us as we crossed the Forum. Why do you not go over and talk to him while I am inside."

Hebe beamed with pleasure and scampered off. Beautiful Flavia accosted a clerk with a load of boxes and asked where she might find Brutus Abstemius."

"Down the corridor. Third door on the left."

Flavia entered the cramped space where Brutus labored over his documents. "I am Flavia Fabulus," she announced.

Brutus stood up from his bench, took one look at her and was smitten.

"I have some minor contract work that needs to be done. Do you think you can help me?"

"I - I, yes, my lady. That is why I am here."

She handed him the contract and explained what needed to be done. He barely looked at it, because he could not take his eyes off Beautiful Flavia.

One week later she returned to pick up the amended contract. Brutus was a wreck. He had not slept. He could barely eat. His already lean frame was gaunt.

"Are you ill?" she inquired.

"I am sick with love, my lady. It is a sickness only you can cure. From this day forward, until you are mine, I shall neither sleep nor eat, but devote all my energies to writing odes of glory in your honor. Though I may waste away to nothing and my body die, my love for you is eternal and will shine brightly as a star in the sky to the end of eternity."

"You really did write those words for the legionary, didn't you?"

"I have been discovered, most beautiful creature. You have revealed me to be a fraud, using the mouth of that brawny soldier to voice my deepest feelings."

"But we had never met at that time. You did not know me."

"You did not know me, mistress, but I have known you. I have pined for your love from a distance for many months. It is only through Cupid's *intervention that we have chanced to meet in person. Otherwise, it never could have happened."*

"I must go now," said Beautiful Flavia. "Weep not. I shall return in one week."

Once again, Brutus neither ate nor slept. He wrote rhapsodically about his love. He was near a state of physical collapse when they next met.

~~~

"Whatever became of that legionary who so fancied you?" said Richli.

"I do not know whether to feel flattered or insulted, but it no longer matters. He has taken up with one of the servants. A better match, I should think."

"Flavia, I will be sailing to Greece tomorrow. I believe the business is in order. I should return in two or three months. Perhaps I will have a surprise for you."

"Wonderful," she said. "You know how I love surprises."

The surprise arrived sooner than either of them expected. The ship on which Richli Deservidus sailed was lost at sea in a storm. There were no survivors.

~~~

Brutus Abstemius maintained a respectful distance from Flavia Fabulus until the prescribed period of mourning had passed. He continued to pine away growing ever more emaciated until the day it was socially acceptable to resume his quest.

"I see that you do truly love me," said Beautiful Flavia. "You may now ask me to be your wife."

"Cupid be praised," gushed Brutus. "My prayers have been answered."

Vesuvius Eruptus continued to pursue the maid Hebe, but she always kept him at a safe distance. The legionary stopped eating; he did not sleep well. In time, his once robust and muscular body shriveled to an empty husk. Though Hebe was quite convinced of his love for her, she was never able to commit to a relationship that would heal his breaking heart.

Brutus Abstemius and his new wife were blissful in their marriage. His appetite returned and he slept well at night. He recovered from his wasted physical state and grew fat with contentment.

"You do not love me anymore," wailed Beautiful Flavia. "If you still did, you would weep in my absence. You would worship the earth on which I walked. You would stay pale and thin."

When Brutus was not engaged with his contracts at the Basilica, he was working on his book, Love Regained.

Beautiful Flavia continued her morning strolls in the Forum in the company of her maidservant Hebe.

"Have you ever noticed that good looking man over there who stares at us every time we come by here?" said Beautiful Flavia to Hebe.

"I have," she replied. "He looks at you like a puppy dog."

Serenity reigned in Pompeii. Beautiful Flavia's new lover grew thinner. So did Vesuvius Eruptus. Brutus grew fat and continued to work on his book, all until. . . the year 79.

~~~

"What a wonderful story, Lady Alice," said Pen enthusiastically. "Elizabeth, we have heard from Lady Alice, do you have a story to tell?"

"I could tell you the story of Ceresia," she said.

Everyone in the room applauded and encouraged her to continue.

"I am not as good at this as Lady Alice," she said, "but I do have my convictions."

~~~

Ceresia stood atop a low hill and surveyed the verdant expanse that was the Valley of Plenty. The sounds she heard were those of twittering birds and the occasional anguished bellow of some large, hoofed creature falling to hunters' spears. The air was redolent with the fragrance of flowers mixed with smoke rising from roasting meat. A shadow, the giggles of children, the murmurs of women gossiping among themselves as they gathered roots and berries from the forest, furnished the idyll.

Not content with her people's lot, Ceresia exhorted them to take more from the land.

"Do not slay the oxen," she said. "They are more valuable to you in front of a plough than on a spit."

But, the people were content, and, at first, paid her no mind.

"I will show you a better way," she insisted.

She urged her husband Phestus to build a smithy. They cut down trees. They made charcoal. They roasted red ore to make iron, which her husband forged into ploughs.

"What do we do with these?" the local hunters inquired.

"I will show you," said Ceresia as she proceeded to harness the oxen to the ploughs. She goaded them forward and the ploughshares dug deep into the loam. Into the furrows she dropped seeds. "Come back later," she said to the hunters. "Come back later and see what I have wrought."

The hunters disappeared into the wood, off to slay their quarry and nearly forgot about the silly woman who made dirt out of grasslands, promising them a better life to come. The rains came and in time rows of green shoots appeared where Ceresia had made her furrows. Their shoots grew tall and green. The season turned and green went to amber. Golden heads laden with grain nodded heavily in the wind.

The hunters were curious, and, sated with roasted venison washed down with good mead made from wild honey, rose from their nap and found their way to the place of Ceresia and her husband. The floor of the valley was lush with primrose and mallow except for the wide gash opened by Ceresia's plough. Row upon row of ripe heads of grain waved in unison at the whim of the breeze.

"Of what use is this?" they asked.

"I will teach you what to do with the fruits of this labor. You will have flour. You will have bread. You will have beer. Beer is ever so much better than mead."

They all laughed. "Nothing is better than mead."

"I will prove it to you," she said. "You men there, spread this cloth between two rows. Good. Now bend the grain over the cloth and beat it with these switches."

The men were in a good mood and gladly sought to humor her. They set about the task and then inspected with some amazement the grain they *had just threshed. A man gathered a handful and let it trickle through his fingers.*

"Pig feed," he said, as he ground a few kernels between his teeth. "You put in a lot of work just to make pig feed, when we can just give them scraps and let them forage for the rest."

"Follow my example," she said, "and you will grow happier and stronger."

"But we are already happy," they rejoined. "We hunt. We kill. We eat. We drink. What more could we want?"

"Wealth and prosperity," she said.

And so the men set about the myriad tasks that would lead them to a better life.

"We will need ploughs," they said.

"My husband Phestus forges the finest ploughs in the valley."

The men descended on the smithy and soon bought up all the ploughs. When the supply ran out and they needed more, the iron mines expanded and the smelters blazed hot. Wages in the mines and factories and the price of ploughs went up. As far as the eye could see across the valley was row upon row of grain fields. The once lovely land was fenced off in a checkerboard of private plots. No longer was the land owned in common by everyone. Game that once grazed the valley floor moved into the forest or to faraway places where there were no ploughs.

The hunters who used to roam the valley now settled into villages next to their fields. They built mills on the river to which they took their harvest to be ground into flour. Bakeries and breweries turned that harvest into the promised bread and beer. Ceresia and Phestus grew rich and built a large house. Their children dressed in fine clothes and paraded through the streets, reminding the peasants of who they were. The sons and daughters of the baker and brewer bragged about their wealth and laughed at the peasant children who used to be their friends.

The hunters set aside their spears to tend to their crops, taking them up only to fight each other over property lines and business disputes. Strife among them increased until one day they banded together, marched to Ceresia's great house, and demanded she listen to their grievances. When she appeared, they all began to shout at once.

"Have I not brought you prosperity?" she said.

"*You brought us prosperity, but not in equal measure to all. When once we were a happy people with little need to own more than a spear to bring down game and a basket in which to collect berries, we are now a people of 'yours' and 'mine.' We are divided between rich and poor. We fight over portions of everything. Gone is the curve of the sickle, now straightened and polished into the sword. Gone is each man bearing his share of the common burden. Some of our people grow fat and lazy, while others are emaciated.*"

"*Calm yourselves,*" *said Ceresia.* "*What would you have me do? I offered you progress and you seized it. I cannot now take it away and return to you an idyll you imagine you once had. We know you cannot step into the same river twice. You waste your time if you try. Look forward instead. Vow not to repeat your mistakes. Turn your unrest into a quest for the future. Remember, that river of tomorrow will not be the same as the river of today.*"

~~~

"That was a fine story, Elizabeth," said Pen, "even though it was a bit subversive. Earl, Lord and Lady Marmion, I have a proposition to make. I would be honored if you would permit your young ladies to take up temporary residence at Kenilworth, where they might continue with their education. It would be at no cost to you and she would be in the excellent company of Charlotte Giveney and the court tutors and masters."

Any sense of competition among the girls vanished as they embraced the offer with enthusiasm.

Chapter Six

Three Maids

With the arrival of three special girls, life at Kenilworth Castle grew merry. Pen had a plan for the future, and in anticipation of its maturation he built living rooms incorporated into the curtain wall across the inner bailey from the keep. It was there he installed his new wards and Lady Ariel. He retained the suite of rooms for himself, Eldric, and Kallias on the first story of the keep.

Pen chose the first day of May, Beltane, the traditional day of celebration of the beginning of summer, to reveal his secret to his wards. He summoned them and Lady Ariel to his private chambers, welcoming them dressed in a purple satin robe and sandals.

"I have chosen you to become members of my inner circle," he began. "We have only one hard rule, and that is what you see, learn, and hear inside these precincts is privileged information and must never be revealed to anyone on the outside. I must have your solemn oath on that. Do you agree, Charlotte, Alice, and Elizabeth?"

The three girls were flattered and somewhat confused, but they all readily agreed to the conditions. Eldric and Kallias positioned themselves, one on each side of Pen. Eldric untied the sash and let it fall. He then took one lapel and Kallias took the other. They opened the robe to the gasps of the three onlookers. Before them stood the prince, the Duke of Warwick, the Earl of Snowdonia, the heir to the English throne, in the form of a finely toned athletic young woman – a woman with a beard.

"Before you faint," said Pen. "Kallias, do the honors."

Kallias stepped forward and removed the hair and makeup he had applied to Pen's face every day since he became a member of the court. Pen shook her head to loosen her abundant golden hair.

"This is the secret, young women, the secret you have sworn never to reveal. I am not a man at all and never have been, just a young woman, except for my royal lineage, not unlike yourselves. Of this fact, the king is unaware. For reasons of state I have chosen to perpetuate this masquerade. Perhaps in the future the matter will become clearer to you. But, for now, we have work to do. If I have read each of you correctly, I think we have much in common."

"But your lordship, your ladyship," said Charlotte. "How shall we address you?"

"Among ourselves you may use 'your ladyship,' if you choose. Elsewhere, I shall be in disguise and you must address me as always as a man. Later, as you will learn, we shall have to adopt different rules."

"Dress me, Eldric," said Pen. That done, he said, "You may leave us now. Girls, you stay."

Three young women about in their mid teens and Pen at twenty sat in a circle facing each other. They were similarly dressed in colorful loose-fitting robes tied with sashes at the waist worn over cotton lawn chemises.

"We are now sisters," said Pen. "Today, I am not your sovereign, but your friend."

Their sense of relief was palpable. The absence of men was a veil lifted. Then they all started talking at once.

"My guardian presented me today in the hope that your ladyship would choose me to be your wife," said Alice. "Can you imagine anything funnier than that?"

The girls had trouble at first shifting their sense of propriety from one subordinate to a lord to one of embracing a sister. There was a clash of values that demanded of them the highest degree of discipline of thought and action. To include Pen in their circle of trust required the violation of a tradition of the separation of classes imbued from the cradle. But Pen needed them as much as the girls needed each other, and the future monarch had to earn their trust as much as they had to earn hers.

"You are all well schooled," said Pen, "but I have plans for our future that will bear fruit only if you all agree. There is work to be done in the world. We are not destined to sit by the hearth weaving and telling stories to our children, unless those stories are of substance and adventure. We are women who will make a difference."

"Your ladyship," Charlotte ventured to say. "I am of an age to wed and I have feelings for a boy in my village. What am I to do?"

"I too have feelings, Charlotte. That should not surprise you. We will come to terms with it. I ask you to place your trust in me. We are one. If you will pledge yourself to me and your sisters, you will come to realize all that is the best in you."

"There is a page, your ladyship, in my father's own court," said Elizabeth. "He is a very sweet boy and I have great fondness for him."

"Little Alice, my friend Alice," said Pen. "What about you?"

Alice broke into tears as she confessed that her love was for the prince, or the princess, or whoever Pen really was.

~~~

Pen, as the prince, gathered his flock to an upper room in the keep. Joining them was Sir Llewellyn ap Rhudd and Sir Guy de Lacy.

"Ladies, you will be shocked by what I present to you today. Lying to the east is the empire of Genghis Khan. He is dead, but his descendants are not. We, of the stodgy west, have clung to our traditional costumes, but the great marauder has taught us how to dress to be mounted warriors. As properly reared young ladies you have been trained in the side-saddle tradition. We will change that. You will learn to ride astride, and Sir Guy will be your instructor. Don't gasp. I understand certain proprieties regarding our sex. Khan's gift to us is trousers."

"What are trousers?" Elizabeth asked timidly.

"Trousers are like braies only made for outerwear."

"That's nasty," said Elizabeth.

"You will be wearing short braies underneath," said Pen. "You will get used to them and actually find them quite comfortable. The next thing for you to do is go to the castle dressmaker where the seamstress will take your measurements. I have ordered a shipment of split calfskin leather for your riding trousers. When they are ready your new equestrian training with Sir Guy will begin. In the meantime, Sir Llewellyn will begin your archery training. It has become quite fashionable for the ladies to engage in the sport. What Sir Llewellyn will teach you goes well beyond that. Ladies, the other half of your new double life begins."

~~~

 The bowyer shop turned out a supply of longbows four and one-half feet in length with a pull of twenty-five pounds. They were matched to the small stature of Pen's merry recruits. They dressed in their usual chemises with ankle-length robes tied around the waist. For purposes of their archery training they donned snug-fitting knee-length kirtles* and tied up their long hair to keep it out of the way.

Training began with the usual exercises to increase upper body strength.

"I can't do this," Alice complained.

"Yes, you can," said the daughter of Leamington. "You just are not used to doing much physical work."

The prince stepped in and said. "I know you won't disappoint me. I promise that your work will be rewarded." He nocked an arrow and loosed it at a wooden target at the far end of the keep, where it stuck with a thud and vibrated for a moment, like the chastening finger of a stern schoolmaster. "You, too, will be able to do that," he said, "but only if you work hard enough. You have not changed your mind about your decision, have you?"

"No, your grace," said Elizabeth sheepishly. "I will try harder."

The three girls quickly got into the rhythm of their daily workouts. They pulled on empty bows and learned to nock the arrow and pull again. As they grew stronger and their archery skills advanced, Sir Llewellyn began their instruction in the fine art of swordplay. They began with wooden replicas, but soon graduated to specially crafted swords similar to Pen's. They would practice with each other and then drop their swords to continue the exercise with only a dagger. They were light, lithe, and quick on their feet and soon mastered the martial arts to Pen's satisfaction.

When they finally got over their embarrassment at riding astride dressed in their new riding trousers, they made rapid gains in horsemanship. After a year of training, Pen announced they had arrived at graduation day.

A small banquet for the girls and a few selected members of the court was held in the great hall. The prince stepped down from the dais and summoned the three forward. They bowed and knelt before him.

"This is your graduation day," he said. "I am very proud of the hard work you have put in and the great progress you have made. Here, today, we establish a new order, and you are its founding members. We are the Monks of Arden. I have asked you to present yourselves in your working attire. This is how you will be dressed when we set out on our missions. Over your surcoat and kirtle you will wear the distinctive forest green monk's cowl I present to you today. Each of you also receives a custom-made bow with ivory inlays, and a matching sword and dagger with baldric. Sir Guy and Sir Llewellyn distributed the gifts and everyone in the hall and raised a cup in salute to the pioneering young women.

Solemnly, they put on their weapons and covered themselves with their cowls. To an outsider, they would have looked like three small monks dressed in habits of an unusual color. To an insider, they looked like clever young adventurers ready for whatever Fate had in store for them.

~~~

Grooms steadied their mounts as the Monks of Arden swung themselves up into the saddle. Pen, as the prince, took the lead. He was accompanied by Sir Guy and his squire on one side, and Eldric, who served as Pen's squire on the other side. Sir Guy served as garrison commander at Kenilworth, but first and foremost, by order of the king, he was Pen's principal bodyguard. Charlotte, Elizabeth, and Alice rode behind and Sir Llewellyn brought up the rear. All wore their trademark forest green cowls. The only sign they were not just a group of unusually prosperous looking monks was a small crest of the House of Plantagenet visible on Pen's horse's caparison.

The band of eight headed west through the forest on a path to Henley-in-Arden seven miles away, tracking poachers reported by the gamekeeper to be in the area. Pen wished this to be a training exercise for his wards, who were taking all this quite seriously.

A side path a few miles in led to a small clearing, where Pen proposed they set up a small camp. The wards joined the squires in gathering firewood as Pen and his two knights looked on. Sir Guy instructed them in the art of building a fire ring and makeshift lean-to shelters. They were proud of what they had accomplished and were busy giggling and congratulating themselves when two men-at-arms appeared at the edge of the clearing. Sir Guy and Sir Llewellyn instinctively rose to the occasion, weapons at the ready.

Pen watched his knights, his wards, and the squires to see how they would react to the situation. Pen had seen to it that they were well-trained. They quickly abandoned their frivolity, seized their weapons and formed a defensive line.

"Monks," demanded the lead intruder. "Who are you?"

Pen stood in silence beside his horse. The men spotted the Plantagenet crest. "Your grace," they said as they nearly tumbled off their horses in surprise. "We did not recognize you at first." Pen stepped forward and threw back his hood. The men knelt before him. "You may rise," he said. "What brings you into the forest today?"

"Lady Caroline de Montfort of Beaudesert Castle required an outing. My men and I are accompanying her."

"Where is she?" said Pen, as a young woman on horseback in the company of her lady's maid came to the fore. Pen offered her a hand as she dismounted.

"I am Lady Caroline, your grace" she said.

"The pleasure is mine, Lady Caroline. "I am Pen Plantagenet."

"My father has spoken highly of you, your grace."

"And how is he? I hope he bears me no ill will after that fracas with your Uncle Henry."

"My father was not a sympathizer, your grace. They were barely related, and even that connection is lost to history."

"You may stand down," said Pen to the Monks. "Please join us, Lady Caroline. We are roasting a pig we will gladly share with you and your men."

"You are most gracious."

"These are my wards, Charlotte Giveney, Lady Elizabeth Marmion, and Lady Alice de Toeni. We call ourselves the Monks of Arden."

Lady Caroline was statuesque and exhibited considerable equestrian skill as she rode up.

"I see that your wards are armed. I, too, have received some modest training in the martial arts."

"Your grace," said Charlotte. "I propose a contest. Let us find out how skilful she truly is."

"Do you accept the challenge, Lady Caroline?" said Pen.

"I do," she said, "though my humble skills will surely be put to shame by your wards."

"We shall soon find out," said Alice.

Eldric fashioned a wooden target and set it up at the edge of the clearing fifty paces from where they were gathered.

"Sir Llewellyn, a bow and arrows for Lady Caroline."

The wards removed their cowls to display their girded bodies.

"I shall have to make do," said Lady Caroline. "Agnes, bind me."

The maid fetched a wide leather belt with crossed straps that went over the shoulders. On the right side a stiff leather gusset inserted between the belt and strap pressed her right breast flat against her body. The wards looked at Lady Caroline and at each other, nodding in approval of her special garment. "I am ready," she said.

Lady Caroline tested the bow. "This will do nicely," she said. A sense of confidence in her own prowess was clearly evident.

The four young women stood in line and took turns sending arrows to the target. After three rounds, a dozen arrows were clustered so tightly in a small circle that three of the arrows had been split by ones that followed.

"I cannot declare a winner," said Pen. "This was a very fine contest. You are a woman of talent, Lady Caroline. Are you also schooled?"

"I am, your grace. My father has hired the finest tutors from London to instruct me and my brothers. He feels it is unfair to penalize women, denying them an education on account of their sex."

"We all live rather some distance from the intellectual centers of England. To what use do you intend to put your learning?"

"I am becoming a writer," said Lady Caroline. "Becoming?" said Pen.

"Yes, your grace. I have been collecting folk tales from the people of the villages."

"Would you do us the honor of telling one of your stories?"

"It would be my honor, your grace."

~~~

This is a love story. The forest begins here and goes all the way up to there. The forest is home to many creatures, some large, some small, some good, and some very bad. Mr. Marmot was a good and happy creature who spent his days in search of Miss Marmotte who had escaped his attentions some time before. Mr. Marmot was happy because he was fond of Miss Marmotte and he had special talent. Unlike most others of his kind, he could make music on his toenails. He could play simple tunes of ten different notes or, if he felt particularly exuberant, he could lie on his back and strum tunes with twenty notes. He had composed several serenades in praise of Miss Marmotte, which he performed by strumming several toenails at once.

Mr. Woody, the wood thrush, and Mr. Thumper, the rabbit, often joined him to form a musical ensemble that delighted all the creatures of the forest. He hoped that the lure of the beautiful music would bring Miss Marmotte back to him.

Mr. Marmot shuffled along a path that led him to a river. As he got closer, he heard the sound of water splashing. He crept forward, just to be on the safe side, and peeked through the bushes at the source of the sound.

Mr. Marmot stood on the edge of a precipice, over which tumbled a waterfall. Below was a furry gray creature with a bulbous pink nose and a long naked tail. He was tumbling an oaken cask in the water and singing loudly out of tune. Mr. Marmot, who was accustomed to fine music, wrinkled his nose at the sound. He shouted at the creature hoping the distraction might cause him to cease making that awful noise. It did.

"Hello, sir," said the creature. "I am Mr. O. Possum, and who might you be?"

"I am Mr. Marmot," he said, "and I am looking for Miss Marmotte. You would not perchance have seen her, would you?"

"I am afraid not, sir. I am busy scrubbing out this cask, from which I have recently drawn a very fine wine." Mr. O. Possum reached into his pouch and withdrew a bladder of liquid. He bit off the stopper and handed

it to Mr. Marmot. "Come down and try this," he said. "There's nothing finer."

Mr. Marmot obliged him and tipped the bladder up in front of his face. A ruby red liquid squirted out and he lapped it up eagerly. "Hmm," he said. "You are certainly a master winemaker. May I offer you in return some bread and cheese?"

"Thank you, kindly," said Mr. O. Possum, as he swallowed his repast. "Very good. Goes well with the wine, if I may say so."

"You may say so," said Mr. Marmot, "and I agree."

Mr. Marmot drank some more and soon began to sing to the accompaniment of his toenails. "My love is lost. She leaves me destitute. I am drunk on her smile and only joyful in her presence. Come back to me. Come back to me, Miss Marmotte."

~~~

Miss Marmotte tripped along the path, deep in her thoughts, paying no attention to her surroundings and oblivious to the distress she was causing Mr. Marmot. Quite by accident she stepped on Mr. Snake, who was minding his own business as he warmed himself in the sun.. Both he and Miss Marmotte were startled out of their wits, and Mr. Snake, as nature had instructed him, lashed out and bit Miss Marmotte, who died on the spot.

"O my goodness. O dear. What has happened?" he said as he looked at the lifeless body. "O well, what is done is done. At least she won't be sneaking up on old Mr. Snake again."

~~~

Mr. Marmot knew right away what had happened, even though they were far apart. The angels of death wafted Miss Marmotte's body above the trees and spirited her off to a resting place among the fallen leaves. Bereft, Mr. Marmot wandered aimlessly believing that somehow he would find Miss Marmotte again.

"Marmot, Marmot," he heard. Soft voices reached his ears. They were of the Misses Mousie who scampered across his path bearing garlands of flowers. "Marmot, Marmot," they called again and again.

"The forest god has sent us, Mr. Marmot," they said.

"Can you help me?" Mr. Marmot wailed. "I am so unhappy. I miss her so. I want her back."

The Misses Mousie danced a circle around his legs, and before he could stop himself, he began strumming on his toenails, playing a quiet serenade. Mr. Woody was in the trees and chimed in with an obligato. Mr. Thumper beat out the rhythm with his hind feet. It was a beautiful sound. Mr. Marmot's spirits rose, but only a little.

Mr. Marmot must have drifted off in sleep, because he awoke to find his companions were nowhere to be seen. He ambled forward and soon found himself among berry bushes heavy with ripe, red fruit, and nut trees sagging under the weight of their burden. Until he saw the plenty surrounding him, in his loss he had not thought of food. His stomach growled, reminding him that the spirit must be sustained by the body. At first he nibbled at the fruit and nuts, but soon was gorging himself at nature's table of plenty.

"My friends," he called out. "Join me, and we shall make music." One by one, woodland creatures came out of hiding: a porcupine, a pangolin, tiny shrews, a vixen and her cubs, and a chorus of bullfrogs joined the ensemble. Mr. Marmot began to play. The Misses Mousie resumed their singing, and soon the voice of a mighty chorus was rising above the tree tops.

"We know where Miss Marmotte is," they sang, "and we will take you there." The grand, singing parade moved deeper into the wood, until they came to a large opening in the earth.

"Follow me," said Mr. Pangolin, as he headed into the burrow. "Old Mr. Badger used to live here, but he was ill-tempered and one day wandered off, never to be heard from again."

Mr. Pangolin's armor clattered noisily as he disappeared into the tunnel. Mr. Marmot followed. Though it was dark, Mr. Pangolin and Mr. Marmot were quite accustomed to finding their way around underground. They descended deeper and deeper, far deeper than Mr. Marmot had ever gone. They made shuffling sounds as they descended, and much to Mr. Marmot's shock, they heard a growl. The growl turned into a sharp bark.

"Don't worry about him," said Mr. Pangolin. "That's just Mr. Mastiff who guards the place. He tried to take me on once. I gave him a good lashing and he's been sweet and gentle ever since."

Unseen hands propelled them forward. "Miss Marmotte, Miss Marmotte," he called. Mr. Marmot sensed that he was in a room. A faint *light from an unseen source illuminated the area, and he saw that it was true. Not only was he in an underground room, but standing before him were two creatures covered in shaggy red hair.*

"Mr. Marmot," he said. "I am the Emperor Orang from the Kingdom of Samudra. This is my wife, the empress. A dispatch from above informs me that you are seeking your lost love, Miss Marmotte. Is that correct?"

"Indeed, I am, your majesty."

"Perhaps we can help you. What do you have to offer me in return?"

"I am a great musician," said Mr. Marmot as he flipped over on his back and began to strum his toenails.

"Stop, stop," said the emperor, covering his ears. "We have no need of music down here, or singing, or poetry, or any of that nonsense; and only a jester would strum his toenails in the presence of his sovereign."

"My sister once picked up a set of Pan Pipes," said the empress. "She has no talent. She made such an awful noise that my husband was soured on music and the arts after that."

"You may play and sing well enough, but you have no place down here. Now, be gone. Out of here before I set Mr. Mastiff on you."

The empress laid a hand on the emperor's arm to calm him and beseeched him to grant Mr. Marmot clemency.

"My wife, Empress Orang, has moved me to grant your wish – not in the name of music or poetry, you understand, but in the name of love, only love. Now, you must leave my kingdom immediately. Scamper to the forest floor above, do not look back and Miss Marmotte will follow you."

"O, thank you majesty," said Mr. Marmot. "How can I ever repay you?"

"Enough, enough. Be gone now, and don't look back until you're on the surface."

Mr. Marmot sensed he was getting near the entrance to the tunnel. Roots and bulbs protruded from the walls. Is she behind me? he thought. She must be. He turned to look.

"O, Mr. Marmot, what have you done? You looked back. They're pulling me, pulling me down. Hold on to me."

Mr. Marmot reached for Miss Marmotte in time to watch her vanish in a puff of smoke. He returned to the tunnel, bent on trying again, but was met by nothing. Down, down he went until he was stopped at the edge of dank and foul-smelling river beyond which was more nothing. Mr.

Marmot returned to the top and waited by the entrance for a year. He played no music, sang no songs; only pined for his lost love.

When he finally gave up, bereft, dispirited, Mr. Marmot shuffled off into the depths of the forest. By chance he wandered into a circle where Mr. and Mrs. Wolf were teaching their cubs to hunt. The wolves pricked up their ears. "This is where you get to practice your skills," Mrs. Wolf whispered to her young.

Mrs. Wolf gave the signal and they all converged on their hapless prey. Mr. Marmot did not try to get away. He did not scream. All that was heard was, "I am coming, Miss Marmotte, I am coming."

~~~

A prompt exchange of documents between Pen and de Montfort paved the way for Caroline to be admitted to the circle of warriors at Kenilworth. Upon her arrival, she joined the others in their physical training with an emphasis on the use of sword, dagger, and lance, areas of deficiency compared to her comrades.

Chapter Seven

Monks Chase

Pen summoned his chamberlain Lord Philip Ardsley and seneschal Sir Malcolm Edwards to his privy chambers.

"Gentlemen," he said, "I have need of a hunting lodge. I have identified a large clearing in the Arden several miles to the east where it is to be built. I have sent for Paolo di Firenze, Italian master builder, to oversee the project."

Pen began a charcoal sketch of his plan on a large sheet of paper. "A stream suitable for diversion runs along this side of the clearing. After the moat and pond have been excavated, you can surround the bailey with a wooden palisade. This will not be a fortress. The protection should only be substantial enough to discourage poachers and outlaws. The buildings, of course, will be inside: the gatehouse, hall, kitchen, stables, the gaol, the guest house, the Monks' quarters, and a small chapel. After all the construction has been completed, a temporary coffer dam placed downstream will fill the moat and pond."

"Do you have a preference for where we recruit the laborers?" said Sir Malcolm.

"The villages, of course, but they are to be paid a small wage. The workers have mouths to feed. I've secured their good will and would not want to lose it. They will be required to work one week each month until it is completed, which, given the fact of its modest size, should not take more than six months."

"Shall I prepare documents for the barons and landholders?"

"Yes," said Pen. "You will inform them that their tenants' labor will serve in lieu of ten percent of their annual royal assessment. The king is in good health today, but I wish to keep the political landscape clear for the eventual royal succession."

~~~

Once a month during the period of the hunting lodge construction, the Monks rode out to survey the forest. The rest of the time they spent in training and their studies in the arts, religion, philosophy, and mathematics with tutors from Oxford.

The young women reveled in their new life and the companionship of others like themselves that came with it. Only Alice had trouble making the adjustment.

"I know I am just being a silly girl," she said to Charlotte, "but I am still in love with the prince who never was. Her grace is not shy about our seeing her in her bath, and when I do, it makes me feel worse than ever."

"If I tell you something," said Charlotte, "you must swear on the bones of St. John never to tell anyone what you heard."

"What is it?"

"Swear?"

"Swear."

"I think there is something going on between her ladyship and Sir Guy. He has been looking at her funny lately."

"But he is her bodyguard. He is supposed to look at her. What's 'funny'?"

"Well, he looks at her like that cute squire Oswald looks at me when he gets the chance."

Caroline and Elizabeth joined the conversation.

"You have noticed it, too, haven't you, girls?"

"Noticed what?"

"The way Sir Guy looks at her ladyship. Alice does not see it."

"Oh, Alice only has eyes for Pen," said Caroline. "She does not see much else. Is that not right, darling?"

"I am embarrassed," said Alice.

"Don't be," said Elizabeth. "Cedric's brother Robert looks cow-eyes at me, and I look cow-eyes right back at him. In fact, he asked me to meet him behind the stables this very night."

The other three girls rushed to her giggling. "Are you going to do it?"

"If I can sneak by Lady Ariel, I will."

"She is a sound sleeper. She won't wake if you are quiet about it."

~~~

"Members of the court are gossiping about us, Sir Guy," said Pen.

"What are they saying, your lordship?"

"Lady Ariel told me she overheard them. The wards think we are lovers. If that were not bad enough, others in the court think the wards are my concubines."

"Lovers? You and I?" said Sir Guy as he burst out laughing. "Your lordship, I assure you that I live my life according to the strictest tenets of the chivalric code. Some day I may choose a wife to comfort me in old age, but a prince's lover? That is beyond all absurdity. I hope you do not take seriously the prattling of young girls and court busybodies. The wards are fine little warriors and good students, but they are still young girls with young girls' imaginations."

"Guy, a woman knows these things. We can read a man like a book. You are sending out some kind of signal they are picking up. Come, sit next to me."

"Yes, your grace. If I may say so, I believe you just misspoke yourself. You said 'we' when you must have meant 'they.'"

"You can stop pretending, Guy. I said 'we' and I meant 'we.' Tug on my beard."

"O my God," he said. "It comes off."

"Give me your hand,"

Pen pressed his palm against her breast. "You see, I do not have hair on my face and my voice is not deep and now you know the reason."

"I suspected something, your grace, but was never sure what it was. You are really a woman, aren't you?"

"I am. The wards and my yeoman know the truth. Kallias maintains my disguise. You are a good man, Sir Guy. I know you will not reveal this secret. It is imperative that my brother Edward, in particular, remain ignorant of the fact. Sir Geoffrey forced me to learn to fight and ride like a man, but he was always disappointed that I was not as strong as the other men. He never knew why. I am not suited to the joust, but I can handle a sword and a bow better than most, as you well know.

"From now on you must be careful in my presence. The girls have picked up on something, so be on guard lest others do the same. I wish to keep that badger in its burrow as along as possible."

~~~

"You are nothing but a usurper," sputtered Lord Ardsley. "I am chamberlain. I am his grace's confidant and adviser. Not you."

"Calm yourself, Ardsley," said Sir Guy. "The king appointed me the prince's bodyguard. I take that very seriously."

"It is no secret at court that Prince Edward and Piers Gaveston are more than just friends" said Ardsley. "And now there's talk about you and his lordship. What is with that family? How will princes who shun women carry on the family line? Edward is offensive and Penfelyn is wispy. And you, high-browed chivalric knight, you are an embarrassment."

"Lord Ardsley, I ought to thrash you for your remarks. Better yet, you should feel the point of my sword, but that is out of the question. The prince would have to find a new chamberlain and I would probably be out of a job. But keep it up and you and I will have it out one way or another."

"The royal succession is at stake here," said Ardsley. "Perhaps his lordship can be persuaded to take a mistress to straighten out his thinking."

~~~

"Lord Ardsley has his back up over what he perceives as my taking his place in your favor," said Sir Guy. "He thinks you should take a mistress in order to divert your attention from other men."

"I do intend to take a lover," said Pen, "but not in the way the chamberlain thinks."

Sir Guy's lightheartedness slipped at the implication.

"Do not be dispirited," said Pen. "My lover is to be you."

Sir Guy reacted with a mixture of anticipation and confusion.

"I cannot go on forever pretending to be what I am not, denying myself God-given pleasures when something can be done about it. But, I am still the prince and first in line in the royal succession. If I were a man, a bastard child here or there would be of little consequence. Being a woman, the story is quite different. I shall not become pregnant. That is an order. Do you understand? I have consulted Lady Ariel on this matter, and it is quite possible, yea imperative, that you deposit your man's spume far from my body. A pregnancy would be good for neither of us."

"My lady, I am both flattered and taken aback at your proposition. Be confident that the consequences of which you speak could never be a product of our union. When I was a boy, I suffered from inflammation of the stones, which rendered me unable to sire a child. Alas, I shall never experience the joys of fatherhood; the comfort of a wife, perhaps, but never of sons or daughters of my own."

~~~

Much to the delight of Sir Guy, and to the satisfaction of both, the consummation was accomplished with great felicity.

~~~

The completion of the royal hunting lodge called for a naming ceremony, a good excuse for a celebration. Pen had decided on the name Monks Chase.

Lord Philip Ardsley sent invitations to the Earl of Warwick, to Lord Philip Marmion and his wife, the de Montforts, the Giveneys, and to Abbot Robert de Hockele of Stonele Monastery, who would offer God's blessing. The word spread through Kenilworth, giving rise to much jockeying for position among the courtiers to see who would be invited.

There was never any question that the Monks would be in attendance along with Lady Ariel, Sir Llewellyn, Sir Guy, Eldric and Kallias, but the chamberlain and seneschal would remain behind to attend to the daily business of the castle. The prince appointed Gwyn de Lacy steward of the lodge. Sir Guy selected seven men-at-arms on foot and a mounted crossbowman and two mounted archers as an escort. Kenilworth's imperious cook Basil Brewet selected two kitchen helpers, two scullions, and four servitors to inaugurate the lodge's new kitchen. The wagoner had his two helpers. A dozen squires served the two knights with the mounted guards doing double duty as grooms in service to the nobles and guests.

Warwick, the Marmions, the de Montforts, and the abbot were all accompanied by their retinues, for a total of nearly a hundred people when added to the Kenilworth contingent. The early fall weather was splendid as the group made its way to the lodge. The court piper played a merry tune to the drummer's beat as they approached the palisade. Arriving at midday, Pen and the nobles crossed the east bridge at the gatehouse. The guards used the south bridge nearer the stables.

Pen and the honored guests emerged from the gatehouse onto the bailey to view the rustic splendor of the great hall rising two stories before them. To the right was the kitchen and to the left the Monks' quarters and guest house. The small chapel was located behind the residences at the northeast corner of the lodge. The men dismounted and helped the women down from their horses.

"Very impressive, your grace," said Lord Philip.

The Monks, dressed in ladies' attire, joined the other women as the men gathered to discuss the day's schedule.

"Ladies," said Lady Ariel. "If you will follow me I will give you a tour. You will want to see the quarters specially designed for your daughters and wards."

"Your girls' chaperone is showing the women around," said Pen to the men. "The naming ceremony will begin in one hour, followed by a brief entertainment and the banquet. In the meantime, we will tour the buildings and stables. As you can see, the lodge is of quite modest size. I built it for use by small hunting parties. I shall invite you back later for a stag hunt."

The abbot wandered among the guests, nodding and chatting until the hour of the ceremony arrived.

"Lords and ladies," said Pen. "I invite you now to gather at the entrance to the chapel. We are far too many in number to all fit inside and so the abbot will conduct the ceremony outside."

Standing before the small crowd, the abbot made the sign of the cross. "*In nomine Patris, et Filii, et Spirtus Sancti. Amen.* Inasmuch as God the Creator has blessed our sceptred isle with this beautiful Arden Forest filled with abundant game, and inasmuch as God has declared our destiny in the Book of Genesis, chapter one, verse twenty-six, as follows: *Let us make man in our image, after our likeness: and let him have dominion over the fish of the sea, and over the fowl of the air, and over the cattle, and over all the earth, and over every creeping thing that creepeth upon the earth*, go forth, Noble Lords, and slay the stag, slay the bear, slay the boar in His name. Today, his grace, Penfelyn Plantagenet, Duke of Warwick and Earl of Snowdonia, has declared this hunting lodge Monks Chase. God go with you and good hunting. *In nomine Patris, et Filii, et Spirtus Sancti. Amen.*"

~~~

Inside the great hall, in the rear was a small elevated balcony for the musicians. Pen had brought a few members of the Kenilworth Consort to play the panpipes, flute, harp, tambourine, and drum. They began playing as the guests arrived.

The banquet in the great hall was preceded by a robing ceremony. The consort played a two-bar fanfare before each presentation. Each of the servants received a white linen tunic, surcoat, and a mantle dyed russet. Leather girdles studded with bronze badges matched the brooches given to close the tunic to complete the costume. Men and women dressed similarly, although the women's robes were invariably longer. As a token of his esteem, Pen presented his noble guests with similar ensembles made of Lincoln scarlet, Samite and Sendal. Their brooches were of gold set with semi-precious stones.

The ceremony was accompanied by great bonhomie, and the good-natured socializing accompanied by the musical ensemble allowed the wards to slip off to their quarters next door. There, they shed their women's robes and donned warrior gear complete with their trademark dark green cowls. They changed quickly and returned to the hall before they were missed. The heads of the noble guests all turned toward the door as they made their entrance to an orchestral fanfare. Silently, they marched to a drumbeat in single file to line up behind an unusually low table on the dais.

"Where is Elizabeth?" Lady Marmion whispered to her husband.

Before he could answer, Pen said, "Ladies and gentlemen, honored guests, may I present the Monks of Arden."

Another fanfare sounded. The wards' faces had been hidden deep inside their hoods. On an unspoken command they executed a left-face in unison. One by one Pen lifted off their green mantles to reveal taut-bodied young female warriors clad in close-fitting surcoats and short kirtles* over leather riding breeches and boots. Each wore her archer's baldric with dagger and sword and carried her custom-made bow.

The guests let out a collective gasp. Lady Frances fainted.

"Lest you be deceived that your daughters and wards may have sacrificed a proper education at the temple of martial arts," said Pen as the Monks left the dais and exited the hall through a side door, "we present for your entertainment a small drama they have composed that draws on a popular legend chosen from among their literary texts. Mothers, you may take a breath as we set the scene."

Lady Frances revived and the other noble ladies composed themselves in the presence of the royal prince, not the least bit calmed by the obviously high spirits and robust good health displayed by their girls.

The panpiper, flutist and harpist played a quiet melody, as two men quickly placed over the low table on the dais a heavy tapestry that hung to the floor. They moved offstage and returned carrying a fabric screen held upright by its frame to block the view by the audience. They stood motionless for several seconds and exited stage left.

"We call this play, The Rescue of Cleodolinda," said Pen, and he too left the stage.

The audience heard a disturbance outside the stage door left. The drummer played a steady somber beat and the tambourine player shook his instrument in a rising crescendo. Snorting and growling followed the commotion as a large dragon crawled through the door and onto the stage. It had four twisted limbs and two black wings. The tail was long and screw-shaped. It was covered in hard green scales. An issue of smoke followed the sound of a great breath being drawn in. Each time it snorted, a new puff of smoke issued from under the stage tapestry.

The effect enchanted the audience. Lady Caroline, dressed in an ermine-trimmed robe and wearing a crown, entered to the accompaniment of a fanfare and took her place upstage from the dragon, which continued to puff smoke as she spoke. Each puff of smoke was followed by a vigorous shaking of the tambourine.

"Silene, my cherished peaceable kingdom, is in great peril," she declaimed. "This demon from Hell will not cease its depredations without a daily sacrifice of two sheep. This we have done faithfully, but now we run out of sheep."

"All right then," said the dragon to the sound of the tambourine. "Send me one of your maidens each day and you shall remain safe."

"I shall do it. If a king cannot protect his people, what good is he?" The king detached a purse from his girdle and thrust his hand deep inside. He rustled around for a few seconds then withdrew his hand to display a token.

"This token bears the name of the daughter of Theobaldus."

Alice came onstage to the tune of a single piper, wearing a white surcoat over her chemise. She bowed to the king, then flung herself down on the dais behind the dragon. "This I do for my people," she cried.

"Woe be unto us," said the king after a brief pause. "Another day has passed and another maiden must be sacrificed." He produced a token from his purse and announced that it bore the name of the daughter of Ambrosius.

Charlotte Giveney came onstage attired similarly to her predecessor, and flung herself down in sacrifice to the dragon.

The king, who had been dry-eyed throughout the season of the sacrifices of the town maidens, began to weep. "Alas," he cried, "we have run out of maidens to give. The only one remaining is my beloved daughter Cleodolinda. I am inconsolable."

Elizabeth Marmion as Cleodolinda entered from stage left, dressed in the rich robes of a princess. The king exited with tears steaming down his cheeks.

"Foul beast, I give myself to you in the name of the people of Silene. May you choke on my bones."

Just as she was about to fling herself down, the sound of hoof beats was heard coming from behind the audience. The musical ensemble joined in a fanfare. Through the main entrance to the hall rode Pen on horseback. He carried a lance and wore a white mantle emblazoned with a red Maltese cross. He spurred his horse to the front, a distance of not more than thirty paces. "Hold Princess," he said, raising his lance high in the air.

"Sir knight," she pleaded. "Go back, lest we perish together in the monster's maw."

"Perish I may," said the knight, "but perish you shall not. Go back inside the city wall where you will be safe. Leave this task to me."

"Aha," said the dragon. "At last someone worthy of my talents. Stupid sheep are tough and bleat. Fair maidens are tender and weep. I shall toy with you for a while before I send you off to your maker," and with that he emitted a great plume of smoke that enveloped the knight.

The knight gasped for air. His horse reared. "You will have to do better than that," he said.

The dragon howled louder and blew more clouds of smoke, each time to the rising and falling sound of the tambourine. The knight, growing weaker, knew he had to make his move before he expired, so he charged forward to the foot of the dais and plunged his lance downward where it stuck, imbedded in the wood. The dragon howled and writhed, and then went silent.

The consort played a quiet theme. The king and Cleodolinda came back on stage. "You have saved my daughter and my kingdom, sir knight. Whatever I have is yours."

"I'll take Cleodolinda," said the knight. The audience cheered.

Elizabeth and Charlotte rose from where they had concealed themselves on the floor behind the stage. Two stagehands lifted off the dragon's skin to reveal the presence of Eldric and Kallias. And finally, a sooty-faced scullion emerged from under the stage carrying his smoke machine.

The prince and his company smiled and bowed to their appreciative audience. The mothers' and guardians' fears had been laid to rest, although Lady Frances was overheard to say, "I still do not approve of women wearing breeches."

~~~

"I invite you all," said Pen to his guests, "up the steps to the library and reading room where the Monks are tutored when we are away from the castle. This gives the kitchen staff an opportunity to set out the banquet, which I trust you will enjoy."

In deference to their parents and guardians, the Monks laid aside their warrior costumes and donned the formal robes of refined young ladies. Being of an age between childhood and full womanhood, they let their hair fall free, a style they would not be permitted in polite company when they reached their seniority.

In the library, the prince seated himself in his padded chair set on a low pedestal. The guests then found their places on benches and at the small tables that served as desks for the wards. Thick tapestries depicting hunting scenes covered the walls. Shelves were home to a collection of twenty-five illuminated volumes, including a Latin grammar, Plato, the works of Boethius, Dante, and Petrarch, and the philosophy of Averroes.

~~~

Gwyn de Lacy was all puffed up over the good fortune of having been reunited with his cousin Sir Guy and now named steward of Monks Chase. As the hall emptied, he ordered servants to clear the dais, bring in the trestles, and set up the dining tables in a long open loop. The servants went about their tasks, and de Lacy went to the kitchen to check on the food preparation.

"You, cook, get a move on," he said to Brewet. "We must not keep the masters waiting."

"Mr. de Lacy," said the cook. "You are nothing but a braying country ass. You do not order me about, nor do you order about my kitchen staff. I have been cook to his lordship since he arrived at Kenilworth. You slunk in here on your cousin's coattails. You are no more than a sniveling peasant who, like a turd, has floated to the top of a bucket of slops. A hunting lodge is not a castle. So, get off that high horse. You are steward of a campground, nothing more. Now, fetch more wood for the fire."

"Fetch your own damned wood," said de Lacy. "Just do your job and we won't have any more trouble."

The hall was a hundred feet long and thirty feet wide. The walls were hung with tapestries depicting dogs chasing stags, Actaeon spying on Artemis bathing, bucolic country scenes, and nobles preparing for the hunt. The wall coverings protected the interior from drafts coming through cracks in the wooden construction, as well as softening the sounds of activities inside.

To the left of the dais near the door leading to the kitchen was a sideboard on which were placed ewers for dispensing water for the guests. Pen showed his sense of humor when he procured a silver ewer in the shape of a warhorse which, when seized by the tail, could be tipped up to allow the water to issue from the mouth. Other vessels included wine pitchers, basins, bowls, platters, plates, salt cellars, and spice and candy dispensers.

Gwyn ordered trenchers on plates to be placed all around. Each diner was given a spoon. Diners without their own knives were supplied with one. The centerpiece of the banquet was whole roasted stag on a wheeled trolley. It was complete with antlers and crabapples for eyes, and mounted on a handcart of its own, so that all the diners would face it.

The wards joined the prince at the head table set on the dais in front of and above the others.

"May I serve your lordship," said the head carver.

"Something from the haunch," said Pen.

The servitors distributed the meat, first to the head table, and then to the rest. The guests drew their knives, and holding the meat on one hand cut it with the other. Servitors brought bowls of beans boiled with bacon, and pantlers baskets of bread. Gwyn poured wine all around.

Throughout the dining, the guests were treated to soft music by the consort. When the main courses were finished, servitors brought sugared fruit for dessert. At the end of the meal, they removed the trenchers, plates, cups and spoons, and the abbot concluded with the saying of grace.

Chapter Eight

A Day of Reckoning

A courier from London galloped up to the Kenilworth gate, demanding an audience with the prince. Sir Malcolm sounded the gong that would summon Lord Philip, Edward, and other members of the court. The chamberlain stepped forward to receive the dispatch.

"Wait for a reply," he said to the courier.

Lord Philip, Prince Edward, and Piers Gaveston hurried to Pen's privy chamber.

"A dispatch from London, your grace," said the chamberlain, handing it to the prince.

"It is from the queen consort," said Pen. "She reports that the king is in rapidly declining health, but is determined to make another raid on the Scots. We are to come quickly. Signed, Marguerite of France." The prince hastily penned a reply and handed it to the chamberlain who took it to the courier.

"We must leave immediately," said Pen. "A day of reckoning is upon us."

The prince ordered fast horses for a journey that would take two days. The next morning, he, Edward, Gaveston, Eldric, Sir Guy, and six mounted men-at-arms set out for Windsor. They covered half the distance the first day, sending a rider ahead to notify a shocked innkeeper in the village of Aylesbury that the prince and his retinue would be arriving within the hour.

The innkeeper's boy ran to the church and told the warden to ring the bell. Quickly the street filled with people wondering nervously what was happening.

"Get the pigs and dogs out of the street," commanded the reeve. "There is a haunch on the spit over at the tavern. Clear the place out and put out the tables. Anyone have any silver? Grooms, where are they? Someone go to the stables and fetch them, and tell them to clean the mud and manure off their boots."

"The prince is coming," someone whispered.

Pen could see through the trees that everyone in town was scurrying about in preparation for his arrival, and so he slowed the procession to a leisurely walk in order not to startle the populace overmuch. It was not every day that the villagers saw eleven richly caparisoned royal riders come through town.

The entourage entered the village between wagons parked in neat parallel rows. The villagers, hastily dressed in their finest, lined up on each side and bowed as the prince passed by. Pen reigned up in the middle of town.

"A farthing to each child, and a penny to their parents," he said to Eldric, who dismounted and opened his purse.

The anticipation of the crowd was palpable. One child tried to rush Eldric, but his mother yanked him back by the hair. He almost tumbled backward as Eldric approached him, smiled, and handed him a coin. The lines of parents and children remained orderly. The prince dismounted, and as he strolled down the middle of the street, he watched as eager mothers shoved their nubile daughters forward to grab his attention. Young blondes and brunettes smiled shyly, curtseying to the prince as he walked by. They were little informed of what their parents expected of them in these circumstances and so their thoughts tended to wander through imaginary romances of their own creation. One saw Pen as a prince in shining armor who would rescue her from a common fate and whisk her off to the princely life in a castle. Another glowered as she looked down, imagining Pen to be an oppressive sovereign who would grind her and her family into perpetual poverty.

One by one the girls, even those with the darkest imaginations, warmed to the prince as he addressed them individually. He was a noble with charm they could not resist.

Pen, for his part, unmoved by their shy smiles, examined every girl as a possible candidate to join the Monks of Arden.

*　*　*

Upon his arrival at Windsor, the two princes were taken directly to the Rose Tower, since the king's great chamber had recently burned. The Rose Tower was part of the greater royal residence with its own special entrance from the courtyard. The king occupied a suite of nine rooms, and the queen consort a suite of two. The princes presented themselves to the king.

"My sons," he said. "You have come to join my campaign in Scotland. God bless you."

Queen Consort Marguerite joined the audience. "Edward, I sent for them. You are not well and should not be going off to war again. You need to talk with your sons."

"I am quite fit, my dear," he said, which set off a spell of coughing.

"You don't sound well, Father," said Pen.

"A few days in the saddle, and I will be as good as new. My sons, you are now of age. Today we hold a private ceremony to confer upon you the title of knight."

With difficulty, Longshanks hoisted his six-foot-two frame from where he sat to his full height. "Go, prepare yourselves."

The chamberlain escorted the princes to an adjoining room. There they were dressed in white vestures covered by red robes, with black hose and shoes. Bishop Augustus Ballantyne welcomed them to the royal chapel where they prayed.

The bishop offered his blessing. "*In nomine Patris, et Filii, et Spirtus Sancti. Amen.* Lord, bless these two young noblemen of spotless character, heirs to the kingdom, keepers of thy Covenant. May their lives be long and illustrious. *In nomine Patris, et Filii, et Spirtus Sancti. Amen.*"

Upon the princes' exit, the court armorer delivered two swords and shields to the bishop who blessed them. The swords were straight, broad, and double-edged. The cross-pieces were curved toward the blades. Rounds were heavily jeweled and decorated with the lion rampant signifying the House of Plantagenet, as were the shields. Having completed the blessing, the bishop turned them over to the castellan Sir Arnaud, who would maintain custody until the presentation.

The seneschal announced the entrance of the king and Marguerite. Piers Gaveston followed. King Edward sat beside the altar in a chair upholstered in red velvet. The queen consort stood at his right side. Sir Arnaud took his place to the king's left. The king took the sword and shield intended for Pen. The bishop administered the Oath Knighthood. *The knight does not traffic with traitors. He treats women with respect and never gives them false advice. The knight swears to observe all feasts and holy days and to attend Mass every day. Above all, the knight swears undying allegiance to his sovereign.*

"Kneel," said the king to Pen. He turned the sword to its flat side and firmly tapped Pen on the shoulder. "I dub thee Sir Knight."

Pen rose and Prince Edward took his place where the ceremony was repeated. Sir Edward was ecstatic, Sir Pen reserved.

"Your brother will inherit this throne," said the king to Sir Edward. "My wife thinks sooner rather than later. I prefer to be optimistic. I hope that your years at Kenilworth have stiffened your spine, else you will be a royal flop. When the time comes, I propose to send you off to be abbot at Combe abbey in Warwickshire. There, you will serve your sovereign by providing shelter for travelers, doing good works of charity, seeing to the religious education of the country boys, and overseeing the copying of documents and keeping the history of the realm. And be sure to take Gaveston with you."

~~~

Sir Pen and his closest associates retired to the royal apartments. "The time has come. We must prepare ourselves," he said.

Sir Pen summoned Sir Edward and Piers Gaveston, and in the company of Sir Guy, requested an audience with the king and Marguerite.

"Father, and Your Ladyship, I have something of great importance to tell you. For the first fifteen years of my life I accepted the role of your son and heir-apparent to the throne, but then I had a revelation which I have kept secret from all save a few."

"Like Paul on the road to Damascus?" said Marguerite.

"Not exactly, Your Ladyship. It was of a different sort. For fifteen years you treated me royally. I have received the benefit of education, training in the martial arts, and the privilege of serving as master of Kenilworth Castle. I cannot imagine a finer set of opportunities than you have afforded me."

The king coughed up sputum and with a raspy voice said, "You are well-prepared, my son. You are an intelligent and humane young man who will serve your people well."

"Father, I believe myself to be intelligent and humane, but all is not as it seems. A few years ago, campaigning in Wales, an old woman found me and begged for refuge from the conflict. I granted her succor, and she in return told me a remarkable tale, the last piece of a puzzle. For many years I had felt there was something different about me, something that made me uncomfortable, but that I could not explain. As I grew older, the explanation was revealed to me.

"My life with boys had excluded me from the common intercourse that exists among girls. But then I discovered the origin of my unease. The old woman told me she had been present at the time you were making war on Llewellyn ap Gwynedd, that she was midwife to Llewellyn's queen, who had just given birth. The king wanted a son, and so too did you, Father. As the victor entitled to the spoils of war, you had that newborn child snatched from its mother's arms. Alphonso was dead, and at that time you had no male heir. Here lay the solution to your problem.

"You assigned the role of mother to Queen Eleanor, and she raised me as her natural son. All the duties of infant care were assigned to servants. The queen was not very attentive to this child as he grew. I believe you had the right to designate me as your successor until my brother Edward came along. You made the decision to maintain the fiction of my birth and relegate your natural son to a secondary role as younger son."

"I admit that this is all true," said the king. "Why do you choose to make it a public matter now?"

"Because of a further complication, Father. What was not revealed to you was a secret I have kept until now. The reason man-things did not sit well with me is that, not only am I not your son, I am not a man at all, and never have been. I am a woman, Father."

The disclosure sent the king into a spell of coughing. Marguerite, recovering from her shock, went to her husband to comfort him.

Sir Edward exploded. "My brother, the queen?" he roared.

Gaveston was overcome by a fit of laughter. "O, the irony," he said, wiping tears from his eyes.

The old king began to settle down, to try to come to terms with his situation. "No woman can succeed me on the throne," he proclaimed. "You are of royal Welsh blood, Pen, and so I could choose you to take the throne if you were a man, but I also have a legitimate son and he must succeed me as Edward II. I pray for my country."

"I freely resign from any claim to the throne," said Pen, "in exchange for Kenilworth Castle and the Arden Forest."

"It is done," said the king, "but my heart is broken."

~~~

The death of Edward I on his last military campaign against the Scots was followed by a period of public mourning, during which time young Edward was quickly crowned the new sovereign. But trouble erupted when he acted on his obligation to marry a brood sow for the sake of the succession. Leaving England in the hands of a regent, his friend and counselor Piers Gaveston, he departed for Boulogne to seek the hand of twelve-year-old piglet Isabella of France.

Gaveston was a commoner. The new king's father would have been furious at the notion of such a man serving as regent. Playing the symbolic role of Edward I were the Earl of Lancaster and his allies, who watched Gaveston feeding into the king's folly. Taking advantage of the king's absence, they seized Gaveston and turned him over to two Welshmen who took him to Blacklow Hill. One ran him through with his sword. The other lopped off his head.

~~~

Thomas Plantagenet, second Earl of Lancaster, master of five earldoms and one of the richest and most powerful men in England, was childless, but he had bastard sons whom he called to Pontrefact Castle in Yorkshire.

"Your days as squires are behind you," he said. "You are now knights trained in the art of war and bound by the chivalric tradition. Go forth and test your prowess in the great melee* at Windsor. I no longer have the strength to participate. You will go and acquit yourselves on the fields of mock battle, but be cautious and ever alert. To say the king was not pleased when I sent his favorite playmate Gaveston to his heavenly reward, would be an understatement. He will send his best cavaliers against you and, should you die, he will not grieve."

The two sons, accompanied by eight more knights from Lancaster's guard, departed for Windsor. They arrived, paid their fees, and found themselves assigned to the *loyal opposition*. On the other side were the king's men. The field was a one-half mile square. The village of Argyll on one side favored the king's men and the village of Somer on the other cheered the opposition.

"Your royal highness," said Sir Geoffrey to the king, "Your cousin has sent his two bastards to the tourney."

"Any others from their camp?" said the king.

"Eight others, I am informed. That makes ten of them altogether."

"That's half the field. Anything else?"

"My sources tell me that Lancaster wants to test his men against ours. He may be negotiating with the Despensers and the barons. We must be watchful."

"Ten men don't make an army," said the king.

At the king's request, Pen and her wards joined the royal spectators. All five dressed in conventional women's robes in order not to draw undo attention to themselves. Pen drew the expected stares from courtiers who knew something of her story. Nothing official was ever said, but the topic was the subject of much gossip in the court. Pen was accompanied by Sir Guy, now her husband and prince consort. The wards were beautiful women of marriageable age, which did not go unnoticed by the young knights present for the tourney.

The tourney opened with ceremonies in front of the canopied reviewing stand on the Argyll side where the royal guests would view the action. Trumpeters announced the arrival of the king and the diminutive queen consort Isabella of France. Upon their arrival they exchanged pleasantries with Pen and Sir Guy.

A trumpet fanfare announced the parade of contestants, twenty knights astride their caparisoned warm-blood chargers. Hoots and howls from the other side of the field at Somer were directed at the royal combatants. They were kept at bay and under control by members of the castle garrison who patrolled the edges of the playing field.

The King of Arms announced each contestant by name. It was understood that certain royal princes participated using false names in order not to interfere in fair fights because of differences in station. Though of royal blood, the Lancaster boys fought under their own names.

Each knight was equipped with a blunted lance of soft wood that was supposed to splinter upon direct impact with its target. Even so, a broken lance could still have a sharp point upon which the adversary might be impaled. Each knight carried a shield and wore a baldric, from which were suspended a blunted sword on one side and a dagger on the other. For protection, they wore leather breeches and hauberks that reached the knees.

When the parade of knights finished, the king rose to announce the rules. "The twenty knights of the royal House of Plantagenet will line up in front of this stand. The knights of the loyal opposition will line up across the field facing them. Upon the sounding of the trumpets, the lines will charge towards each other. After the first pass with lances couched, opponents of unhorsed competitors will dismount and commence hand-to-hand combat. After the first pass, it is every knight for himself. The deliberate killing of an opponent will be frowned upon by the king. Winners are entitled to take the horse and equipment from a vanquished foe. The fallen may offer money in exchange for clemency. Fighting will continue for six hours, whereupon the trumpets will be sounded and all combat will cease. Failure to abide by these rules will be met with a serious royal rebuke. Take your places and let the melee begin."

The knights tipped their lances to the king and separated into two lines facing each other. The trumpets sounded and the knights galloped toward the center of the field in a rising cloud of dust.

"Long live King Edward," Sir Allyn of Thetford yelled as he clashed with Lancaster's Gregory Lovejoy, a tall and powerful contestant who splintered his lance in a glancing blow to Sir Allyn's chest. Lovejoy wheeled his horse and quickly dismounted. Sir Allyn's varlets* steadied the knight as he stumbled off his horse to the ground. Both men's squires spirited the horses away from the heart of the fray and the two men beat each other with their swords. Within five minutes, Sir Allyn, amidst whistles and taunts from the spectators, was down, and Lovejoy was grappling with his shield. He tore it away and started working on his armor when Sir Allyn's varlets swarmed him. In retaliation, Lovejoy's varlets joined in, and the ensuing brawl had to be broken up by King of Arm's marshals. Lovejoy raised his sword above his head and with two hands prepared to deliver a potentially fatal blow to his opponent when the marshals stepped in and declared him the winner. Reluctantly, Sir Allyn's squire relinquished his horse to Lovejoy's men, and the fallen knight gave up his arms and armor to the victor.

"Poor showing," said Pen to her husband.

"Not well trained. No talent for close combat," said Sir Guy. "You would cut him down in a minute."

"But Guy, no fair princess would ever engage in such activities, would she?"

"Not just any fair princess, Penny. Not just any."

The wards paid scant attention to the actual combat, instead, focused their attention on the contestants and their assistants.

"Look at him," said Caroline, unconsciously raising her hand to point.

The unlucky lad, who like so many others, was taken by the presence of the young beauties, caught the gesture, which diverted his attention from his task of steadying Sir Norwood Gallant in the saddle. At that moment of inattention the horse's head flung around and hit him between the shoulder blades, sending him sprawling in the dust. Had his fellow varlets not dragged him to safety he would have been trampled.

The wards, seemingly unaware of the danger to the young man, laughed at the indignity of it all, reveling in their power to command attention in the midst of a noisy brawl.

What began as an orderly encounter of two rows of men-at-arms, deteriorated into the confusion of nineteen separate battles among pairs of antagonists, each oblivious to the presence of the others, who raced from one corner of the course to the next in their violent pursuit of conquest. Every half hour or so, varlets dragged another beaten warrior from the field, as his triumphant opponent pranced on horseback before the spectators, waving the spoils of victory in the air for their approval.

When the king's man won, cheers went up from the royal viewing stand, and hoots and howls of disapproval arose from the opposition spectators. When the opposition man won, the roles reversed. After six hours of unremitting combat, the warriors grew noticeably weary, as did the spectators on both sides. Many who had been drinking all day had fallen asleep, and their collective enthusiasm was on the wane.

Finally, the King of Arms called for the trumpeters to stop the action. Some of the fighters were so swept up in the violence they heard nothing and kept flailing away at each other. Even the young varlets attending knights on opposing teams found themselves caught up in the competition. They picked their own fights when they were not attending their masters.

Roger Somery took a special interest in Robert of Sudeley, the young man who had been knocked down because he could not take his eyes off the wards. Thinking him vulnerable, Roger tried to take young Robert by surprise by pouncing on his back in an attempt to wrestle him to the ground. In a move of surprising agility, Robert turned the tables on Roger, who ended up flat on his back in the dirt. Referees from the Windsor garrison finally broke them up and the dusty and dirty survivors assembled in front of the king's reviewing stand.

The once proud and elegantly caparisoned knights and gentlemen looked like refugees from the fall of Troy. They bled and they limped, some on foot, and others on horseback led by their squires.

Everyone cheered at the singular moment when spectators on both sides were of one mind. The warriors had put on a splendid show, and the king was prepared to reward them for their effort, even the Lancasters. Into the hand of each fighter's representative, an assistant to the King of Arms placed one pound, whereupon the king declared the tourney at an end and everyone dispersed.

~~~

Pen and Sir Guy gathered their entourage together for the return to Kenilworth.

"Beware of the Lancaster boys," said Sir Geoffrey to Sir Guy.

The guards from the Kenilworth garrison assembled in the upper ward awaiting the princess and prince consort. Lady Ariel's special wagon was readied below the royal apartments. Her attendants carried bundles upstairs to the princess and the wards, and returned with similar bundles they placed inside the wagon.

Footmen held six horses caparisoned in dark green in a line between the guards in the lead and the wagon in the rear. Readied for departure, six figures dressed as the Monks of Arden exited the building and mounted their horses. Sir Guy took the lead, directed the group through the gate, and headed south.

~~~

The Lancaster boys cleaned themselves up after the melee and headed to London in the company of several friends. Having surveyed the royal spectators at the tourney, they had seen opportunity. The most direct route south was by way of the old Roman road Watling Street out of Southwark. Conveniently, Southwark also hosted an assortment of inns, brothels, and stews, where the young men might find comfort as they discussed their plans.

The abbess of the Castle upon the Hope Inn welcomed the group of well-dressed and obviously affluent knights and gentlemen, offering them food, drink, accommodation, and companionship.

"What are you called, wench?" said Viscount Henry Plantagenet to a buxom young woman who immediately sidled up to him.

"Madeleine, your lordship."

"Well," he said. "Your abbess runs a first class establishment here. Are you a first class whore?"

"Nuthin' but the best, sir. How would you have me?"

Lord Henry broke out in laughter. "Any way but up, I would say."

"By that I presume you mean the *grande horizontale*?"

"That I would," he roared.

Other coquettes gathered around to join the merriment. Barmaids brought pitchers of ale which the men insisted on sharing with the women. Boards of bread and cheese appeared. They ate and drank until two by two the men and women began to totter off to the rooms on the first story.

The abbess intercepted Lord Henry on his way to his ease. "I am pleased the needs of you and your friends are being met at my establishment, my lord. Without meaning to distract you from your pleasures, I would consider it a gentlemanly gesture for you to deposit five shillings in advance, and then we shall not speak of it again."

"Why, you old harlot," he said. "Run a tight ship here, don't you?" He reached into his purse and withdrew the coins, which he slapped onto her outstretched palm.

"You are a gentlemen, my lord, and don't forget a little something extra for the working girls."

~~~

The next morning the Lancaster boys rolled out of bed hung over and alone. They checked their purses and found them short, but most of their funds remained intact. Lord Henry silenced their grumbling. "What do you drunken sots expect? The abbess sees to it they don't rob you blind. She has a lot of competition and wants your business on the return trip."

"O well, what the hell. I saw quality on the reviewing stand," said Lord Edmund. "We may be the earl's bastards, but we still have standing."

"I'm going to be sick," said Geoffrey Lighthouse, as he threw up on the floor.

"That will be another penny," said the abbess to Lord Henry.

"I noticed the newly-minted princess had four comely maids at her side," said Sir Peter Hornsby. "Do you know who they are? They were not dressed like servants."

"They looked like four miniature little princesses to me," said Sir Edmund.

"I don't know who they are," said Lord Henry, "but there is one way to find out. They are on the way to Kenilworth."

"When did they leave?" said Sir Lawrence.

"I think they left Windsor ahead of us yesterday," said Lord Henry. "They're probably halfway to Kenilworth by this time."

"Better to intercept them on their way than to go through the formalities at the castle," said Gregory Lovejoy.

Princess Pen's entourage took its time, moving at a leisurely pace to their stopover at Aylesbury. Not so the Lancaster boys, who headed south at a fast clip, beating them to the town.

"Something is not right here," said Sir Guy to Pen as they reached the outskirts of the town. "Where are the village greeters?"

The road through Aylesbury was deserted, until two knights caparisoned in black, one on each side, rode the middle to face Sir Guy, who signaled the caravan to stop as eight more knights and men-at-arms joined the Lancasters.

"Lord Henry and Lord Edmund," said Sir Guy.

Lancaster's men lined up in a formidable-looking row spanning the width of the road; Sir Guy's men did likewise, facing them.

"What is your business with us?" said Sir Guy.

"Purely social," said Lord Henry with a smile. "We were only seeking an introduction to the beautiful young ladies in your company on the reviewing stand at the tourney. By the way, where are they?"

"You must be referring to our wards," said Sir Guy signaling to the princess. "They are among us."

Sir Guy's archers and crossbowmen fixed their attention on the row of Lancaster's men. Five figures cloaked in dark green mantles dismounted from their horses. Princess Pen threw off her cloak.

"My wife, the princess," said Sir Guy. She posed in her fighting gear, shield in one hand bow in the other. The Lancaster boys were taken aback. At the same time, the other four figures cast aside their cloaks to reveal similar costumes. "The Monks of Arden, gentlemen."

"I am Lady Caroline."

"I am Charlotte Giveney."

"I am Lady Elizabeth."

"I am Lady Alice."

"If you value your lives, you would be wise to step aside now," said Sir Guy. "We shall occupy both inns here. I am sure you will be able to find comfortable spots for yourselves in the forest."

~~~

The next morning Lancaster's men were nowhere to be found. Pen's entourage continued on to Kenilworth and arrived without further incident. One week later a dispatch arrived. Lords Henry and Edmund requested an audience with the princess, who replied that she would receive them at the hunting lodge in ten days.

On the ninth day, the Monks secretly left Kenilworth on a scouting mission. They hid in the forest surrounding Aylesbury and watched as Lancaster's group entered the village. With Lord Henry in the lead, one hundred men-at-arms proceeded quietly in single file through the middle of town.

"It is as I suspected," said Pen. "They have more on their minds than a simple social call. We must return to the castle as quickly as possible to prepare their welcome."

Sir Guy mustered the garrison. The gamekeeper served as eyes and ears in the forest, and when he announced the approach of Lancaster and his men, Sir Guy set up a hidden perimeter of two hundred soldiers around the hunting lodge.

"I heard about this Monks Chase," Sir Henry joked to his brother. "Flimsy wooden construction. This will be easier than I thought."

"I would expect them to be more careful about defending themselves but, so what. The little princess is not likely to have much knowledge of such things," said Lord Edmund.

"Her husband, Sir Guy, is garrison commander. Do not underestimate him," said his brother.

"Four pretty maids, all in a row," said Lord Henry. "What shall we do with them?"

"I believe in fairness, brother. Two apiece. How does that sound?"

"It sounds fair to me, Edmund, but being your older brother, I get first choice."

"They were quite fetching outfitted in their little warrior costumes. Each one is more beautiful than the next. How can I lose?"

~~~

All was silent at Monks Chase. No birds sang. A startled deer leapt from its cover and bounded away. As the Lancaster brothers approached the gate, a single bird call was heard.

Lord Henry rode up to the gate and banged on it with the tip of his lance. "Anybody home?" he laughed.

"Perhaps we're early," said his brother. "Why don't we go inside and wait?"

One of Lancaster's men tried the gate. It was not locked. He opened it and the troop of one hundred entered the compound.

"Hello," said Lord Edmund. "Anyone here?"

Sir Guy on horseback seemed to appear out of nowhere as one of his men closed and locked the gate. "We've been expecting you," he said.

"We come in peace," said Lord Henry.

"Is this a social call, then?" said Sir Guy.

"That it is, Sir Guy. That it is, indeed."

"The forest can be a dangerous place, Lord Henry. I see that you have come well protected."

"A gentleman cannot be too careful," said Lord Edmund. "These are parlous times."

"Let me get straight to the point, Sir Guy. We are here for the young ladies, the ones you so cunningly dressed as tiny warriors."

"You mean the Monks of Arden."

Yes, of course. That is what you called them. I trust they are here."

"That they are, Lord Henry. You said you are here for them. What exactly are your intentions?"

"I propose to take them off your hands. Since you have a wife now, you will have less need of them. We can provide for them handsomely, if you agree."

"So, you propose to take the young ladies off to your lair. What are you offering in exchange? Surely, you don't believe you can just march in, take them, and march out."

"That would hardly be the gentlemanly thing to do," said Lord Edmund. "As a token of our gratitude, we have a small purse that will add to your coffers. In addition, we convey to you the warmest regards from our father, your wife's cousin, the Earl of Lancaster Thomas Plantagenet."

"Yes, indeed, our cousin, friend of the barons," said Sir Guy.

"May we see them now? The ladies, I mean?"

Lancaster's soldiers milled about aimlessly, not sure what to do with no one to fight.

"Monks come forward," said Sir Guy.

Five robed figures exited the keep and lined up in front of the brothers, who quickly dismounted to address them.

"Ladies, may we see you?"

Pen removed her habit and handed it to Eldric at her side.

"Your grace," said the brothers, bowing weakly. One by one the Monks cast aside their habits. Five young women, armed to the teeth, stood facing them. The brothers dropped to one knee.

"I am Henry Plantagenet."

"And I am Edmund Plantagenet. We would be honored if you would accompany us to Pontefract Castle."

The brothers rose and advanced toward them. Their soldiers sprang into action and formed a dense semicircle around them. The Monks did not move. That lone bird call was heard again and two hundred armed men on horseback ringing the compound readied their weapons.

"Tell your men to stand down," said Sir Guy. "You are surrounded. Look around you."

The brothers evaluated the trap they had fallen into and signaled their commander to have the troops stand down.

"Unless you are prepared to watch your men cut down in a swarm of arrows," said Sir Guy, "I suggest they leave the compound at once."

Gwyn de Lacy opened the gate. Lancaster's men lowered their weapons and filed out under the watchful eyes of the Monks Chase garrison.

"You won this round, Sir Guy, so we'll just be on our way," said Lord Henry, attempting to mount his horse.

"Not so fast," said Sir Guy. "Seize them."

"You seem to harbor some serious misapprehensions," said Pen.

"It would seem so, your ladyship," said Lord Henry weakly.

"My wards will not be leaving with you. They have more important things to do than be your servants and whores." Pen had a brief, whispered conversation with her husband. "Secure them to the wall," she ordered.

Sir Guy's men tied the terrified brothers to the wooden wall of the keep, their arms and legs tied at the wrists and ankles with ropes, arrayed like the spokes of a wheel.

The Monks stood in a row twenty paces in front of them. Eldric took their shields and each stuck five arrows into the ground in front of them. They nocked their arrows and took aim at the brothers. Pen loosed hers first and was followed by the others. Less than half a minute later none remained on the ground. Each Monk had shot five arrows at the brothers at a rate of one every five seconds. Urine ran over the boot tops of each brother. They were unscratched, but each had been outlined by a dozen arrows.

Pen handed her bow to Eldric and marched up to the men. She drew her sword. It flashed through the air four times. Each pass cut one of the ropes binding the brothers' wrists.

"Go," she said, "and do not look back. Tell your father, my dear cousin, of the force he will encounter should he and his barons seek to overthrow the king."

The Lancaster boys quickly loosed their ankles and sped out the gate, leaving behind only their silhouettes in arrows and puddles where they had been shackled.

Chapter Nine

Peripeteia

The gamekeeper at Kenilworth notified seneschal Sir Malcolm Edwards of the approach of a troupe of minstrels on the road from Aylesbury. Begging admission to entertain the court, they promised songs, poems, and dances. Lord Philip ordered that they be given refreshments of bread and beer.

Sir Guy inspected the band. He and a sergeant went through their meager belongings looking for weapons. Satisfied they posed no physical threat to the princess, Sir Guy signaled to Lord Philip approval to admit them into the great hall.

The princess and the Monks gathered on the dais at the front. Members of the court formed a semi-circle open at the entrance. Acrobats doing flips and cartwheels heralded the approach of the main troupe. They were followed by the musicians, marching to the beat of tabor* and tambourine. Jongleurs* playing lute, viol, and tabor-pipe* took positions at the foot of the dais. Four men quickly laid down a platform on the dirt floor of the hall. Four women wearing wooden clogs stood in a row on the platform before the dais. The tabor and tambourine set up a heavy beat. The dancers picked it up and began their noisy percussive dance. The other musicians joined to create a tuneful musical background.

At the conclusion of the dance and with the hearty approval of the audience, the women retired and a bard took his place on the platform.

"Wales is home to many poems, songs, and tales," he began. "Let me sing to you of the stolen princess Gwenllian, a story passed on to me by an old woman cloistered in the Cistercian monastery at Garth Ceyln.

> *God's breath shrouded Snowdon's jagged teeth*
> *As He chose to loose murderous hordes*
> *On a king betrayed by countrymen*
> *Who cast their lot with English lords.*
>
> *That Wales might have princess Gwen*
> *His queen in labor gave her life;*
> *But dark soon descended at Orewin Bridge*
> *Where King Llewellyn joined his wife.*
>
> *His body was interred in the church of Cwmhir,*
> *With his head on a pike at the Tower;*
> *They buried Eleanor at Garth Celyn,*
> *And Gwenllian vanished forever."*

Pen listened to the story, but the bard interrupted her thought by inviting the audience to join in an estampie.* Pen and Sir Guy remained in their places. The wards joined other members of the court as the musicians struck up a lively tune.

In lines with hands joined, the dancers hopped in time to the beat of the tabor. After a time the older people began to drop out to catch their breath. The younger the dancers, the longer they were able to go on, but after twenty minutes of laughing and hopping around, the musicians brought the dance to a conclusion.

The bard stepped forward to address the princess. "I hope you have enjoyed our performance. We serve at your pleasure. God save King Edward and Princess Penfelyn."

The troupe bowed out. Lord Philip gave them a purse and instructed the kitchen staff present for the festivities to supply them with comestibles for the rest of their journey.

"Bring me the bard before he leaves," said Pen to Lord Philip.

In the royal presence, the bard bowed. "I am at your service, your ladyship."

"I wish to know more about the old woman at the monastery where you got your most interesting story."

"Yes, your ladyship. She told me she was midwife to Queen Eleanor at the birth of her only daughter Gwenllian. The infant was first mistaken for a boy. A surgeon proved otherwise. The queen died in childbirth, as everyone knows and Llewellyn died in battle half a year later. The siege laid upon the castle by your father brought down the Welsh monarchy. The infant Gwenllian disappeared and was never heard from again. Perhaps her tiny bones lie interred in the castle ruins. Who knows?"

~~~

Pen retreated to her apartments at Kenilworth.

"What may I do for you, your ladyship?" said Lady Ariel. "You appear to be deep in thought."

"My heart has grown heavy," said the princess, "since I heard the bard retell much of what I already heard some years ago from the very woman who had passed it on to him."

"But, m'lady, what is it that so weighs you down?"

"A name, Lady Ariel. A name. I have always been known as Penfelyn, the one with the golden hair. The appellation was attached to me from the very beginning of my captivity. But surely I am Gwenllian, the abducted daughter of Llewellyn, not Penfelyn. King Edward snatched me from the bosom of reality and put me in a virtual cage. A cloak of ignorance covered my eyes. He locked me away in a make-believe world. Not only did he rob me of my father and my identity, but my heritage was taken from me as well. You see, Lady Ariel, my erstwhile brother Edward is not the rightful Prince of Wales. Were I a man the title would belong to me. I am Gwenllian of Wales, hereditary sovereign of Gwynedd."

~~~

The embarrassing rout of the effete Lords Henry and Edmund by the Princess Penfeyln infuriated Lancaster. He summoned the young lords, his advisors, and his castellan Sir Robert FitzAlan to his council chambers in Pontefract Castle.

"I intend to wipe this blot off my record. You will not be worthy of your name until you learn how to overcome an armed opponent. You let a handful of women send you home with your tail between your legs like a whipped puppy. What use was all that military training? Did you leave it at the gate? You will become men, or you will become corpses."

"But Father . . ."

"Do not 'but Father' me. I am giving you an opportunity to redeem yourselves. Resistance must be challenged with overwhelming force. In my name you will travel to the castles of four of my most powerful barons. Each will provide knights,* lances,* and yeoman archers. Sir Robert will command his own troops and serve as overall commander for the operation. We will take Kenilworth Castle. Questions?"

"How soon should we be ready?" said Sir Robert. "I will need time to send scouts to Kenilworth."

"You will have two months to prepare," said Lancaster.

The young lords accompanied by Sir Robert arrived at Barnard Castle the following week. They were promptly admitted to the great hall, where they were met by Baron Richard Balliol.

"Lord Richard, greetings," said Lord Henry. "I hope you are well."

"And you, Lord Henry."

"We bear a request from the earl that you provide a contingent to be part of a small military force." Lord Edmund presented him with a sealed order.

"I require," he read, "that you assemble five knights, ten lances, and twenty-five archers to present themselves at Pontefract Castle thirty days from this date. Their commander is to be paid according to your discretion. Your bannerets* shall be paid four shillings per day, regular knights two shillings, men-at-arms one shilling, archers and infantry two pence. They will be part of a company that will secure Kenilworth Castle from its current occupants under the leadership of the Lords Henry and Edmund. Their obligation will continue for a period of two months."

Sir Robert and the lords made the rounds of Bowes, York, and Conisbrough Castles to deliver similar requests to the barons, de Montfort, Malebisse and Warenne, respectively. They returned with commitments to a total force of seven hundred thirty men. The inclusion of wagon masters and muleteers swelled the force to nearly a thousand.

~~~

Abelard and Son, textile manufacturers, were principals in the rise of the trade in Coventry and hereditary suppliers of fabrics to the nobility. They readied their quarterly delivery to Kenilworth Castle.

"Try not to be too late returning," said James Abelard to his son Thomas. "You will be safer traveling in daylight, and you know how your mother worries when you are out."

"Kenilworth is only five miles away," said Thomas. "I will make the delivery and be back before you know I have been gone."

"Perhaps you should take an armed escort with you."

"That will not be necessary," said Thomas. "I will be safe. Do not worry."

Thomas left Coventry with a wagonload of fabric, woolens, russet, and cotton lawn for the castle. Two servants armed only with daggers in their belts accompanied him. Halfway between Coventry and Fosse Way, they were halted by three armed riders.

"We are just simple merchants," said Thomas. "We have no money, just cloth for the castle."

The riders raised crossbows and sent bolts into the bosoms of the three men. The assailants stripped the corpses and covered themselves with their rustic robes. Tying their horses to the wagon, they proceeded toward the castle. When they were near, they tethered the horses out of sight in the wood. Their leader studied the merchant's documents and a quarter hour later they presented themselves at the Kenilworth Castle gate.

"I do not recognize you," said the gatekeeper.

"Abelard and Son are very busy just now. We are temporary drivers hired in order that your delivery should not be delayed. Here is our paperwork."

The gatekeeper examined the documents and waved them in. They crossed the causeway, driving the team as slowly as possible in order not to arouse suspicion. They noted that the castle was situated within a double moat. To the west was a large lake created by damming the streams that fed the moat.

A guard escorted them to the tailor shop where the keeper of the wardrobe received the goods. "I ordered linen. This is cotton," he said.

"I am sorry, sir, but we are just humble delivery men. We would not know anything about that."

"Abelard's son usually makes the deliveries. He would have known."

Two of the wagoneers began to wander around. "Stop," said the guard. "Stay with your wagon."

The leader concluded the transaction with the keeper of the wardrobe and signaled his men to prepare to leave. Keeping their heads low, they proceeded slowly toward the gate, but in their eagerness to quit the castle, they began to speed up. "Not so fast," ordered the guard, but they continued to drive the slow wagon as fast as it would go. "Stop," he said. At this point Lancaster's men panicked and bailed out of the wagon. They ran hell-bent through the gate, heading for their horses. Two of them made it. The gatekeeper caught the third.

A sergeant from the garrison took charge and delivered the man to the gaol located under the great stone keep. Guards removed his cloak. Underneath he was wearing a gambeson identified with the Lancaster crest.

"Fetch Sir Guy," said the sergeant, as they transferred the prisoner to the interrogation room.

"This man gained entrance to the castle grounds impersonating an agent from Abelard and Son in Coventry," said the sergeant. "His two confederates got away. They had horses within reach tethered outside the castle grounds."

"Strip him and tie him to the post," said Sir Guy. "Who are you?"

"Just a poor peasant, sir," said the man.

"Give him ten lashes. Maybe that will loosen his tongue."

"Just following orders. Doing our job," the man blubbered.

"Did Lancaster give you your orders?" said Sir Guy.

"Yes, sir."

"Tell me," Sir Guy demanded.

"They will kill me if I talk."

"I will kill you if you don't."

"We were just to look around, sir."

"Men who sneak in and just look around are called spies. Are you a spy? I might let you keep body and soul together if you talk."

The man said nothing.

"Ten more lashes," said Sir Guy.

"Please, sir," the man pleaded. "They're coming to take the castle."

"When?"

"Now," he said and went on to spill out all the details.

"Hang him."

"But you gave me your word."

"I lied."

~~~

Sir Guy hastily conferred with the princess, who convened a meeting with the principal members of the court.

"We are under attack," he announced. "It is Lancaster. He is sending his bastard sons to avenge their humiliation at the hands of the princess and her wards. A thousand men will be on their way from Pontefract as soon as Lancaster digests the report from the two spies who escaped. We have very little time."

"I will need four of your fastest riders," said the princess. "They will deliver dispatches to Warwick, Tamworth, Beaudesert, and Leamington as quickly as possible."

The messages were similar. Kenilworth coming under attack. Need reinforcements as soon as possible. Lord Philip Marmion, Lord Thurstan de Montfort, Earl William de Beauchamp, and Robert Giveney delivered their responses in person. But for Giveney, they were unanimous. "We want our daughters and wards back and out of harm's way."

"We are the Monks of Arden," said Lady Alice de Toeni.

"We are pledged to Princess Penfelyn," echoed Lady Caroline de Montfort.

"We will not abandon her in her time of need," said Charlotte Giveney. "We fight better than most men. You should have seen those whimpering bastards just before we drove them out of Monks Chase."

"Yes," said Warwick, "and that is why they are so dangerous. A thousand men will overcome the garrison and they will end up having their way with you in spite of your defiance."

"We cannot cut and run, Father," said Lady Caroline. "You gladly gave us up to be educated and trained here. It has been done. We have created a new heritage that we must defend, and defend it we shall."

With the Monks standing in solidarity behind the princess, all their guardians could do was agree to send what reinforcements they could muster on short notice. Each noble pledged to send archers, infantrymen, and a knight-commander for a total three hundred fighting men including the garrison at Kenilworth. Mayor Giveney promised to send fifty yeoman-archers who had no combat experience, but had become first class bowmen through years of practice.

Wagonloads of supplies soon began to emerge from the forest: wheat, oats, salted meat, and sheaves of arrows. Some of the foresters remained at the castle, while others melted back into the dense wood. Every able-bodied man within the castle grounds went to work to erect temporary scaffolds inside the north and east walls. Sir Guy posted scouts along Fosse Way with instructions to report Lancaster's position and not to fire on them.

With arrival of the volunteers, the population of Kenilworth swelled to six hundred. Women and children were dispersed into the forest to ride out the conflict with yeoman families and other trusted protectors. The Monks were the only women who remained to fight.

The first scout arrived at six a.m. with the news that the leading elements of the Lancastrian force were five miles away. Half an hour later, a second scout arrived to report that Lancaster's men were moving into the wood and aligning themselves in a semicircle to the north and east of the castle grounds.

A knight-herald presented himself at the far end of the causeway and, holding aloft a white banner, shouted to the gatekeeper, "I request an audience with your commander in the name of Thomas Plantagenet, Ninth Earl of Lancaster."

After conferring with his officers, Sir Guy ordered the gatekeeper to signal the herald to come to the gate, which was not to be opened.

"I am Sir Lawrence Camelback," the herald announced. "The Lords Henry and Edmund, in the name of sparing two noble military forces an unnecessary loss of life, will gladly accept your unconditional surrender of Kenilworth Castle. Lay down your arms and you will be treated with the greatest respect and deference due your king."

"I am Sir Guy de Lacy, commander of this garrison. You may thank the lords for their offer, but I regret to inform them I shall have to decline. If you choose to lay siege to the castle, it will cost you grievously in blood and treasure, and the bastard sons will have to face the earl in yet another humiliating defeat. Good morning, Sir Lawrence."

~~~

Two men felled a large oak tree. The sound was beyond earshot of the castle. When they finished trimming, they were left with a heavy section of trunk three feet in diameter and twenty feet long. At the same time, carpenters were busy fashioning a cradle on wheels onto which the trunk was loaded. One end of the trunk protruded three feet beyond the end of the cradle. Muleteers harnessed six animals to the cradle and towed it from the wood to the road to the castle. Approaching the far end of the causeway, they reversed the position of the mules so they were pushing the heavy ram instead of towing it.

~~~

Sir Guy ordered his archers to the scaffold. "Stay close to the wall," he ordered. "They will be raining arrows."

The shower of arrows began. Sir Guy's archers hugged the wall as they clattered to the earth without effect inside the bailey. Sir Guy's archers returned the fire after the first volley. Infantrymen inside the castle walls raced to retrieve spent arrows before the next volley arrived. In a show of bravado, the Lancasters sent a banneret and trumpeter in view of the gate house. Both were cut down in a volley of arrows shot from inside the Kenilworth curtain wall. The exchange of fire continued with each side sustaining losses. At this point Sir Lawrence ordered the battering ram into position at the end of the causeway where they began their slow advance toward the gate. Knights and mounted cavalry on both sides prepared to face each other. Lancaster's infantrymen and muleteers were somewhat protected from the Kenilworth archers by the mass of the battering ram.

"Aim for the mules," Sir Guy ordered. A few arrows found their mark but failed to slow the advance. Sir Guy deployed his cavalry in a split formation with half to the left and half to right of the gate. He then ordered his pike men to form into three tight linear schiltrons in the center.

In a final push, Lancaster's men rammed the gate and knocked it down, following which infantry and cavalrymen swarmed through the breach. The horsemen charged the schiltrons which held fast, running their pikes through horses and riders alike. Lancaster's cavalry fell into disarray as Sir Guy's closed in on their flanks. Gradually, Lancaster's men began to fall back. As Sir Guy's archers and infantrymen pressed their counterattack, Sir Lawrence was forced to send his men into a full retreat. Many of his men were lost as they jammed the exit where the gate once had been. The fighting subsided and Sir Lawrence vanished into the wood to confer with his lords.

The next few days were marked by minor skirmishes. At Sir Guy's request, the princess and the Monks stayed out of the fray, giving him an opportunity to take a measure of his attackers' force. Kenilworth men brought the battering ram inside the castle walls and then set about to repair the gate.

The castle was bounded to the west and south by a large artificial lake, which limited accessibility by an attacker to a full half of its perimeter. Geoffrey de Clinton had built the great square tower two hundred years earlier. Before the lake was filled, he constructed a stone tunnel beneath what would become the lake bed. By cleverly creating a system of drains that fed into a long pipe reaching to a point beyond the castle grounds at a lower elevation than the floor of the tunnel, he assured that the inevitable leaks from the lake overhead would not permanently flood the tunnel. It was through this tunnel that Sir Guy dispatched scouts to find out what the Lancasters were up to following their retreat. The word that came back was not good.

"They have sent for reinforcements," said the scout, "perhaps thousands."

Sir Guy consulted with his wife and his captains. "We will not be able to withstand an attack by a force that large," he said.

"What do you suggest?" said the princess.

"We have no more resources to call upon," he said. "We shall have to quit the castle or we will all be slain."

"We will live to fight again," said the princess. "We must begin the evacuation immediately before their reinforcements arrive. Come with me, Sir Guy."

"We have time to get everyone out," said Sir Guy. "We certainly cannot go out the main gate. Our men will have to use the tunnel. You, princess, must go with your wards. I will remain with my cavalrymen and knights. We must make a show of resistance before they discover the castle to be abandoned."

"But, my husband," Pen protested, "You will be killed."

"I am your husband, but I am also your bodyguard, appointed by King Edward to keep you safe. You are my sovereign, but I have a duty to protect you to the best of my ability. To hold off the attackers until you have found safety is my sovereign duty. I cannot do less. Spread the word," he said to his officers. "Access to the tunnel is through the tower basement. Your men should gather at the tower and be prepared to leave immediately. They will have to make their way back to their farms through the forest, taking great care to avoid detection by Lancaster's lookouts. The princess and her wards will be escorted by armed guards to the hunting lodge. But everyone must be vigilant. Sir Lawrence may figure out where you are. If he goes to the lodge, you must get away as quickly as possible. You must not let the lord bastards take you captive."

During the next fortnight, everyone but the skeleton force had departed. Simultaneously, a force of several hundred armed men moved south from Pontefract Castle to Kenilworth. Sir Lawrence deployed his men in concentric ranks of archers and infantrymen. Half a dozen archers inside the castle walls created the illusion of many. Sir Lawrence assembled his cavalrymen at the far end of the causeway. Seeing the battering ram gone and the gate replaced, he pondered his next move. Unexpectedly, the gate swung open. Inside stood a row of knights and armed horsemen facing Lancaster's men at the other end of the causeway. He signaled his knights to charge. They galloped across the causeway, followed by a surge of roaring cavalrymen and infantry. The knights clashed in thunderous collisions of horses, men, and weapons. Lancaster's cavalrymen and foot soldiers poured in through the gate, but found no one to fight. Vastly outnumbered, Sir Guy and his small contingent valiantly succumbed. One by one they fell until the only men left standing were the Lancastrian attackers. When the brief skirmish was over, the Lords Henry and Edmund presented themselves to the scene.

"We are vindicated," Lord Henry crowed.

"To the tower," said Lord Edmund. "We must find the princess and her little friends. We have a score to settle."

~~~

A bereft Princess Penfelyn and her wards made their way through the forest to Monks Chase. "In times like these, I wonder if I will have the strength to go on," she lamented.

The women huddled close together inside the entrance to the Monks' quarters dormitory. "We have escaped the boy bastards this time," said Charlotte, "but this was the location of their great infamy. It will not take long for them to figure out where we are."

"Their army will be returning to Pontefract," said Lady Caroline. "They will move north past us not five miles to the west."

"I cannot imagine they would not at least send a scout to check on this place," said Lady Alice.

"Could we hide out here?" Elizabeth asked timidly.

"They would find us in a trice," said the princess. "We must decide whether we want to leave before they discover us, or after."

"But where would we go?" said Elizabeth.

"We own the Arden Forest," said the princess. "They do not, and it is there we must regroup. If we don't waste any time, we can easily get away. Once they have passed by, perhaps we can return. This will be our first survival test. We will have Eldric, Kallias, Gwyn de Lacy, Lady Ariel and a handful of guards to accompany us. Beyond them, we will be on our own."

~~~

Word of the disaster at Kenilworth reached the wards' families and set off a wave of grieving and self abasement. "Why couldn't I keep her safe?" was the common refrain. "I never should have let her take up with that strange prince or princess, or whatever she is."

Warwick, Marmion, de Montfort, and the humble Robert Giveney arrived red-eyed at the ravished castle. Rotting corpses of horses and their riders lay strewn about. A handful of dead archers and infantrymen played the role of buzzard bait. The men tearfully pored over the remains hoping to retrieve the bodies of their daughters and wards, but they were nowhere to be found. They searched the square tower. Giveney descended to the basement where he discovered the entrance to the tunnel. He summoned the others. "They got away," he said. "I am sure of it."

"Where does it lead?" said Warwick.

"I don't know, my lord, but I intend to find out." With that, he plunged into the darkness followed by two of their armed guards. Minutes later they emerged three hundred yards away on the other side of the lake. He yelled and waved to the men who had stayed behind to watch from the curtain wall. "This is it," he exclaimed. "This was their escape route. They live. All we have to do is find them."

~~~

"Hundreds of soldiers and five thousand pounds later," thundered Lancaster, "and this is what you have to show for it? You are as stupid as your whore mother. I'd rather she gave me the pox than you two."

"They all got away through a tunnel under the lake," said Lord Henry. "Sir Lawrence and his men killed the princess's husband and the few men-at-arms left behind to cover their escape. The women are at large."

"What about that hunting lodge where they rubbed your faces in the dirt?"

"We had it checked out on our way back," said Lord Edmund. "There was no sign of them."

"Did you leave a sentry at the lodge?"

"No, your lordship," said Lord Henry.

"Did it not occur to you they might be hiding in the wood waiting for you to leave so they could go back?"

"No, sir, but I will dispatch a squad immediately."

~~~

The princess and her retinue returned to Monks Chase. "There is no sign that they left anyone behind to spy on us," she said.

"The Lancaster boys might not be quick enough to think of that," said Lady Caroline, "but their father would."

Pen retired to her room. The wards had glimpsed the wave of grief that swept over her face when she realized her husband was going to sacrifice his life for hers, but they had never seen her weep. Unable to contain herself any longer, she buried her face in Lady Ariel's lap and sobbed. Lady Ariel patted her back. "There, there now. Let it all out. I am here with you."

In time, her sorrow assuaged, she regained her composure. "I must meet with my Monks," she said. "We have to plan our defense against the Lancasters."

Everyone met in the hall. "We have precious few days to get organized," she said. "We must expect that the earl will send agents to watch for our return."

"What do you suggest we do?" said Charlotte.

"I have an idea," said Lady Caroline. "Let them think the lodge is empty. Sooner or later they will venture past the gatehouse, perhaps even set themselves up inside the compound where it would be more comfortable than camping out on the forest floor."

"Good idea," said the princess. "When they get too comfortable, they will get careless, and we will be able to seize them."

"We can hold them in the gaol as a temporary measure," said Lady Alice.

"Squire Gwyn de Lacy," said Pen. "You are the new head man. It will be your responsibility to supervise the guards and servants, such as they are. Yeoman Eldric will see to the needs of the wards. My lady-in-waiting will continue to be Lady Ariel. You Monks must wear minimal fighting gear. Carry your weapons with you at all times. "

"We will need some provisions," said Pen. "We have beer, but little else."

"My father's house is only five miles away," said Charlotte. "He will give us bread. I can take a man with me and get there and back before sundown."

"Off with you then," said Pen. "Squire Gwyn, choose an escort and send them on their way. We haven't much time; a few days at most, I would guess."

"We need meat, your ladyship," said Squire Gwyn.

"Take two men and a wagon and a bowman outside," said Pen. "Bring us a stag."

"I'll do it," said Elizabeth. "I've seen them browsing on the other side of the moat. I should be able to bring one down easily."

Pen smiled and agreed to let Elizabeth go out and practice her hunting skills. Once outside the compound, the drivers continued a short way into the forest and parked the wagon. Elizabeth dismounted and approached a patch of meadow that adjoined the moat. She concealed herself and waited. She was nearly invisible in her dark green habit and cowl. After half an hour had passed, a fine young buck presented himself at the water's edge. He lowered his head and prepared to drink. Elizabeth took careful aim, but before she could release her shaft she heard a twig snap. The noise startled the deer who bounded off. She withdrew into the shadows and surveyed the surrounding forest.

A man was lurking in the vicinity of a large oak tree fifty yards away. With Elizabeth now out of sight, he stepped into the clear for a better look, offering her an unobstructed view of him. He was not a peasant out for a stroll in the wood. On his tunic was the crest of the House of Lancaster.

What would Pen have me do? she thought. I cannot let this spy report back to his confederates. She cast off her habit and rose to her full height. In the seconds the man stood motionless, transfixed by what he saw, Elizabeth drew back and sent an arrow straight through the crest. The man fell dead without uttering a sound. Elizabeth summoned the drivers. "Put him in the wagon," she said. "We must return to the lodge immediately."

~~~

The petite figure in a green habit that rode down the main street of Leamington was immediately recognized as Charlotte Giveney. She dismounted and moments later her father and mother along with a dozen villagers swarmed into the street to greet her. Tears streamed down the cheeks of Mayor Robert at the realization his daughter was alive and well.

"You are back," said her father. "Can you stay?"

Charlotte explained the urgency of her mission. Her father sent a man to the bakery to fetch sacks of bread. "Will you need anything else, my dear?"

"A little bit of salted meat will do," she said. "But I must hurry. I cannot tell you where I will be. What you do not know you cannot be forced to reveal. I promise to return again, often, but for now I must say good bye."

Charlotte and her escort slung the sacks of provisions over the backs of their mounts, just behind their saddles and departed for the lodge.

~~~

Looking at the corpse, the shock of recognition spread across Pen's face. "They are already here. You have done well, Elizabeth. Very well, indeed. You did not shirk your duty. You have given us a chance to get away to safety."

Charlotte returned with the bread and meat. Pen described the current situation to her and suggested they eat something before packing up to leave the compound.

"What shall I do with this body, your ladyship?" said Squire Gwyn.

"Hang him from the gate so the rest of them can see him when they show up. It will serve as a reminder to the Lancaster boys of what they are up against."

Chapter Ten

Lancaster Agonistes

Princess Penfelyn instructed her followers that she was to be addressed henceforth by her birth name, Gwenllian ap Llewellyn. She pulled together their loosely organized resources, and she and her retinue began their journey to Wroxeter fifty miles away. Gwen and the four Monks rode single file ahead of supply wagons pulled by teams of mules. Lady Ariel, Eldric, and Kallias rode with the princess. Gone were Sir Guy and his knights. Gone was the garrison. Pen's small armed force was now led by Squire Gwyn de Lacy. Ten mounted light cavalry rode in front and five more protected the rear.

The first half of their journey was uneventful. At the end of the day they made camp near the old Roman site of Letocetum at the village of Wall. Services for commercial travelers had grown up around this intersection of the Roman roads of Watling and Icknield Streets since they were built centuries earlier.

The crossroads in the marches* was a hub of commerce. Wagonloads of wool from the highlands in the north passed cargoes of leather and worked metal moving up from the south. At the same time, primary goods like cattle, skins, fleeces and cheese moved from west to east. Coming from the opposite direction were goods that included necessities like salt, wheat and iron.

Locals approached Gwen's entourage with caution overcome by curiosity at who had come to town displaying the Plantagenet crest.

"Make way for Princess Gwenllian," said Squire Gwyn, bursting with pride at his new charge. The gawkers pulled off their caps and dropped to one knee.

A man distinguished from the others by a gold sash around his waist and a large medallion around his neck stepped forward. "I am Roger of Cadell, your ladyship, and I speak for the people. May we be of service?"

Gwen dismounted and threw off her monk's habit. The crowd drew in a collective breath and instinctively stepped back at the sight of a beautiful, fair-haired young woman dressed as a warrior knight. "I am Gwenllian ap Llewellyn," she announced, "rightful heir to the throne of Gwynedd usurped by my brother the king. I am gathering a force to reclaim my patrimony. I am in need of archers and infantrymen to join the campaign, and I pay very well. Who among you are ready to volunteer?"

Gwen's augmented force arrived at Wroxeter, five miles south of Shrewsbury, the following day. The Earldom of Shrewsbury was forfeit in 1102. Absent a powerful lord, the sheriff collected the king's fees on behalf of the justiciar* of Chester Edmund fitz Alan. The sheriff, confused by the princess's name and having received word of Gwen's presence in the march, assembled a contingent of armed deputies, who rode down from Shrewsbury to face them.

The sheriff, seeing he was badly outnumbered, elected to use diplomacy rather than confrontation. "I am the king's representative, my lady," he said to Gwen. "And you are . . . you are . . . a Welsh princess?"

"I am Gwenllian ap Llewellyn, sheriff, formerly Princess Penfelyn Plantagenet. The king is my brother."

Gwen hated associating herself with Edward in this way, but called on the defunct kinship to strengthen her negotiating position.

"Your ladyship," said the sheriff, bowing obsequiously. "I see that you are traveling. The king will be pleased to hear that you are well. May I inform him of your destination?"

"You may not. What you do not know you cannot report. Tell him we are in Shrewsbury buying wool."

"Thank you, your ladyship," said the sheriff bowing out. "Please send word if there is anything I can do to make your visit more pleasant."

The sheriff and his men departed for Shrewsbury and Shrewsbury Castle, which housed the shire offices. He sent two dispatches, one to the king and one to Lancaster.

~~~

"I have bigger fish to fry," said the earl to his bastard sons, "like her brother the king, for example. I have given you every opportunity to do something useful with your lives. You are a pair of wastrels who are unlikely ever to amount to much. Go chase those girls or boys, or whatever they are if you want to, but do not expect either my help or my blessing. The best thing you can do for your father is to stay out from underfoot. Now, go."

The Lancaster boys still had a small group of hangers-on who caroused with them: Sir Peter Hornsby, Sir Lawrence Camelback, Geoffrey Lighthouse, and Gregory Lovejoy.

"According to the sheriff, they are heading toward Chester," said Lord Edmund. "If we leave now we can make it to Newcastle-under-Lyme by sundown. With luck we should be able to intercept them tomorrow."

~~~

Gwen understood that the sheriff would dispatch a fast courier to Pontefract Castle with intelligence on her whereabouts, so she posted lookouts around the camp perimeter to await the inevitable arrival of the Lancaster boys.

"We are on a sacred mission," she said to her followers. "The earl's bastard gadflies will continue to vex us until we settle with them once and for all. To reclaim a throne will demand all our attention. We do not need them pestering us along the way."

~~~

The Pontefract Six rode north on London Road to the castle, where they were given accommodations. They paid their respects to Baron

Richard Clayton, and, leaving their coin and valuables in the custody of the chamberlain, decamped for an evening at Madame Claudette's Roadhouse for Weary Travelers.

The abbess was short and plump and wore a red silk robe over a full-length kirtle closed at the neck with a silver brooch. "Gentlemen," she said. "Welcome to my establishment."

"I am Lord Henry Plantagenet. My father is the Earl of Lancaster."

"Your lordship," she declared, dropping to one knee.

"Bring your best beer and wenches," said Lord Edmund.

"Of course, your lordship." She snapped her fingers in the direction of the staff awaiting her orders. Men quickly erected a trestle table in the middle of the room and moved benches for seating to either side. Serving wenches brought tankards and pitchers of beer. They hovered over the men. Their kirtles were open at the neck, secured only by a girdle at the waist. Their ample breasts swung freely as they moved about the task of appealing to the men's base instincts.

The six men laughed and joked with the women. Their voices grew louder as the drinking proceeded. Soon they were grabbing at buttocks and breasts. The women responded by sitting on their laps and running their fingers through the men's hair. As the evening wore on, couples took turns retiring to the small adjacent rooms to consummate the ritual. By midnight, the men were pleasantly intoxicated, and with their carnal appetites satiated, they paid the abbess and returned to the castle to sleep it off.

~~~

"The boys will be here soon," said Gwen. "We would have heard by now if they were bringing an army to take us by force. The earl holds them in such low regard that I doubt he would send them off with much more than their dimmed wits to serve them."

"They know that the Monks are a formidable fighting force," said Squire Gwyn. "If they are short-handed, they are not likely to attempt a frontal military assault."

"The boys are not quick enough to feel chastened by their previous defeat," said Gwen. "They might decide to try out their irresistible charm on us instead of pressing daggers to our throats."

"They draw near," said the lookout as he rushed into the encampment.

~~~

A mile away six armed men rode up to a farmhouse and ordered the occupants outside.

"This will do," said Lord Henry. "Seize the man and the boy."

Geoffrey Lighthouse and Gregory Lovejoy leapt from their horses and grabbed the two.

"Stop, please," shrieked the wife. "They are my husband and son. What do you want?"

"I am Lord Henry Plantagenet, and I am commandeering your house in the name of the Earl of Lancaster." He gestured with the back of his hand to Lighthouse and Lovejoy. "Take them into the forest."

The farmer's wife begged for mercy to be shown her family. "Be quiet," said Lord Henry as he dismounted. "Take her inside."

The four men and the wife entered the house where they discovered two children huddled by the hearth. "Get up," said Sir Lawrence. Two terrified girls in their mid-teens rose to their full height of five feet, barely reaching the shoulders of their tormentors. "Very nice," said Lord Edmund. "You shall make for some fine entertainment tonight. Now, get moving. Fetch us bread and drink."

The girls and their mother, in shock, went about robotically complying with the lords wishes.

"What have we here?" said Lovejoy, holding up a dark glass jug of amber-colored liquid. He pulled the stopper and took a sniff. "Mead!" he said. "How fine a fragrance."

"Cups all around," said Lighthouse to the girls. Lovejoy took a long draught from the jug, then filled the cups of his brethren. "To women and the good life," he toasted.

The men drained their cups. "More, more," they demanded.

"Fetch another jug," said Lord Henry to the wife. The men grew merrier and the women, their spirits crushed, grew flaccid and apathetic. They were as disembodied beings passed around from man to man like rag dolls. The men were in full rut. The women's faces glistened with tears, which inflamed the men's passions further. Quite overpowered, the women could do little more than yield. The wife accepted her fate compliantly but fainted at the sight of her daughters being ravished in front of her eyes.

Lord Edmund shook her. "Wake up, good woman," he said. "Now is not the time for sleep. This is a time for celebration. We need more bread, more drink, more wood for the fire. Go fetch."

The wife rose groggily. The men freed her daughters, and the three slowly moved toward the rear entrance of the house. "Hurry up, now," said Lord Henry. "Great things await us." Once out the back door, the women gathered up their robes and ran as fast as they could into the forest. They ran and ran through familiar dells, racing down paths that would take them as far away as possible.

The sight of the bodies of her husband and son hanging from a great oak tree sent the wife into spasms of sobbing. Her daughters, clenching their jaws, seized their mother's arms, bearing her forward. They had not gone another fifty yards when an armed man appeared in front of them, causing them to collapse in their tracks.

"Why are you fleeing?" said the man. "What terrible fate has befallen you?"

"Just kill us," the wife pleaded. "We are lost anyway. Do with us what you will."

"Please arise," he said, "and follow me. Princess Gwenllian will give you succor."

Gwen was appalled at the women's story. "We have been expecting this bunch. I will send men for the bodies of your husband and son. We will give them a Christian burial. As for the ones who did this to you, how many were there?"

"Six, your ladyship."

"It is as I thought," said Gwen. "Did they identify themselves?"

"They said they were the Earl of Lancaster's men."

~~~

"They should have been back by now," said Lord Henry. "Geoffrey, go find out what is taking them so long."

Moments later, Lighthouse returned to inform the lords that the women had taken flight. They were nowhere to be found. "Well, find them," Lord Henry roared. "After them, the lot of you. Brother, you stay here."

Hornsby, Camelback, Lighthouse and Lovejoy lit torches and plunged into the darkness, not having the faintest idea where they were going. They stumbled across the path to the tree where they had killed the farmer and his son, but the bodies were missing.

"They were dead," said Lovejoy. "We killed them both."

"Be careful," said Lighthouse. "Whoever cut them down knows we are here."

The men stood four abreast, torches held high and arms at the ready as they looked around for any movement that might betray the presence of an adversary.

"What is that?" said Hornsby. The men squinted into the darkness ahead, detecting the silhouettes of four berobed figures moving silently toward them from the shadows. Instinctively, the men placed their hands on the pommels of their swords.

"Who is it? Who are you?" Sir Lawrence demanded to know. The four figures stepped into the light and discarded their dark green habits to reveal their warrior garb.

"We are the Monks of Arden, gentlemen," said Lady Caroline. "I believe we have met before."

The four men, recalling their last encounter with these women, were stricken with horror. The Monks raised their bows in unison and loosed four arrows that found their marks in four ignoble hearts. The men crumpled soundlessly to the ground. The Monks retrieved their habits and vanished into the darkness.

"It is done," Lady Caroline reported.

"Good work. Now, you and I shall sweep up the remaining dregs," said Gwen.

~~~

The princess and Lady Caroline rustled about in a trunk full of fine clothes. "Just killing them with a couple of arrows does not do the lords proper justice," said Gwen. "I have an amusing idea. We shall meet them dressed in smocks and silk kirtles and wearing fine leather boots with our hair up in lace nets."

~~~

"Hornsby, Camelback, where are you?" Lord Henry called out but got no reply. "The women are gone. The men are gone. What is going on here?"

"Sir, sir. Can you help us?" came a woman's voice from the darkness. "I believe we may be lost."

"Come closer," said Lord Henry. "Edmund. Come here."

The brothers stood at the back door and watched as two finely dressed young women came into view. "Lord Henry. Lord Edmund. Do you remember me?"

"Princess Penfelyn. I cannot believe my eyes."

"I am she, your lordship only now I have taken my birth name, Gwenllian ap Llewellyn. May I present Lady Caroline de Montfort?"

"The formidable ladies in green," said Lord Henry. "What a bit of luck. We have been looking for you."

"So you have. So you have, and now you have found us."

"How did you get past my men? They were out looking for the women who live here, but everyone seems to have disappeared."

"They are back at our encampment enjoying the hospitality offered by my friends. I have decided to offer you the hand of peace. We should not be enemies. Your father, the earl, is plotting against our common enemy the king. We are on the same side and should be enjoying each others' company instead of bickering among ourselves. Would you not agree?"

"Wholeheartedly," said Lord Henry. "And my brother Edmund agrees."

"We would be pleased if you would join us inside," said Lord Edmund. "We have a fire and delicious mead."

"We would be honored," said Gwen. "Come, Caroline."

Once inside, they shared bread and cheese washed down with copious amounts of mead, or so the men thought. The women had perfected the trick of seeming to drink but not actually consuming more than a few drops at a time. As the men continued to drink they grew frisky, having warmed themselves up on the farmer's wife and daughters.

"Lady Caroline, the farmer's bedroom is just through that door. Would you care to join me there?"

"O, yes, my lord, but," she looked around the room and spotted a glass jug in the corner. "We must have more mead."

"I could not agree more," said Lord Edmund. "More mead it is."

Lady Caroline took the jug and two cups and followed Lord Edmund into the bedroom. They sat on the edge of the bed. Lady Caroline let him explore her body with his hands.

"You are a wanton woman, Lady Caroline. My type. Are you as wanton as the whores in Stoke?"

"I may be even more so," said Caroline. "Lie back."

Lord Edmund's breathing grew shallow and rapid as his excitement rose.

"You must have more mead, my lord," she said. Turning her back to him she emptied the contents of a phial secreted in her clothing into his cup. "Here, my lord. Enjoy. Now, did that woman in Stoke sit on your face? I can sit on your face. How would you like that?"

"I would like that," he mumbled as she lifted her smock and straddled his chest.

"Like this?" she said.

"Like that," he said as he dozed off. "Like tha. . ."

Lady Caroline slid herself closer to his face. She grabbed a handful of hair, lifted his head and pulled out his pillow. Seizing his chin in one hand, she righted his head so that his sightless eyes were pointed directly at the ceiling. She put the pillow over his face and lifted her hips just enough to be able to slide onto the pillow where she let her full weight settle. "There, there, my lord."

Edmund's brain soon ran out of oxygen and in a final surge for survival sent an impulse down his body, raising the mightiest erection he had ever had. "Too bad you will not be around to enjoy that," Caroline said.

Meanwhile, in the other room, Gwen and Henry were engaged in a bit of sport.

"Have you ever played horsey, my lord?" said Gwen.

"Horsey, horsey. No, no. Teach me to play horsey," he said.

"Take off all your clothes," she ordered. "You must not be wearing anything except your boots."

"Yes, yes, princess," he said as he hurriedly stripped.

"Now down on all fours," she said.

"All fours, yes. Like this?"

"You are a quick study, my lord. You are my horse and I am your rider."

"Yes, yes," said Henry as his excitement rose.

Gwen hoisted her robe and straddled the man's bare back. "Now whinny and neigh. You are a happy horse," she said.

Henry made strange noises.

"You do not sound like a horse. I am sure you can do better than that." She gave him a whack on the buttock with the flat of her hand. He kept trying to make horse sounds but to little avail. "You do not believe you are a horse. You must have a bridle. Real horses have bridles."

"Yes, princess. I need a bridle."

Gwen seized a length of rope and quickly tied a noose in one end. She gyrated her hips while slipping the noose over his head. She tugged on the rope. "Do you like the bridle?"

"I like the bridle."

Gwen took the other end of the rope and laid a few stripes on his backside. Lord Henry was so ecstatic he almost fell into a swoon. "Giddy up, giddy up," she said. She glanced at the bedroom door where Lady Caroline was standing. They nodded to each other and Caroline took the end of the rope from Gwen. She heaved it up over a rafter and pulled it taut. Henry began to choke. Gwen dismounted from her horsey's back and the two of them hoisted him into the air. He grabbed at the rope around his neck seeking to free himself but succeeded only in exposing the naked front of his body to the women's wrath.

"Is that not the funniest thing you ever saw?" said Caroline. "His brother did the same thing when I suffocated him."

Lord Henry's legs flailed in the air but quietened after several minutes. From thenceforward, the two brothers slept soundlessly into eternity. Princess Gwen and Lady Caroline returned to their camp.

"I think we can move forward with our mission, now," she said.

~~~

The farmer's wife and daughters were bereft. "We cannot manage the farm on our own," she lamented. "What are we to do?"

"First," said Gwen. "Tell me your names."

"I am Helen Bradford. My husband was James Bradford and our son was James. My daughters are Anne and Mary."

The girls dropped to one knee. "Your ladyship, thank you for rescuing us from the wolves," said Anne. "We are at your service."

"If you are certain you do not want to return, you are welcome to join us. Ours is not an easy life, but at least you will be safe."

"Thank you, your ladyship," said Helen. "We can cook and clean. We will earn our keep."

Gwen chuckled aloud. "Clean what? We sleep in tents made from animal hides and cook over a campfire. You would certainly be helpful. Do not worry about your keep. Your keep is our keep."

"You are a princess," Helen dared to note. "May I ask why you are living in the forest?"

"I am Princess Gwenllian ap Llewellyn, heir to the Welsh throne. I was once sister to the king, but am no longer."

The women looked at her quizzically.

"I am the daughter of Llewellyn, the late king of Gwynedd. When I was an infant I was kidnapped by the king's father Edward I and raised disguised as his son. As an adult I have chosen to reclaim the throne in opposition to the king who would have it for his own. As for the Lancasters, they were a cruel and worthless pair who sought to take me and my wards captive. They learned to their chagrin that we are warriors. We humiliated the Lancasters, and they brought an army down to storm my castle in Warwickshire. They killed my husband and sacked the castle, but we escaped. So you see, your revenge on those cowards is also my revenge. We are women, we are strong, and we survive."

The Monks stepped forward. "I am Lady Caroline."

"I am Charlotte Giveney."

"I am Lady Alice."

"I am Lady Elizabeth."

"We are the Monks of Arden," said Princess Gwenllian.

~~~

"We are about to enter hostile territory," said Gwen. "To engage in open conflict on our journey to Beaumaris would be to jeopardize our mission."

"Princess," said Kallias. "You have used me recently. Perhaps I can help you now. If you forge ahead obviously armed to the teeth, you will invite a confrontation. Suppose we change our appearance to that of merchants. I can make that happen."

"That is an interesting idea," said Gwen. "It would reduce the threat from Edward's men. The only other hazard would be bandits, and we could deal with them."

"Our numbers are growing," said Kallias, "and I will need some assistance."

"Perhaps we can draft the Bradford girls as trainees in the art of disguise," said Gwen. "Would that interest you, girls?"

"It would, your ladyship" said Anne. "Mother?"

"Yes," said Helen. "It is important work, and I think you should do it. Mary? How about you?"

"I will gladly help in any way I can."

~~~

"We must keep moving," said Gwen. "We will have to take our chances with our adversaries until Kallias has finished his work."

"We are not far from Wrexham, I believe," said Kallias. "We can dispatch men and a wagon to the town for certain supplies I will need for my work. In the meantime, the girls and I will work on the facial disguises."

Anne and Mary rode with Kallias in a covered wagon, where he opened his magic box of secrets to them. "The warrior women," he began, "will have to be disguised. Word is out that the Monks are moving through the area. They would be quickly recognized in their green habits. I will show you how to make the Monks look like men and all of us look like merchants."

The girls giggled at the prospect.

Princess Gwen ordered the band to proceed to Ruabon twelve miles to the northwest. "Ruabon is a staunchly Welsh village off the main route between Wroxeter and Chester," she said. "We will stop long enough for Kallias to prepare our disguises for the journey into hostile territory."

Kallias set Helen Bradford and two servant girls to work cutting and stitching fabric for new robes. "They must not look new," he cautioned. "rub some dirt into them, especially along the hems."

"Are you ready for the Monks?" said Gwen.

"I am, your ladyship. Seat yourselves in a row on this fallen log and put back your cowls. Loosen your hair and we will begin."

Gwen, Alice, Charlotte, Elizabeth, and Caroline sat for the transformation.

"With your permission," said Kallias, "I will trim a few strands of hair from your heads while Mary and Anne apply the base makeup. They have collected oak galls which I have extracted. Mary, pour a little sour wine* into the extract."

"It turned so dark," she exclaimed.

"You just made iron gall ink," said Kallias. "Now dip your cotton squares into the ink. Rub it into the skin on the inside of your forearm and tell me what you see."

"It stains my skin," said Anne. "What shall I do with it next?"

"Give me your square," he said to Anne. "With your permission, your ladyship, I will apply this to the skin of your face. We must make any strangers believe that you are a man. We begin by darkening your skin a shade with the ink. Close your eyes, your ladyship."

Kallias smoothed the ink over her face and indicated to Anne and Mary that they should follow suit on the other four. "Not too dark," he cautioned. "Just enough to make them look weatherworn."

Kallias's palette consisted of vermilion from cinnabar, charcoal, a yellow dye extracted from wild mignonette, chalk, and the dull blue of woad.* Kallias showed the girls how to use blue to subdue the reddishness of the lips. They mixed together woad, vermilion, and charcoal with chalk and applied it lightly around the eyes, along the jaw line, and to the top of the forehead to create the illusion of depth to their features. "That was the easy part," he said. "Your ladyship, as you know the next step will take some time. Monks, be patient."

Kallias had snipped samples of hair from each of the women, which they held in their hands during the procedure. He cut the strands into segments half an inch long. Using special tweezers from his *bag of magic tricks*, Kallias and the two girls painstakingly glued strands of hair between the women's brows, across their upper lips, and on their chins and cheeks.

"Charlotte, you make such a cute boy," Alice laughed. "Kiss me."

"Hold still, please," said Kallias. "You will have plenty of time to admire each other when we are finished."

"Mrs. Bradford," said Kallias. "Are the robes ready?"

"They are," she said.

"Everybody," said Gwen. "Gather round."

The mounted cavalry wore leather cuirasses and leggings. "Give them the black robes," said Gwen. "Conceal your arms until you need to use them."

The drivers and other servants were already outfitted in the rustic robes of peasants. The Bradfords and other women wore kirtles over shirts. They were issued the russet robes.

"The Monks, Squire Gwyn, and my yeomen shall conceal their arms beneath woad," said Gwen. "A word of caution to all of you regarding how to address each other. We must not betray our true identities if we are accosted by territorial authorities. You will call me Mrs. De Wynne. The squire will be Mr. Ambrose and Lady Ariel, Mrs. Shore. The Monks will mingle among the servants and be addressed only by their first names. Cavalrymen and servants will use their own names. The ruse should allow us to make our way to Garth Celyn unmolested."

Early the next morning, the merchant caravan continued on its journey. Kallias touched up the Monks' makeup and they broke camp. Thirty-seven travelers accompanied two wagons disguised with merchandise bought at Wroxeter. "We must try to reach Deganwy where I have kinsmen who will join us," said Gwen.

~~~

Though William Wallace was dead, his hatred of the English lived on. His followers shared common cause with the Welsh in seeking independence. However, such sympathies were not intense enough to discourage roving bands of rogue Highlanders from swooping down from the Cumbrian mountains to lighten the purses of unwary travelers to the south.

"Hold on there," came a booming voice from the wood at the side of the road. A large man dressed in close-fitting trousers and wearing an ancient Wallace tartan surcoat of orange and dark brown stepped out. He was armed with a spear in one hand and a small shield in the other. Squire Gwyn signaled the caravan to a halt. The Monks and the cavalry went on alert.

"What is your business with us?" said the squire.

"My business is to relieve you of your money and your merchandise," he said.

"Ha," Gwyn snorted. "You look fierce, but how do you propose to overcome twenty-six travelers single-handedly?"

The man whistled and twenty similarly armed men emerged from the cover of the wood. Bristling with spears, they moved to surround the caravan. "My men will collect your purses, and we will take your wagons."

"Are you sure of this?" said Gwyn.

"I am sure, and are those two young girls I see? I will have them as well."

"I see by your tartans that you are followers of William Wallace," said Gwyn. "Do you know why he lost his fight with the English?"

"What does that have to do with your surrendering your goods to me?"

"Just this," said Gwyn, casting off his outer robe to reveal himself as a man at arms. The Monks and the cavalry followed suit and brought their bows to the ready. "You are no match for Welsh bowmen, something Wallace learned to his regret."

One of the bandits tried to throw a spear and as he drew back took an arrow in the chest from a cavalryman's bow. He fell forward as the rest of the band melted back into the forest.

"You will join your friend face down in the dirt if I ever see you again," Gwyn shouted as the leader followed his men.

Unruffled by the encounter, the Monks and cavalrymen gathered up their mean attire and the caravan continued on toward Northop Hall.

"That is one gang of thieves that knows we are not merchants," said Squire Gwyn. "Do you think the word will go out on us?"

"Who would they tell?" said Gwen. "They are outlaws. They have no friends here. They might catch up to sympathizers up north. By that time we will be long gone."

Chapter Eleven

Odyssey

"Guy, Guy," said Gwen, peering into the darkness of the forest. She called her retinue to a halt and dismounted.

"No one is there, your ladyship," said Lady Ariel, perplexed by her peculiar behavior.

"But I saw him," she insisted.

"Guy is dead, my dear one. I am so sorry." Lady Ariel dismounted as Gwen wandered toward the shadows cast by the trees. She caught up to the grieving woman and took her by the arm. Gwen pulled away and continued on.

"Guy, Guy," she pleaded. "Show yourself. I am your wife. You know me as Penny. I know you are in there, my love. I took back my given name, but you can still call me Penny. Come, join us. I will reclaim the throne in Gwynedd. I shall be queen and you shall be my prince consort."

Lady Ariel remained close at hand as the distraught woman continued her conversation with the phantom in her head.

"Come to me, my darling," Gwen said as she started to undress.

At this point, Lady Ariel stepped in and wrapped her arms securely around the princess. At first Gwen resisted, but then relaxed and allowed herself to melt into Lady Ariel's embrace. "We must get back to the others, your ladyship."

~~~

The Celtic mound upon which stood the holy enclosure of Eurgain rose before the merchant caravan as it approached Northop.

"My cousin Dafydd Lawgoch hides here in the guise of an abbot," said Gwen to Squire Gwyn.

As they drew closer, the sounds of the village grew louder. Farm houses built of wood lay on both sides of the road. Their orientation bore no relation to the right-of-way, but rather appeared to face in whatever direction suited the fancy of the builder at the time of construction. Dogs ran out yapping at the passing caravan. Above the din could be heard the sharp, rhythmic singing of the blacksmith's hammer on his anvil. Wagon and cart traffic increased and lent the sounds of wheels rolling over stones and squishing through muddy ruts. Peddlers and tinkers shouted at each other as the density of the street traffic increased.

Under the watchful eye of the guards, Squire Gwyn directed his wagons to a row of shops. He separated himself from his make-believe merchants, leaving Eldric and the Bradfords to haggle with the locals. Gwyn, as Mr. Ambrose, led the women to the abbey where they were greeted by a prior with a puzzled look on his face.

"I am Prior Portman. What do you want?"

"I am Mr. Ambrose, a lowly textile merchant. This is Mrs. De Wynn, her companion Mrs. Shore, and her attendants."

"There is nothing I can help you with here. You must return to the village where the other merchants do their business."

Gwen threw back her hood to reveal her face and flowing golden hair. "I would like to see the abbot, Prior."

"The abbot does not deal with merchants. As I told Mr. Ambrose, you must return to the village."

Gwen flung off her robe, revealing herself to be a woman of status.

"My lady," said the prior. "Who are you really, Mrs. De Wynne?"

"I am Princess Gwenllian ap Llewellyn, heir to the throne of Gwynedd. Your abbot is my cousin Dafydd Lawgoch."

"I beg your pardon, your ladyship," said the prior laconically. "Please follow me."

~~~

The prior conducted Gwen and her companions to the parlor where they were greeted by the abbot. "Your ladyship, the prior tells me you are my cousin Gwenllian."

"That is correct, Dafydd, if I may use the familiar. I was kidnapped by Edward as an infant and spirited away from Gwynedd. That is why we have never met."

"My cousin Gwenllian is rotting away at the Lincolnshire priories, So, tell me, who are you truly?"

"I am that woman, Dafydd. The story of my exile to Lincolnshire was concocted by the king to cover his perfidy. He tried to have me raised as his son, stupid man, something bound to be revealed I was not."

"Do you have any proof of your identity?"

"Nothing but my word."

"How can I know you are not an imposter?"

"Have you heard a story circulating related to the Earl of Lancaster?"

"Yes, indeed," said the abbot. "It is said the lascivious pair of bastard sons got their comeuppance not far from here. It seems they had a bit of a history of chasing after the king's sister and her wards."

"Whom you see before you, abbot," said Gwen. She motioned to the wards who shed their habits and stood in formation for the abbot's inspection. "We are the Monks of Arden."

"Your notoriety precedes you, your ladyship," said the abbot. "What do you want of me?"

"I intend to return to Gwynedd to reclaim the throne denied me by my erstwhile brother. I wish you to provide fifty men at arms and join me in this quest. Our cousin Owain is imprisoned in Bristol Castle. We shall free him, and he will bring with him more recruits as we make a final assault on Garth Celyn. North Wales will be restored to its former glory."

Lady Ariel had a worried look on her face.

The abbot crossed himself. "I am afraid, your ladyship," he said, "that I am not who you think I am."

"O, but you are. I am sure of it," Gwen replied, undeterred. "As a child, I was put in the care of women who told me of our storied past, the glories of the princes of Gwynedd. You and I and our cousin Owain are of that blood."

"There is little I am able to do in support of your quest," said the abbot. "Prior Portman, have the shepherd select ten sheep for the princess's group."

"You are truly generous," said Gwen. "Lady Ariel, give the abbot ten gold florins,* one for each man."

"Yes, your ladyship."

"I wish I could do more, princess," said the abbot knowingly, "but to do more is not within my power. Godspeed."

~~~

The old Roman commercial road followed the coastline of the Irish Sea.

"I cannot tell you," said Gwen to Lady Ariel as they moved on, "how disappointed I am that my cousin could not accompany us on our journey. I understand he has heavy responsibilities, but what could be more important than regaining our patrimony?"

"He believes your patrimony has been lost to the English king, your ladyship. Too many Welsh have become Englishmen."

"Be of good cheer, Lady Ariel. All is not lost, and our army has grown by ten more men-at-arms."

"Yes, your ladyship."

"We shall arrive at Flint Castle before sundown," said Gwen. "My cousin Madog ap Maredudd is castellan. He will join us with many men-at-arms."

The castle lay at the edge of the River Dee estuary. "Another monument to my brother's treachery," Gwen sniffed. "We must trust that Madog is not unbreakably loyal to him."

Squire Gwyn signaled the caravan to a halt as they approached the gatehouse. "You will proceed to the borough, presenting yourselves as cloth merchants while the princess negotiates for men and arms."

Squire Gwyn led the Monks toward the gatehouse. At the edge of the moat, he shouted to the gatekeeper, "Lower the drawbridge for Princess Gwenllian."

The gatekeeper summoned the castellan, who viewed the group from an upper window. Squire Gwyn removed his peasant robe to reveal himself as the princess's armed guardian. "We come in peace," said Gwyn. "The princess requests an audience with Madog ap Maredudd."

"Come forward," said the castellan.

The drawbridge creaked into place, and the small group moved to the large wooden gate. It swung open as they approached. The castellan, backed by six mounted men-at-arms, blocked their further entry. "Who are you?" he demanded to know.

Gwen removed her habit and peeled off her disguise. "I am your cousin Gwenllian ap Llwellyn, Madog ap Maredudd."

"You must have me confused with someone else. I am Sir Geoffrey Gallant."

"You are my cousin, sir."

"I do not think so," said Sir Geoffrey.

"This is Flint Castle, another grotesque monument to my kidnapper's infamy. Surely you remember the days of the glorious Welsh nobility from which you are descended. You cannot have rolled over in fealty to this despot."

"The despot, as you call him, is my king, your ladyship. Your story is known throughout the kingdom. We are assured you are in competent hands. The king has issued orders that you are not to be harmed in any way."

Gwen exploded. "In competent hands? Not harmed in any way? I am the princess. How dare you patronize me? This is my husband Sir Guy de Lacy," she said, pointing to Squire Gwyn, who made eye contact with Sir Geoffrey and subtly shook his head.

Sir Geoffrey summoned grooms who took charge of his guests' horses. He escorted them over the tower moat to the entrance of the immense donjon* located a few paces to the right. Inside, the keep was divided into concentric galleries around an open central area, conveying the sense of the tower as a hollow cylinder. The castellan turned the guests over to the steward, who led them up a spiral staircase to a series of rooms.

"Please refresh yourselves," he said. "A meal will be prepared for your enjoyment. I will send a servant for you in an hour."

Gwen and Lady Ariel retired to one room and the wards to another. Squire Gwyn left the keep and sought out the castellan.

"The princess is not well," said Gwyn to Sir Geoffrey. "The death of her husband at the hands of the Lancasters left her bereft. At first she seemed to be coping fairly well but lately she has been seeing her late husband in the shadows. As you witnessed, she even believes at times that I am Sir Guy."

"It is well that the baron is away," said Sir Geoffrey. "It will make it easier for me to resolve the problem."

~~~

"The princess does not concern herself overmuch with us anymore," lamented Caroline to her sisters as they waited in their room for dinner.

Alice, picking up on a tremor in their hitherto rock solid relationship with the princess, ventured to admit that she was growing weary of the life. "I want to get married, have a husband, have children."

"The princess is barren and quite mad," said Elizabeth. "We owe her much . . . but how much?"

"Please, sisters, let us not talk of mutiny," said Charlotte.

"I agree," said Elizabeth.

"You are all of noble birth," said Charlotte. "The princess lifted me out of the peasantry. Among us, I have gained the most. My debt to the princess is greater than yours."

"There is very little more she can do for us," said Caroline. "How much should we be expected to do for her in return?"

"Since the death of Sir Guy she no longer engages us in private conversation," said Alice. "Lady Ariel and Squire Gwyn have enclosed her in a protective shield. She trained us as scholars and warriors. Now we differ little from Squire Gwyn's men. What can we do beyond serving as four more armed guards?"

"If Sir Geoffrey is to be believed," said Caroline, "she has little to fear for her physical safety, apart from rogues and bandits, and I doubt that Squire Gwyn's men would have much problem with their likes."

A knock on the door was followed by the announcement that their meal was ready.

~~~

The great hall rose from the inner bailey to a height of two stories. The kitchen sat apart, connected to the back entrance of the hall by a covered walk. Servants escorted the guests to a dining area in the great hall, where they all sat on one side of trestle tables. The tables were covered with a white cloth with a secondary cloth offset to the diners' side that covered their laps and was used to wipe their hands during the meal. Each place setting consisted of a trencher* and a spoon. Sir Geoffrey joined them in the communal setting unmarked by the usual formalities accorded noble guests.

Using their fingers. the guests took pieces of boiled mutton from common bowls and teased it apart on their plates using their own all-purpose daggers. A servant circulated behind the guests with a bowl and ewer for the guests to wash their hands between courses.

The pantler* provided table bread and the butler, wine. The diners also had a small variety of vegetables to choose from. The meal was finished off with oven-fresh mulberry tarts.

"You are very kind to have provided such a fine banquet for me and my people," said Gwen. "We are refreshed and received new strength to soldier on in our quest."

"It is my honor and pleasure, princess," said Sir Geoffrey.

"I would consider it my honor, Sir Geoffrey, if you would select fifty of your finest men-at-arms to accompany us. Upon resurrection of the old order you will be amply rewarded."

"What is your plan, princess?"

"My cousin Owain is being held captive in Bristol Castle. I will assemble a fleet to sail south from Anglesey, and then proceed up Bristol Channel to the castle where I shall free him to join us. I will purchase more ships in Swansea, and we will sail back to Beaumaris, from which I will launch my final assault on Garth Celyn."

"That sounds like an ambitious plan, princess," said Sir Geoffrey.

"You, my cousin, will help make it all possible."

"Now that I understand your plan, perhaps there is a way I can help. I will give you a cog* built at the boat works here on the estuary. My duties at Flint preclude my accompanying you on your mission, but the boat will be safe and will take you where you want to go."

~~~

The cog, rechristened *Llewellyn's Revenge* by the princess, displaced thirty tons. Wide and seaworthy, it bore a single mast and a square-rigged sail. Decks were present fore and aft with a small cabin for the Monks, Lady Ariel, and the Bradfords. The servants and crew slept wherever they could find a place. A few chickens and sheep were put aboard a small, sail-rigged tender towed behind the cog.

With all aboard, the princess bade farewell to Sir Geoffrey, and her crew rowed the cog slowly out into the estuary where they caught the wind to propel them onward to the Irish Sea. The wind from the northeast was brisk and chilly, but it pushed the *fleet* on its way at a speed of three knots. Their success at sea came about because Sir Geoffrey had lent them a seasoned coastal captain and four able bodied seaman, in part to see the princess safely on her journey, and, in part to ensure that he got his ship back in one piece.

~~~

Near the end of the first day, the magnificent limestone cliffs of the Great Orme at Llandudno came into view. Seven miles out to sea, they appeared as a white line on the horizon. The captain steered the ship closer to shore to take advantage of the protection offered by Llandudno Bay. Two of the four young Monks leaned over the gunwale heaving into the waves.

"We will be in calmer waters very soon," said Lady Caroline. "Perhaps even onshore for a while. It is the perfect cure for mal de mer. You will soon grow used to the sea and the sickness will go away."

"I don't want to do this anymore," said Alice tearfully.

"If you still feel that way when we get to Bristol, we will talk to the princess about it. It's only three days' ride to Warwick from there."

Charlotte looked pasty. The color had drained from her face and she had dribble down the front of her robe. "A fine lot of pirates we would make," she declared.

"We are a long way from Bristol," said Elizabeth. "We need to talk about this with the princess before we get there."

The princess and her party boarded tenders that met the *Revenge* as it sailed toward the Llandudno harbor. The princess insisted on standing in the bow like a figurehead as she entered her domain. Squire Gwyn steadied her from behind.

"My cousin Llywelyn ap Iorwerth is the Bishop of Bangor, lord of the Manor of Gogarth," said the princess. "He will join our cause."

The landlubbers, including Gwen's uncomplaining servants, gratefully stepped ashore, and it was the end of only the first day. They all hoped to prolong their stay on shore as long as possible. The remaining journey for them would be long and miserable. The next day at sea would take them to Holy Island, forty miles on.

The princess stepped ashore and announced she was there to see the bishop. The Gogarth reeve was notified of the presence at the waterfront of a woman claiming to be the bishop's cousin.

"I am Madog ap Hywell," he said as he approached her. "What is your business with the bishop?"

"I prefer to discuss that with him," she said.

"The bishop does not grant an audience to just anyone. Who are you?"

"I am Gwenllian ap Llewellyn, rightful heir to the throne of Gwynedd," she said, casting aside the oilskin she wore at sea. "Inform the bishop of that fact. I wish to see him at his earliest convenience."

The reeve looked at her skeptically. "Very well, your ladyship. Follow me."

~~~

Gwen and her followers made similar stops at Holy Island, the nearly abandoned outpost on Bardsey Island, Ramsey Island (after two days at sea), across St. Brides Bay to Skomer, Lundy Island, and the tiny settlement at Weston-super-Mare that put them within striking distance of Bristol Castle fifteen miles inland.

"This has been the most miserable voyage of my entire life," Elizabeth moaned as they disembarked. "Everyone sick all the time. Everything I ate went over the side. I lost weight. I would not have the strength to fight off an attack of butterflies."

"At least we all made it safely," said the ever-reassuring Lady Caroline. "We are close to Princess Gwen's destination. We shall learn soon what her next move will be."

"Land," exclaimed Alice. "*Terra firma*. I want to go home."

"Fine job," said Gwen to the captain. "Perhaps I will make you admiral of my fleet. Squire Gwyn, bring the army ashore, and you Monks, buck up, we are almost there."

Gwen's army was thirty-seven strong, not counting the sheep she believed to be archers. Their encampment at Weston attracted curious local onlookers. The sheep milled around bleating. Chickens squawked as small boys poked at them with sticks through the bars of their cages.

"We will establish our base camp here," said the princess to Squire Gwyn. "Tomorrow we re-board the ships and sail into the port of Bristol. From there I will send an envoy to the castle demanding their immediate surrender of my cousin Owain."

Squire Gwyn moved slowly toward Princess Gwen.

"Did I not make myself clear?" she said.

"Indeed, your ladyship. However, we are but a tiny force. We would not have a chance standing up to the castle garrison. Perhaps a better approach would be to use some quiet diplomacy."

"The time for diplomacy is past. These English understand only force." The pitch of her voice rose as she scanned the beach. "Look at my fleet. Look around you at my army." Gwen's gaze darted from point to point as her level of agitation rose.

Gwyn moved closer to her. "You may be my husband," she screamed, "but I am your queen and sovereign." Lady Ariel moved toward her in the hope of defusing what was rapidly becoming a crisis, but she was not quick enough.

"If you will not honor me, sir, then you must die," and with that, she drew her dagger and plunged it into Squire Gwyn's chest.

Lady Ariel and the Monks were stunned into silence. The Monks regained their discipline and quickly disarmed the princess. "You have killed Squire Gwyn," said Lady Caroline.

"Squire Gwyn, Squire Gwyn? That is my husband killed by the Lancasters." She knelt beside the body. "What have they done to you, my love?"

The crowd of townsfolk that had witnessed the spectacle were as taken aback as were members of the princess's retinue. A loud murmur ran through the audience. One man hurried away unnoticed. A few minutes later a man dressed in a velvet robe and wearing a medallion around his neck rode up on horseback. He looked down at the body and dismounted.

"I am Sir Richard Camden, sheriff of Gloucestershire. Who are you?" he said to the princess.

The Monks remained grouped around Gwen. "I am Gwenllian ap Llewellyn, heir to the throne of Gwynedd, and these are the Monks of Arden."

"Who did this?" said the sheriff, looking down at Squire Gwyn's body.

"The bastard sons of the Earl of Lancaster," said Gwen.

"Hmm. Being dead, I wonder how they could have done this. Where are they?"

Lady Ariel caught the attention of the sheriff and shook her head.

"I am here to free my cousin Owain from the clutches of the odious man I used to know as my brother, your king, Edward."

"Princess, it will be necessary for you to accompany me to the castle."

"Very well," said Gwen. "I am sure we can expedite his release, and then I can be on my way to reclaim my throne. Perhaps you can be persuaded to join us. You would be amply rewarded."

~~~

Bristol Castle was built on a prominence between the Rivers Avon and Frome. The magnificent keep housed the great hall as well as the chambers of the court and those of the First Earl of Gloucester, Hugh de Audley. His wife Margaret de Clare was the widow of the despised Piers Gaveston.

"Gwenllian, Gwenllian," said Lady Gloucester when they were introduced. "I sense something familiar. My late husband used to speak of a boy Penfelyn raised in the king's household. Strange episode. I heard that the boy was actually a girl and later changed his name to . . . to Gwenllian. You were that boy, were you not?"

"I am she," said Gwen.

"The sheriff informs me that you got into some sort of altercation with one of your men, and that he ended up dead."

"He was my faithless husband, my lord," said Gwen.

Lady Ariel raised her hand. "I am Lady Ariel Shore, my lord. The old king Edward made me companion to the princess during the early days of her childhood. So well concealed was the truth of her sex that even I did not know Penfelyn was a girl for several years. She gathered around her the four warrior women you see before you. They call themselves the Monks of Arden. They are formidable fighters, as the Lancasters discovered to their chagrin when they sought to take them as concubines. Some years ago the princess had married her bodyguard Sir Guy de Lacy, who gave up his life in her defense when they were attacked by an overwhelming Lancastrian force. My princess has been slipping away ever since."

"So she killed the man, Squire Gwyn, was it?"

"She did," said Lady Ariel, "but she believed the squire to be her dead husband. She cannot understand that she killed anyone since her husband was already long gone. I beg you to take her state into consideration. Her ladyship is not responsible for her actions."

"You Monks, as you call yourselves," said the earl. "Lady Gloucester will conduct you to a comfortable upper chamber. The princess and Lady Ariel will occupy an adjacent room to be locked and guarded at all times, until I decide on the disposition of this case. We shall discuss it further after the doctors have examined her."

~~~

The gatehouse keeper admitted two men dressed in long, black hooded robes. One carried a large book, the other a small leather case. The chamberlain conducted them to the earl's privy chambers.

"I have a mad woman upstairs," said Gloucester. "She has committed a murder."

"Do you wish that we should examine her, my lord?" said one of the doctors.

"I do. But be advised she is not a commoner. Though out of power she is one of the last three surviving princes of Wales. I have the other two in my dungeon."

"Do you have any special instructions, my lord?"

"She is to be handled with care by order of the king from whom she has received special protection. She is deemed to be harmless, and so I am forbidden from detaining her."

"Did she kill anyone of importance?"

"No. Just some squire in her company. All I call upon you to do is bring her back to her senses, so I can send her on her way. I have more pressing matters at hand."

The guard announced the arrival of the doctors. Lady Ariel opened the door. The doctors went in and surveyed the room. It was furnished with a bed, a small table and ewer, and a bench. Gwen was disheveled but came to attention as the two men entered. She eyed them warily. Lady Ariel held her by the elbow.

"We are doctors, your ladyship," said one. "The earl informs us that you may not have been feeling well. Would you agree?"

The other doctor watched the proceedings and leafed slowly through the great book, turning pages forward, hesitating, then flipping back.

"I see that you have come to join me in the pursuit of the throne that is rightfully mine," said Gwen.

"Perhaps, your ladyship, but first the earl has instructed us to examine you."

"Examine me? Examine me for what?"

"For soundness of mind and body, your ladyship."

"Return my weapons, sir, and I shall demonstrate to you the soundness of my body."

"Lady Ariel, you may remove the princess's robes."

Gwen resisted at first, but finally relented. Dressed only in a shirt that reached to her knees, she stood before the two men.

"If you will permit me," said the doctor as he stepped forward and placed his ear against her chest.

"Contumelious old goat," said Gwen.

"Open your mouth, your ladyship."

Gwen complied and stuck out her tongue at the old man.

"Do you have pain?"

"My only pain is your intrusive presence here," she said as she took a swing at the doctor. Her hand grazed the side of his head as he fell back. Lady Ariel tightened her grip on Gwen's arm.

The two doctors retreated to a consultation.

"Excess of blood and yellow bile," said one.

"I agree," said the other. "Guard."

The guard entered the room and set aside his weapons.

"We must bleed the princess," said the doctor. "It is only by relieving her of the pernicious effects of bad blood that she shall be cured."

The other doctor and the guard seized Gwen by the arms and flung her on her back onto the bed. "Lady Ariel, hold her feet."

The doctor opened his case and removed a lancet and a bowl which he placed on the floor below her elbow. Gwen squirmed and howled. She was in such superb physical condition that it was all that three people could do to hold her in submission. Quickly and expertly the doctor opened a large vein inside Gwen's elbow. The dark blood began to flow and soon the basin had received two pints. The color drained from Gwen's face as the doctor secured a bandage to cover the wound.

"That should calm her down," said the doctor. "We may have to repeat the treatment tomorrow. In the meantime, she should drink no wine and be fed only raw greens, barley water, and milk."

The doctors gathered up their gear and bowed out, leaving a weak and pallid princess and her companion to make the best of what had just transpired.

~~~

"I never felt afraid when the princess was leading us," said Alice, "but now?"

Lady Caroline suddenly seemed to stand a bit taller. "Do not be afraid," she said. "She cared for us. Now it is our turn to care for her."

"We must devise a rescue from those doctors," said Elizabeth, "before they kill her."

"I agree," said Lady Caroline. "I shall go to the earl to try to get him to release her into our custody. Charlotte, you must go down to the ship and speak to the captain. You must convince him to stay in port until we have safely spirited away the princess. She cannot be allowed to think she has been abandoned."

~~~

Reluctantly, but with the weight of a few extra pounds in his purse, the captain agreed. With the help of Gwen's servants, his crew emptied the barge of its load of chickens and sheep, which would make his return journey easier.

On her own initiative, Charlotte contracted with a local wagon works to customize a conveyance for their expected northward journey. For the princess, the lead wagon would be canopied and equipped inside with a special pallet on which she could recline, as well as benches to sit on, if she chose. The other would be a conventional supply wagon.

Charlotte reported back to Lady Caroline, who had assumed the role of their de facto leader. The caravan could be ready in as little as two days, if the earl cooperated.

~~~

"You leave me with two choices, Lady Caroline," said the earl. "I cannot hold her as a captive, and I certainly do not want her as a guest. I have better things to do than spoon-feed a mad woman. Since you are preparing to leave us anyway, I have decided to let you do just that. Take her away when all is ready. The sooner, the better."

~~~

Two days later, once again astride her horse, Gwen led her entourage northward. Four men-at-arms supplemented the four Monks as her bodyguards. Eldric the Lesser became the default leader of the small group of the princess's followers. Kallias was gone, having joined a group of traveling actors he found in Bristol. Apart from the Monks, the group of Gwen's female companions was reduced to Lady Ariel and the ever-grateful Bradfords. Everyone understood that from now on Lady Caroline would speak for the princess.

Chapter Twelve

Caroline Mulier Officium

Princess Gwenllian gripped her saddle with both hands. Eldric held the horse's bridle lightly, walking before her, turning his head frequently to assess her steadiness.

"I do feel the least bit light-headed, I admit. For all the misery those doctors put me through, I think they may have done some good."

Eldric grew confident enough to let go of the bridle and mount his own horse that trailed behind. The four Monks immediately fell into a square formation surrounding the princess in case they were needed. The little caravan rumbled northward toward the Arden Forest where they had begun their journey. The old Roman road Fosse Way offered them both direction and a clear path to their destination.

"I do look forward to seeing mama and papa," said Elizabeth.

"As do I," said Charlotte.

Gwen drifted in and out of her own world, oblivious to the conversation taking place around her.

As their second day of travel drew to a close, in search of accommodations, Lady Caroline led the group to Gloucester, recently established and renamed at the site of the old Roman village of Glevum. Gloucester sat at a Roman crossroads linking the iron mines to the west with Cirencester to the east. The air was redolent with the odor of fish and manure. The road was barely wide enough to accommodate the passage of conveyances passing in opposite directions.

Wagonloads of iron ore pulled by teams of mules ground their way eastward. Lady Caroline ordered her followers to hug the right edge as the muleteers urged their weary animals forward on their way to the inland smelters. Her fellow travelers had donned their peasant robes and continued forward in the guise of merchants. They gave rise to no suspicion, blending well into the milieu of commerce that engaged the town.

The Monks concealed their identities within their hooded robes. Gwen had taken a turn for the worse and was confined to her wagon. The stress of having to deal with the princess was beginning to take its toll on Lady Ariel. She sat beside the reclining princess and held her hand, dozing off to the rhythmic rumble of the wagon wheels beneath her. The Bradford women took turns ministering to the princess. When not attending to that duty, they walked alongside the wagon.

Gloucester had a single inn large enough to accommodate everyone. The innkeeper was grateful to receive a higher class of guest than he was accustomed to. "I have three rooms for you," he said. "You will have to do your own cooking."

Mrs. Bradford stepped forward to declare that she was in charge of that department, and that she and her daughters would take care of the evening meal. "With Lady Caroline's permission," she volunteered, "perhaps you and your wife and daughter would care to join us."

The startled innkeeper said nothing for a moment, then accepted the invitation. "I have never before had a guest at my inn who offered to feed me and my family."

Lady Caroline inspected the premises and sent for the princess.

"Lady Ariel," said Mrs. Bradford. "Lady Ariel. We can bring in the princess now."

Lady Ariel was lying peacefully across the princess's breast, still holding her hand. She was still and did not answer. Mrs. Bradford got into the wagon and immediately realized that all was not well. The princess lay in a daze, softly mumbling to herself. Mrs. Bradford raised Lady Ariel's arm but got no response. She hurried back inside the inn and pulled Lady Caroline to the side. "It's Lady Ariel, my lady. I believe she has died."

Lady Caroline was silent at first. Tears formed at the corners of her eyes trickled down her cheeks as she ran to the wagon. "Are you all right, your ladyship?"

"I am very well, thank you," she said. "Lady Ariel is here to watch over me."

"We have lodgings for the night here at the inn. Lady Ariel will come with us and we shall fetch you in a few minutes." Lady Caroline summoned two of the men-at-arms to assist with Lady Ariel's removal. "Do not let on to the princess that anything is amiss."

The men lifted Lady Ariel's body from its resting place against the princess's bosom.

"Can she not walk on her own?" said the princess.

"Lady Ariel is quite tired, your ladyship. We are just giving her some assistance."

The men managed to get the body out of the wagon without disturbance. Members of the traveling group gathered about somberly as they took her inside.

"I am feeling much better now," said the princess, as she got herself down from the wagon and followed them inside. The men lay the body out on a bench. The reality of what had happened finally registered on the princess. She let out a long, anguished howl of grief and flung herself down on the body. "No, no, no," she wailed.

The innkeeper sent for the priest at the abbey of St. Peter.

Lady Caroline and Charlotte lifted the princess off the body and took her to one of the bedrooms. The priest arrived in the company of a deputy shire reeve, who asked them who they were.

"I am Caroline de Montfort. The dead woman is Mrs. Shore. We are wool merchants. Mrs. Shore was nurse to Mrs. De Wynne, who is ill. Mrs. De Wynne has received quite a shock and is resting in another room. Mrs. Shore had been complaining of fatigue before she died. We are all greatly saddened at her passing."

"Where was Mrs. Shore at the time of her death? Was anyone with her?"

There was a long pause before Lady Caroline answered. "Yes, sir. Mrs. De Wynne was with her in the covered area of the wagon."

"The sick woman? I must speak with her."

"She is quite stricken with grief, sir. It would not be a good idea?"

"I will be the judge of that," said the reeve. "Take me to her."

~~~

Gwen lay on her back staring at the ceiling. Her eyes seemed unfocused. Lady Caroline moved to her bedside and looked down at her.

"This is Mrs. De Wynne," she said to the reeve. "You may speak to her, but do not be surprised if she does not answer. She has become an invalid. We women have to take care of all her needs."

The reeve looked at the deranged woman and grunted.

"Are you my husband?" she said.

"No, madam. I am the reeve."

"I don't believe I know anyone by that name, sir. I am . . . I am. . .." Her eyes wandered. "I am very pleased to meet you. I have need of Lady Ariel. Would you fetch her for me?"

"Lady Ariel?" said the reeve to Lady Caroline. "Would that be Mrs. Shore? Why would she use a title when calling for a servant?"

"I must ask you to be discreet, sir," said Lady Caroline. "Mrs. De Wynne is actually Gwenllian ap Llewellyn, heir to the Welsh throne. She travels under the protection of the king."

"And you are?"

"I am Lady Caroline de Montfort. My father is Lord Thurstan de Montfort of Beaudesert Castle. My young companions are noble wards of the princess."

"I must ask you and your retinue to accompany me to the shire office while I investigate this matter further."

Lady Caroline nodded to the Monks who formed a semicircle around the reeve. They opened their habits to reveal the arms and warrior garb worn beneath. "I think not. We are the finest fighters in all of England," she boasted.

The reeve, surprised at the Monks' posturing, opined that perhaps that would not be necessary after all. "There does not appear to be any evidence of foul play. She was old. Death by natural causes, I would say. I must return now. I put you in the priest's hands."

The priest stood over Lady Ariel's lifeless form. "*In nomine Patris, et Filii, et Spiritus Sancti. Amen,*" he intoned as he made the sign of the cross. "Has this woman been baptized?"

"Yes, father," said Lady Caroline, supposing that to be true without any proof.

"We shall transport the body to the church, where it will be examined by the stone mason. A gift of five pounds to the abbey will allow her effigy to be placed close to the altar."

"Two pounds should suffice, Father."

"We are but a poor parish, my lady. For the five we could also recommend her to the pope for sainthood."

"St. Ariel," Caroline pondered. "Mmm . . .three and she goes next to the altar."

"Done, my lady," said the priest.

~~~

Lady Caroline estimated the distance from Gloucester to Beaudesert Castle to be about thirty-five miles, one day's long journey if all went well. They set out at dawn of the morning following Lady Ariel's interment. Princess Gwen's condition was such that she could not be trusted to ride horseback, and so she was restricted to the wagon. Mrs. Bradford sat with her, and the girls walked alongside. Not only was the little band approaching the castles where the wards' parents and protectors lived, they were also entering the vicinity of the home villages of the guards and servants who accompanied them.

One by one, the four men-at-arms who had been Gwen's faithful bodyguards melted into the wood. By the time they were within five miles of Beaudesert Castle, the guards and most of the servants had gone. Lady Caroline had given them leave to take the supply wagon in payment for their service, leaving only Gwen's van*, Eldric, the Monks, and the Bradfords to finish the journey. The driver was allowed to return home which left Eldric with the reins.

~~~

The Normans built Beaudesert Castle shortly after the conquest. They selected an elevated location to begin with, and then excavated around it in an elongated circle, pushing the dirt to the top, leaving a dry moat behind. It was on the motte* they constructed the early wooden fortress.

By the time of the de Montforts, Beaudesert had been upgraded to a stone-built castle enclosed by a curtain wall.

The gatehouse keeper peered down from the heights as the lone wagon grew near. Eldric whipped the mules forward as they climbed the grade leading to the bridge over the moat. The sound of wheels grinding in the gravel of the road gave way to the hollow rumble of hooves and wheels beating their rhythms on the timber causeway. A lone covered van accompanied by five horsemen and two pedestrians pulled up to the gate and stopped.

"Who are you?" the keeper demanded to know.

"I am Eldric the Lesser. I believe you are acquainted with my lady."

The lead rider threw back her hood. "I am Lady Caroline de Montfort."

The gatekeeper was overcome with joy. He ordered the gates opened wide as the motley band made its entrance. Grooms summoned from the stables led the mules to the foot of the bridge to the keep. The chamberlain, upon seeing who had arrived, raced inside to fetch Lord and Lady de Montfort. The liveried staff were beside themselves in their eagerness to welcome Lady Caroline home.

Lady Caroline embraced her old nanny, but rushed forward to throw her arms around her mother and father, who appeared directly behind her.

"My dear, dear Caroline," said de Montfort.

"Come in," said her mother.

"Before I do that," she said, "I must look after my traveling companions. Special issues are involved. It is a very long story I shall retail later. The princess Gwenllian ap Llewellyn is in the van. You knew her one time as Prince Penfelyn."

The de Montforts were nonplussed.

"The princess is very ill, quite mad, in fact. She must be taken to a bedroom where she can lie down. Mrs. Bradford looks after her needs. You will not understand all this until I explain, but that will be for another time."

Mrs. Bradford helped the princess down from the wagon, and, joined by two ladies-in-waiting, escorted her to a first floor room. She looked around, uncomprehending. Spotting Lord de Montfort, she asked, "Are you my husband?"

~~~

"This is the ever-loyal Eldric the Lesser," said Caroline to her parents, "lone male survivor of our journey. He was body servant to the princess from the beginning when she was passed off as a man. The three women in green habits are wards of the princess. You will remember them as Charlotte Giveney, Alice de Toeni, and Elizabeth Marmion. They are my sisters. We are the Monks of Arden. And last but not least are Anne and Mary, Mrs. Bradford's daughters."

Gone was the teen-aged girl who had left home to reside at Kenilworth Castle. In her place was a self-assured young woman clearly in charge of the situation.

"You have changed so, my dear," said her father. "You are not my little girl anymore. We are happy beyond words at your return, but I sense that you may not be staying very long. Am I correct?"

"I and my friends are your guests, father. I love you, but we have work to do. I am working on a plan. In the meantime, Alice, Elizabeth, and Charlotte will want to visit their homes for a few weeks. Princess Gwen, Eldric, the Bradfords, and I will accept your hospitality here at Beaudesert."

~~~

Lady Caroline and the Monks retired to Caroline's former private apartments. The parlor was large enough to accommodate them all in a reasonable degree of comfort. For months, they had been girded for defense and eagerly sought the opportunity to shed their protective arms, gambesons, and trousers. They cast aside their green habits and let their warrior garb fall where they stood. Swords and bows clattered to the floor. Unencumbered by heavy gear, they sounded a collective sigh of relief. They breathed in clean air warm enough for them to be comfortable lounging around in the cotton shirts they wore next to their skin.

"I can breathe again," said Elizabeth, as she slumped down on a padded bench.

"There is a large, invisible presence in this room," said Lady Caroline. "Princess Gwenllian. If it were not for her, we would be sitting around doing needlework, waiting for our parents and guardians to bring suitors to our door."

"That would not be all bad," said Elizabeth.

"I am not saying it would be bad, only that we can do better than play the role of brood sows to perpetuate the patriarchy, however benign it might be."

"Without the princess," said Charlotte, "who among us would have had the gumption to break out of the mold? It would be more than most women could do on their own."

"The princess is not most women," said Alice. "In the beginning she was not a woman at all, at least in her own mind."

"Perhaps that early training made her tougher than if she had spent her girlhood staring at an embroidery hoop," said Lady Caroline. "Regardless, it did not change her inside, and we are deeply in her debt. She was there for us in our time of need, and we must not abandon her in hers."

"Mrs. Bradford's bad luck has become our good fortune," said Charlotte. "Poor Lady Ariel, loyal to the end, finally gave out. Just when the princess needed her the most, Mrs. Bradford was there to take her place."

"And do not forget about her daughters Mary and Anne," said Elizabeth. "They are of the age we were when the princess took us in."

"They are bright and industrious girls," said Lady Caroline. "We are now only four. What do you think?"

"But they are unschooled," Charlotte lamented. "They never had the advantage of being tutored by the Stonele friars as I did."

"Perhaps the situation is not as bad as you portray it," said Lady Caroline. "They read a little, cipher a little, and know their Bible quite well."

"It would take years," said Alice.

"It took years for us, as well," Lady Caroline reminded them. "If I ask him, my father will hire tutors for them. We can help also, and who better than us to train them in swordsmanship, archery, and horsemanship?"

This is all well and good," said Alice, "but what are we about? What are we to do? You told your father we have work to do. What work is that, Caroline?"

"I want us to work where we are needed most. I believe that is what the princess would want for us."

"Caring for the sick; ministering to the poor? God knows of the unmet need there. Is that what she would want?"

"I suppose there is a certain nobility in such pursuits, but they are already being done," Caroline continued. "What is it we can do above all others? What did the princess do for us that rarely, if ever, had been done before? The answer is she brought us together and showed us that we were equal to or better than the boys trained at the castle. What's more, as adults, when we have been forced into conflict with men, the men have learned that we are not to be trifled with, that we have minds, strength, and endurance, and more often than not can beat them at their own games. If their physical prowess exceeds ours, we outsmart them."

"But must we be at war with men all the time," said Elizabeth. "Look at your own father, Caroline. He is a dear man. Your mother seems quite content."

"He is a dear man, and my mother chooses to be content. She does not challenge him. She is subordinate, if not quite submissive all the time. It is her belief in the old myths that allows her the comfort of opinion without the discomfort of thought."

"Caroline," sputtered Charlotte. "How can you be so disrespectful of your mother?"

"I show her no disrespect. I respect her right to choose her role. But for the princess, I would have fallen into that way of thinking. And to the extent you too have fallen away, you place yourselves at the forefront of a new and modern philosophy."

"Surely you do not wish us to follow in Penthesilia's footsteps by cutting off our right breasts, mating with the enemy, and then killing all the boy babies?"

"Very funny, Alice," said Caroline, "but spare me the drama. Nevertheless, the true story of the Amazons is instructive. They were our spiritual forebears. Thinking they must be young men, the Scythians fought the Amazons. They killed many and gathered up their corpses, only to discover they were women. Being men, they were taken aback that they had done battle with a force of women who had inflicted casualties on them in a fair fight. Monks, take note here. The chink in the male armor was exposed. In the realization they had been slaying women in combat, the Scythian men decided to cease their hostilities and encamp their youngest compatriots on the periphery to see what the women would do next. They chose to stop killing the women and simply mimic their activities, do what they did. When the women discovered their presence and sought to chase them way, the men gave ground and fled. When the chase was over, the men returned to their encampment.

"O, those devils. Their ulterior motive was to have children with them, to sire more strong, Scythian babies. Over time, the Amazons concluded that the men were no longer intent on harming them, and let them venture closer. The women had only their weapons and horses and the men had only their weapons and horses. For a time the Scythians kept their distance from the Amazons, surviving by hunting and raiding, but not on each other.

"In the middle of the day, the Amazons would split into groups of one or two and retire to some secluded spot to relieve themselves. The Scythian men watched, their passions inflamed. One brave young man ventured to make contact with one of the women. She did not drive him away, but rather, consented to have intercourse with him. They did not speak to each other because they spoke different languages. They did not need to. The men returned to their camp and spread the word. From then on they met regularly with the Amazons.

"After a time, the Scythian men formed couples with the Amazon women with whom they first had sex. The men found the women's language impossible to master, but the women had no trouble with the men's. The women declared to the men that their customs and attitudes so differed from those of the Scythian women, they would be unable to integrate into their community. The men agreed, and they migrated to a new country and founded the Sauromatian nation. The women spoke Scythian, but only poorly. They continued to hunt on horseback and go to war with or without their husbands. Some, however, had no husbands since, in order to marry, they must have killed a man. They died in old age, barren."

"Not one among us has not killed a man," said Alice. "Are you giving us permission to marry and have children?"

"I am telling you that you do not have to subordinate yourselves either to men or to me. You do not need my permission. Most women do not have that choice. How better to serve than to extend rights of self-determination to that one half of the population that stands in man's shadow? Now, if you so choose, I suggest you go home to visit your families. Think about the legend of the Amazons. When you return we shall chart our future."

Chapter Thirteen

Charlotte

Charlotte Giveney, in the company of two armed guards from the Beaudesert garrison, received a hero's welcome upon her return to Leamington. She concealed her bow and five arrows beneath her clothing but had forgone the rest of her battle gear in favor of traditional robes of a somewhat finer grade than she had worn at her departure. No one who knew her from before could fail to appreciate the fact that she had matured and grown more self-assured.

The Church of St. Peter beckoned to all and so the village grew. News that their benefactor, still known to them as Prince Penfelyn, was gravely ill caused great sadness among the villagers, especially those who had personally met the prince. The local priest Father Benedict conducted a special mass offering prayers for the prince's recovery.

Mayor Robert opened his tavern to the village in celebration of Charlotte's return. He provided bread and cheese for everyone. He roasted pigs. Ale flowed freely. Childhood friends Madeleine, Annabelle, Mary and Antoinette flocked to her. Breathlessly, they wanted to know what it was like to live in a castle.

"Did you see the prince every day?" said Madeleine.

"Were there parties all the time?" said Mary.

"One at a time, please," she said. "I shared good rooms with three other girls. Our days were filled with training in horseback riding and martial arts, along with our education in letters. It was not easy."

Charlotte seemed to stand taller. It was not that she had grown in height since she left but, rather, she stood more erect, was more self-confident. In Leamington, Charlotte was a celebrity returned from a world her friends could only imagine. A visitor from a strange land where she had discovered worldly ways and acquired a vocabulary of thousands of words, she was uneasy in conversations with villagers whose vocabularies rarely exceeded a few hundred. The village had grown, but she had grown more. The simple people with their simple ways were like a constricting girdle from which she instinctively sought release. The pull of family and the old familiars was in a losing battle with the force of knowing she belonged with the Monks.

John, the baker's son, was the first on her doorstep. He held his cap in front of him. "I am very happy to meet you again, Charlotte. We used to play together when we were children. Do you remember?"

"I do, John," she said.

"You are looking very fine today," he said. "Will you . . . will you walk with me?"

"It will be my pleasure," she said after a brief hesitation. The lad missed a hint of reticence in her reply. They proceeded side by side down the main street. The villagers stared at them intently.

"See how everyone looks at us," said John. "You have made me very happy."

"John, my old friend, we are just walking. There is nothing more to it than that."

"I was hoping, now that we are both of age to . . ."

"Please go no further, John. We can remain friends if you wish, but nothing more."

John's hopes were dashed, but he took it stoically. "Too much to hope for," he said with resignation.

~~~

John was but the first. He was followed by the miller's son Edward, the brewer's son Felix, and half a dozen other young men her age who would have given much to wed her.

"Have you thought of marrying?" said her father.

"I have, and it appears that some of my former childhood friends have as well. To marry me off to a local boy would be to consign me to

. . . what I mean to say, Father, is, to marry me off to a local boy could never work. It would make me very unhappy. Soon, I will have to return to Beaudesert Castle, Lady Caroline, and the Monks. I am not sure what my future holds, but I know my future does not lie here."

~~~

The legend of the Monks of Arden grew after the fall of Kenilworth and the death of the Lancaster boys. Few had met them personally, but many knew of their exploits real or imagined.

The young knight Robert de Sudeley, son of the first Baron Sudeley, knew the stories that included extravagant claims of their beauty as well as their physical prowess. The talk within baronial circles was of a mysterious malady that had befallen the king's sister and the return of her followers to Beaudesert Castle. No one was certain whether the princess was dead or alive, but there was a unanimity of opinion that her uniquely trained wards were back in the area. Some said they were the spiritual descendants of the Amazons, if not their actual reincarnation. Sir Robert was possessed of a manly curiosity that compelled him to make sense of all the talk.

Sir Robert wrote to his friend, a lieutenant in the Beaudesert garrison.

"You are correctly informed, Sir Robert," came the reply. "The wards are quite special, my friend. One of them, Charlotte Giveney, is visiting her parents in the village of Leamington right now, not far from you. She is of peasant stock, but do not let that fool you. If you find her, you will see what I mean."

Among Sir Robert's hobbies was raising doves. He took particular pride in the fact that they were all snow white, in contrast to the multicolored pigeons more commonly encountered. The knight was a clever and cautious young man. *I must devise a plan to make contact,* he thought, *and doves will be my messengers.* He summoned one of the keepers from the dovecote and instructed him to take three good flyers to Leamington. He was to surreptitiously feed them for four days and release them.

The doves returned to their roost at Sudeley Castle, where they were deprived of food for three days in order to insure they would return to the place of their last feeding. To the right leg of each, Sir

Robert attached the following note: *A shilling to the man who delivers this message to the mayor's daughter Charlotte.* The keeper took them a quarter mile from the castle and released them. Two immediately returned to the dovecote. One did not.

The following morning Charlotte was awakened from her slumber by little Jimmy Gaunt, who roused everyone in the house with his loud banging on the front door. He was holding a white dove. "Miss Charlotte, Miss Charlotte," he said to Mrs. Giveney at the door. "It is most wondrous. A bird with a message for Charlotte."

Charlotte's mother looked at him, then down at the bird. The boy proffered the note. "It was wrapped around the bird's leg, Missus."

Charlotte soon appeared beside her mother and they read the message. "A shilling? That's a great deal of money, Jimmy. Who was the man who gave it to you?"

"Well," he said. "Nobody gave me any money, but I 'spect he will."

"I'm sure you are right, Jimmy. Thank you for delivering the message."

The boy left with the bird under his arm as Charlotte opened the message that had been folded and refolded before being wrapped around the dove's leg. Written in a tiny and precise hand was the following: *One day in the not so distant past a young varlet attended his knight Sir Norwood Gallant at a melee attended by four fair maidens, one of whom was you. In a moment of inattention, so taken was he by your beauty, that a horse knocked him to the ground in the middle of the fray, and he nearly lost his life. So full of love was he that, had he died that day, his life would have been complete. But he did not die. That young varlet is now his own knight, and he seeks the favor of an audience with his true love. I beg you for a favorable response, which, if you will attach it to the left leg of the dove that brought you this, will return it to me posthaste. Yours i'faith, Sir Robert de Sudeley.*

"Dickie," she called to her little brother. "Run fast and catch up with Jimmy Gaunt. Make sure he still has the bird."

This is quite extraordinary, she thought. *He probably thinks I am a lady instead of a commoner. But, of course, if he believes that, why would he seek me out in the house of villager?* Soon, Dickie returned with Jimmy in tow.

"What is it, Miss Charlotte?"

"I will give you a shilling for the dove," she said. "That will make two shillings for your day's work. I know the man who owes you the other."

"That's very gen'rus, Miss Charlotte. Here. Take him."

Charlotte paid the boy and he left very happy.

"What do you want that bird for?" said Dickie. "Jimmy was going to take it home to his mother for supper. Are you going to fix it for us?"

"Not tonight, little brother. I have other plans."

~~~

Sir: I remember the day we watched you take that tumble. We laughed at your misfortune in our girlish way. I pray now that you did yourself no serious injury. At that time the brutal event was nothing more than entertainment, and you were one of the clowns. I can tell from your message that you are an honorable gentleman, courtly in your ways, and certainly deserving of a hearing, but perhaps just now is too soon. We have not been formally introduced. With respect, Charlotte Giveney.

Charlotte affixed her reply to the dove's left leg and sent it out the window into the sky. The bird rose, wheeled in a large circle to get its bearings, and disappeared in the direction of Sudeley Castle.

Two days later, Charlotte arose in the morning to find a white dove perched on her windowsill. Attached to the right leg was a message.

Miss Giveney: Your reply is my treasure. Today I pledge obedience to your wishes. Though not of noble birth, you have a noble heart. Your exemplary character is part of your inner being and not something acquired as an afterthought to a noble birth. Thus does it exceed the value of a noble acquisition. Better it is that your good character should be an inborn trait integral to your soul than to be a veneer applied by moral tutors. Grant me an audience and grant me your heart. I'faith, Sir Robert de Sudeley.

The exchange of messages continued.

Sir Robert: Are you not speaking at cross-purposes of yourself? You are of the nobility and yet you diminish the quality of nobility by declaring the good character of a commoner to be superior for being inborn. Perhaps, that it may be rarer it is to be more highly prized. With respect, Charlotte Giveney.

Miss Charlotte Giveney: I think that it is a matter of degree, that it is better to woo a commoner of excellent character than a noblewoman of good character. In you, the class of commoners is exalted by virtue of your excellent character, and I pray that you will keep in your heart always the idea that my services are devoted to you and to you alone. I'faith, Sir Robert de Sudeley.

And then the messages stopped. Every morning Charlotte arose in search of the dove, but two weeks passed and there was none.

Miss Charlotte Giveney: Why have you given me no answer in recent weeks? Have I offended you in some way? I no longer eat or sleep. I hunger only for you, for the sustenance of my soul only you can provide. I'faith, Sir Robert de Sudeley.

~~~

Sir Robert summoned the keeper of the dovecote and ordered him to train new flyers for his mission.

"They might be getting lost," he said to the knight.

"It is possible," said Sir Robert. "This time you must take six doves to Leamington to teach them where to fly."

At the village, the trainer attached dummy messages to the left legs of the doves and released them daily, one at a time. Sir Robert, on the edge of despair, waited anxiously every day for their arrival at the castle. Waiting at the dovecote for the second bird, he scanned the horizon. The dove came into view and suddenly began to dodge and weave in terror as a falcon diving from the sky above struck it and flew off with the hapless messenger in its talons. Dangling from the raptor's legs were the telltale jesses identifying it as a trained hunter.

Dudley Castle lay between the village of Leamington and Sudeley Castle, near the flyway used by Sir Robert's doves. By chance one day, as the young knight Sir Roger de Somery of Dudley Castle was engaged in his favorite past time of hawking, one of his prized gyrfalcons brought down a white dove. The court falconer rushed to retrieve the bird where it had landed in a field. The trainer retrieved the dove and saw that something was wrapped around its leg. He rushed it to Sir Roger. It was a message meant for someone he had seen from afar.

Miss Charlotte Giveney, it read: *Help me, dear Charlotte. I am drowning in a sea of tears shed in grief that you have not answered my entreaties. You must allow me to come at once to pay my court. I'faith, Sir Robert de Sudeley.*

Through the timely intervention of the court falconer, the dove escaped lethal injury. Sir Roger instructed the falconer to nurse the bird back into flying condition. Two days later, he released the dove to continue its journey.

Charlotte arose from her bed. Thoughts of Sir Robert having drifted from her mind, she prepared to return to Beaudesert, but her heart leapt anew when on her windowsill she spotted the familiar white dove. She hastened to read the note and vowed to herself to meet this man.

Sir Robert: Your message arrived just as I was losing hope of ever hearing from you again. The uncertainty of this mode of correspondence compels me to give you a positive answer to your request to visit me here in Leamington. I shall look forward to your favorable reply and anticipate with great joy in my heart our meeting in a fortnight. Cupid has struck. With my abiding love, Charlotte Giveney.

Sir Roger's curiosity rose to a fever pitch when he read Charlotte's reply. *I must have a piece of this action*, he thought. *Retribution and conquest in a single grand sweep.* Once again he released the dove to continue its flight, this time to Sudeley Castle.

~~~

"I have a suitor," said Charlotte to her father.

"I hope he is a worthy local lad," he replied. "If you marry, perhaps we can look forward to your staying home instead of running off to be with those other women."

"Father, his name is Sir Robert de Sudeley, a young nobleman I saw once some years ago during a melee at Windsor. He was just a boy at the time, but the moment he laid eyes on me, he was smitten. He was so funny. He almost got killed. . . . Well, it seemed funny at the time."

"A nobleman?" said her father in surprise.

"A nobleman, Father. He will arrive here in two weeks for a formal visit of introduction."

"A nobleman. A nobleman courting my daughter," he mused. "We have a fortnight to prepare. That should be enough time."

Word of the forthcoming event spread quickly throughout the village. The mayor sent runners in search of entertainers. They returned with promises of the appearance of musicians and jongleurs, along with an assortment of acrobats and jugglers.

Charlotte sought out the two bodyguards who had been quartered in the village to accompany her to Coventry, seven miles away. The town was at the center of the cloth industry and was well-populated with seamstresses, clothiers, and boot makers. There she commissioned seamstresses to fashion special clothing for the event: a long front-laced linen kirtle worn over an ankle-length chemise, a hooded robe of green silk, a girdle and baldric woven with golden thread, the end of which hung to the knee, and calfskin boots for her feet.

On the morning of Sir Robert's expected arrival, Mayor Giveney posted lookouts at the entrance to the village to announce the knight's approach. Pennons and banners adorned the fronts of the buildings that lined the central street. Charlotte was radiant in her fine new attire, standing out like a shimmering emerald in the midst of the earth-toned villagers.

"They are coming! They are coming!" shouted the lookout. Excitement rose, not least in Charlotte who fought to maintain a dignified restraint in the manner of her greeting. The acrobats emerged to begin their show with flips and cartwheels. As the lead horse in the knight's procession appeared, the musicians sounded their tabors and tambourines to accompany dancers who formed moving circles and squares and sinuous lines, all swaying to the beat.

Charlotte could barely contain her anticipation. A short parade of caparisoned horses and riders preceded the knight, who finally made his entrance to a fanfare of trumpets. They began their stately parade toward the center of the village where Charlotte waited. Then, without warning, a shout came from the opposite end of the street.

"Ho, there," bellowed the armed rider of a warmblood charger, richly caparisoned in his own right. The village grew silent. Sir Robert's entourage came to a halt. The knight spurred his horse around his riders and took a position at their head to face the challenger. Charlotte stood between them at the edge of the road, momentarily stunned.

"I am Sir Roger de Somery, varlet. We have a score to settle."

"On what account, sir, may I ask?"

"Near the end of a melee at Windsor some years ago, you, a lowly varlet, cowardly attacked me, throwing me to the ground in front of the court of King Edward. Among the guests were noble ladies including Miss Charlotte Giveney who stands before us today. I am here to seek revenge and to claim the hand of Miss Charlotte as the prize."

"I remember it quite clearly, sir. You call me a lowly varlet. As I recall, we both served in that capacity at the time. And as for a cowardly attack, sir, you would be the villain who attacked me from behind without warning. What sort of effete character would dwell for so long on a boyish prank?"

"You have the effrontery to call me effete? For that remark alone I would seek satisfaction." And with that, Sir Roger unsheathed his sword and charged toward Sir Robert. They roared past each other, swords clanging, each missing the mark. They wheeled their horses and dismounted to face each other, their blood rising with each passing second. Charlotte was aghast.

"Stop," she screamed. "I demand that you stop this instant."

The villagers were awestruck at this spectacle, two knights engaged in mortal combat in the middle of their sleepy town. The combatants stared each other down, neither willing to risk yielding his advantage.

"For the honor of Miss Charlotte Giveney," Sir Roger yelled as he charged his opponent. Sir Robert parried the first pass of Sir Roger's sword, and on recovery caught his attacker in the ribs with the flat side of his sword. Sir Roger groaned audibly at the blow and dropped to one knee. Infuriated, he scooped up a fistful of dirt and rose. Throwing the dirt into Sir Robert's eyes set Sir Robert off balance enough that Sir Roger was able to drive his sword through his opponent's chest.

Charlotte rushed to the fallen lover as he bled to death in the middle of the street. She knelt beside him, then looked up at the victor who was crowing over his kill to a crowd that did know whether to run away or to cheer. "You are mine," he said.

As she rose to face him, she cast aside her emerald green robe. She wore a close-fitting kirtle intended for the festivities celebrating her betrothal to the fallen knight. Around her torso was the girdle and baldric from which were suspended her dagger and sword. The fire of love that was once in her eyes changed into the fire of hate. *Do not get emotional*, she remembered Sir Guy having taught her. *You must have all your wits about you in combat.*

Something in Charlotte's expression disturbed Sir Roger. He was not sure what it was. He continued with his self-referential tribute to the conquering hero and lover, but without much conviction. The reason quickly became apparent to him. Charlotte was as cool as ice. The Monk of Arden fixed her gaze on his, not wavering as she unsheathed her weapons. The truth of the legend of these women began to sink into Sir Roger's consciousness. Charlotte stepped toward him and he instinctively stepped backwards. Realizing that he was giving ground to a woman, he stopped his retreat and tentatively raised his sword. Charlotte continued toward him. Sir Roger raised the tip of his sword in her direction, whereupon, in a move too quick to follow with the human eye, she parried the feeble thrust and sent the point of her sword through the knight's throat.

The villagers were silent until Jimmy Gaunt materialized out of the crowd and, looking down at Sir Robert's corpse said, "Now I'll never get my shilling."

Chapter Fourteen

The Lay of Four Knights

Charlotte bade farewell to her family and departed for Tamworth Castle, where she would join Elizabeth Marmion prior to their return to Beaudesert. There, she was met by the chamberlain who explained that Lady Elizabeth had sequestered herself in a cell for a period of contemplation. "I shall take you to her ladyship," he said, "but be prepared. She is in the grip of the black dog."

Her state of melancholy distorted Lady Elizabeth's face. A blank stare rendered it almost featureless. The spark of life had vanished. Charlotte was shocked by her appearance. "Elizabeth, Lady Elizabeth, Your Ladyship," said Charlotte, searching for a way to crack the deathly pallor of the situation.

"I have committed a great wrong," said Elizabeth. "A very great wrong."

"What happened?" said Charlotte, dismayed at her friend's anguish.

"What happened was no sin in the eyes of the Church, but it was wrong nonetheless. On my account, four beautiful young men are dead. Though I intended the best for each of them, the outcome was the worst."

"Death surrounds us," said Charlotte ruefully.

"I have committed the story to paper in tribute to their memory. It is the story of four young knights led to destruction by Love; Love, that great enemy of reason."

~~~

Lord Albert Deville, as I shall call him, was a member of the warrior aristocracy. He granted fiefs to his several vassals, who, in return, owed the lord forty days' military service each year and annual payments of one-tenth of their tenants' harvest, which the knights were obliged to collect. The Festival of Lammas was held by the lord during the first two days of August. It was here, at the end of the growing season, that rents and harvest shares were collected. The lord, in order to keep the good will of the people, provided food, drink, and entertainment for the vassals and their entourages. The entertainment included an hastilude* to be held outside the castle wall. The lord encouraged the knights to select twenty of their most worthy tenants to accompany him to the festival. Naturally, there was great prestige among the peasants attached to being selected for the honor.

Among the dozen vassals attending the festival were four unmarried young knights, each of whom was deeply in love with Lady Beatrice, a woman of extraordinary beauty and intelligence, and one of Lord Deville's many children. She was skilled in needlework as well as in writing poetry. She had become proficient in the aristocratic recreations of horseback riding and archery. She would have been the perfect noblewoman without further embellishment, but Lord Deville also had engaged tutors to instruct her in reading, writing, grammar, theology, and Greek and Roman classics in their original languages, which enhanced her worth and desirability.

The four besotted knights sharpened their fighting skills by participating in melees where they engaged each other in mock battle using blunted weapons. A knight, unhorsed and forced to yield was obliged to surrender his armor, weapons, horse, and sometimes even some land to the victor. However, the four knights of whom I write had been lifelong friends, and none had any intention of taking advantage of another.

Renowned in the Midlands as an annual event, knights from distant manors took their retinues to Milford Castle to participate in the melee, hoping for a chance to enrich themselves in the process by beating their opponents. In addition to the four knights of which I write: Sir Allyn Fitz Gerald, Sir Morgan Hanford, Sir James Burlington, and Sir William Bingham, was Sir Guy de Beauchamp, known to his detractors as "The Black Dog of Arden" for his dark complexion. Also arriving were Sir Henry of Rosemont and the son of the Earl of March, Sir Gideon de Mortimer.

Each principal knight brought ten of his own vassal knights, all of whom were there to participate in the melee.

Lord Albert made the inner bailey of Milford Castle available for the for the erection of trestle tables under large tents. Banners and pennons bearing the crest of Milford fluttered in the breeze. Guests mingled freely on this occasion without regard to rank. Servants distributed quantities of bread, cheese, and roasted pork. Ale flowed freely. The first day was devoted to the tax and harvest collections, lubricated by free food and drink.

Sir Allyn secured an audience with Lady Beatrice in the shelter of the porch in front of the chapel. In the Middle World, there is said to be a beautiful palace of Love with four splendid façades. In each façade is an ornate door. One door is labeled Wisdom, another Justice, and the other two, Restraint and Courage. Sitting on a ivory throne in the center of the palace was Lady Beatrice Deville. Sir Allyn sought entrance through the door labeled Wisdom.

"Lady Beatrice," he said. "You are a paragon among women. It is a truth that smolders in my breast, crying for expression. Its utterance threatens to overwhelm my prudent nature, but if I were not to express the thoughts in my heart, I would deny Virtue her right and deprive the world of knowing the blessing of your worthiness."

"Were you not speaking the truth," she said, "I should blush. As prudence is in your nature, the gracious acceptance of any worthy man's suit is in mine. To cause a man to flee from my skirts would be to heap insult upon goodness, thereby denying my own. "

"Though in the flesh we seldom meet," he said, "you are ever present in my heart. I feel both pain and solace; pain in your absence and solace in your love. My entreaty is a two-edged sword. It is right and good that I should seek ecstasy behind the veil that hides the entrance to your Temple of Love, but it is wise to test our love in other ways. Devotion, simple and total, ought to be proved to create a bond of trust that allows your slave admittance to that sacred place. That which is attained with ease is also lost with ease."

"You are a wise and thoughtful knight, Sir Allyn," she said. "I take your hand. Tap lightly on the temple door and it will be opened to you."

Sir Allyn, dizzy with anticipation, withdrew. No sooner had they parted company than Sir William entered by way of the door marked Courage.

~~~

"My lady," he said. "At last. At last I have realized my greatest wish. Your beauty and worthiness nearly blind me. Take my hand. Show me the way."

"You declare my worthiness, Sir William, but show me your own."

"The worthiness you see in me is but a reflection of yours. Goodness begets goodness. The qualities that elevate you above all other women heap scorn on the notion of rejecting my suit, knowing such an act would subject your lover to great pain. It is not in your nature to be mother to anguish. To become so would be to shake the very foundations of your moral superiority."

"Your words please my ears," said Beatrice. "You are courageous and forthright in your suit. I am resolved never to be a slave to Venus or to endure the torments of lovers. But I am also resolved not to send a worthy suitor flying away in remorse for having misplaced his love."

"I will accept your judgment," he said, "even as I knock on the door to your tunnel of delight. Permit me entrance one time in a gesture to cement our good relations, that I may be encouraged to continue my quest to capture your heart."

Lady Beatrice, doing her best to stay true to her oath to first do no harm while honoring her pledge to avoid romantic entanglements, allowed her robes to be parted in an act of consummation while leaning against a pillar of the church.

Sir William melted into the throng of celebrants, and once out of sight, was replaced by Sir James, who entered the palace through the door marked Restraint.

~~~

"Your greatness and beauty are known to all," said Sir James. "I kneel in all humility before your worthiness. I have loved you from afar, but now in your presence, I feel the flames of my passion to become your servant rising within me. You threaten to unlock in me the vault of secrets known to no other man. Love, the irrepressible locksmith, is forcing open the seal to allow my innermost dreams and desires to spill forth. Should I die on the spot, having been in your divine presence for these few moments, my life would have been complete."

"*Your gracious words fall lovingly on my ears, Sir James. Only a woman with a heart of stone would not be moved. You speak of your innermost dreams and desires. Tell me more.*"

"*Poems yet to be written hang in the air. They are like snowflakes in moonlight, drifting, drifting, begging Providence for the honor of alighting on your breast. I must not reveal all before it is time.*"

"*Though I am pledged not to be the cause of a man's pain,*" said Beatrice, "*to accept you into Love's court would be to send you through the valley of tears; to reject your entreaty would be to do likewise. What am I to do?*"

"*To liken the pain of Love to the torturer's iron,*" said the knight, "*is to understand the exquisite agony of unrequited love, mitigated only by the undying hope for ultimate conquest and acceptance. Your love is the salve upon the wound. It wipes away the pain. It is a deep draught from Lethe's cup. There is only now and henceforth.*"

"*Your words come from the heart,*" Sir James.

"*I find no solace in your being out of my sight,*" he said. "*I pray that you may have a place for me in your heart.*"

"*Your motives and intentions are clear, Sir James. I shall not become Love's inquisitor, one who extracts importuning adulation without end. To be so would be to diminish me in your sight. Give me your hand. Beneath your touch beats a heart overflowing with joy at your suit. Be true to your ideals, and you will continue to be true to mine.*"

Sir James retired as Sir Morgan entered the palace of Love through the door marked Justice.

~~~

"*Sleepless nights plague me, Lady Beatrice. I can neither eat nor think of other than you. You inhabit my soul, imposing on me the exquisite pain of not being in your presence.*"

"*It is not my practice to be a source of pain to any man,*" she said. "*I refuse no man who seeks solace from the burden of unrequited love. You are here. Speak to me. Press your suit. Mine ears are yours.*"

"*Your graciousness is exceeded only by your beauty, my lady. There are but two worlds: Heaven is where you reside; Hell is where you do not. Only you can be the oarsman who carries me away from torment into bliss. All my life I have striven to treat my fellowman with respect and dignity,* yet I remain lost in my sorrow, sorrow so profound that only you, the most worthy princess, can assuage."

"Self-depreciation does not become you, Sir Morgan."

"I beg your indulgence, my lady. I feel Iusticia's fingers closing about my throat."

"Surely you are not as lost as you think. Breathe. Tell me what I want to hear."

"My only hope for redemption is in your Love, Love freely given to one who worships all that you touch, the air that you breathe."

"Come closer," she said. Lady Beatrice took him by the shoulders and pressed her lips to his. "My breath that you so crave will resuscitate your flagging spirits."

Sir Morgan's body swelled.

"I refuse no man who in good faith presses his suit. You are a good man. To send fleeing from my skirts an honorable suitor would be to violate my principles," she said as she parted her robe. "You have found the vessel of healing nectar."

Sir Morgan had never before known such a moment. "Iusticia be praised," he uttered with a grunt. "Iusticia be praised."

~~~

Lady Beatrice dreamed a dream. At the far edge of a wood in the Kingdom of Vulgaria, she watched as a caravan of beautiful women moved northward in single file.

At the head of the procession rode the most beautiful woman of all, dressed in white and wearing a bejeweled diadem. She rode a white horse caparisoned in white silk. The Women of Perfection followed. Servants who skillfully attended to all their needs accompanied them. They all sang her praises as they scattered rose petals along the way.

Similarly, servants attended the next group of women who were nearly as beautiful as the first. However, the servants' best efforts were thwarted and they were ineffectual, because the women could not decide on who would serve them best. The women scattered their attentions like corn among chickens. The servants fell to quarreling among themselves as they all vied for the women's attention.

The sky above the Women of Perfection was sunny and bright as they headed toward the Kingdom of Delight. The sky above the second group was overcast. *The third group of women trailed into the darkness of a storm-clouded southern horizon.*

The women of the last group were all quite beautiful, but their clothes were tattered and their horses broken down. Servants attended them or not, depending on their whim. Lady Beatrice hurried toward the procession and came upon a member of the last group, a lovely brunette with ivory skin and scraggly hair. Her robe was threadbare. The hem was soiled.

"Who are you?" said Lady Beatrice. "Where are you going?"

"My lady," said the woman in a pleasing voice. "We are the dead. The Goddess of Love takes us on our final journey. Our earthly existence was lived entirely in the Kingdom of Vulgaria where you now stand. The reward of a life well-led is to follow the Goddess into the Kingdom of Delights. But not all will gain admittance.

"The beautiful women you see following the Queen of Love are the dutiful lovers who honored God and family, foreswore earthly excess, and led the most exemplary lives. The second group were the well-meaning but disorganized who scattered their attentions, were kind and generous, and denied no man. We of the last group were the harlots who sold ourselves to the lonely hearts who had a few coins to pay for what comfort we had to offer.

"See the northern horizon. See how bright and warm it is. In its center, which you cannot see from here, is an oasis of date palms, flowing sweet springs, and soft earth. Amidst the trees is an ivory throne upon which the Queen of Love will sit. She will invite all those women of the first order to join her in the Kingdom of Delights, but once they are inside, the women of the second order will find they cannot enter. For them instead is an eternity in the second kingdom called Humidity. There the stream of sweet water carelessly overflows its banks, cascading over their feet. The water is very cold. If they seek escape to higher ground, that place is soon flooded as well. Alas, even so mild a torment as this is denied the women of the final order. We, the women of pleasure, must remain in the darkness of the Kingdom of Aridity where our throats are parched and dust swirls around us after each step." The procession continued its northward march and the lovely brunette with the ivory skin waved farewell as she moved on.

"Do not leave," said Lady Beatrice. "Am I dead? What must I do to be with the queen in the Kingdom of Delights?"

And then she awoke.

~ ~ ~

The sun rose on the second day of Lammas. Contestants for the melee assembled in front of the reviewing stand outside the northern curtain wall. The field was a half-mile square and included open land, copses, and a wide stream that ran through the middle. Rising above the northeastern corner of the curtain wall was a tower overlooking the scene from which Lady Beatrice observed the spectacle.

The earl declared that the tournament was for the discipline of the young men and the amusement of the ladies, of whom several dozen had arrived from neighboring manors. Combat would cease after four hours. Eight principal knights accompanied by eighty lower ranking knights and squires paraded onto the field. About two hundred varlets and pages formed a line at the edge of the field next to the reviewing stand and castle wall, prepared to intervene on behalf of their masters should they be needed.

The King of Arms in civil dress distributed weapons to each of the nobly attired contestants. Each received a blunted lance of soft wood and a flat, two-handed sword without a point or sharp edges. He announced that no daggers or other sharpened weapons were allowed. He likewise instructed the spectators that arms and other marshal paraphernalia were prohibited on or around the reviewing stand. The captain of the garrison supplied the field marshals for the tournament, whose responsibility it was to insure that the contestants adhered to the rules and that no one was deliberately subjected to potentially lethal attacks. When a contestant went down before a victorious opponent, the duel was considered to be at an end with a winner and a loser. The loser was required to give up certain possessions at the request of the winner, whereupon the loser would retire from the field and the winner would go back to the fight. Killing an opponent was considered to be a grave offense, not only violating the chivalric code of conduct, but also incurring the wrath of the noble sponsor.

No feuds or blood rivalries among the knights in this tournament were known to exist that might create enmity among them. They were generally friendly with each other and so were expected to comport themselves with honor to the extent that such is possible in a group of lusty young men engaged in a rough and dangerous activity.

Trumpeters on horseback stood at either end of the reviewing stand facing the tournament field. The first fanfare directed the contestants to form rows and assemble in descending order of rank to face the noble spectators. They saluted the earl and waited for the second fanfare that would scatter them across the field of combat. When all were in place, the third fanfare signaled the melee to begin.

Lady Beatrice commanded a broad overview of the tournament field from the window at the top of the tower. She watched as the contestants split into two large groups. Four knights, Allyn, William, Morgan and James, accompanied by their knights and squires, moved as a group to the left and the other four principals faced them from the right about a quarter mile away. As if by signal, the opponents exploded into action, galloping toward each other with lances lowered, whooping and yelling above the percussive din of hoof beats. The melee had begun.

The cavaliers piled into each other at high speed, raising clouds of dust as they charged. Splintered lances mixed with the dust that billowed above the combatants' heads. Unhorsed riders in the middle of the field rose to face their opponents on foot, wielding swords in efforts to fell each other.

One by one, knights of lesser skill fell before their masters, forced to yield, whereupon marshals intervened and declared the winners. The ranks of cavaliers soon thinned, leaving the more successful to fight it out. Fewer men fell with each succeeding hour as the contests became more prolonged and interesting. Sir James the Restrained and Sir Henry of Rosemont sweated and bellowed in mock hostility toward each other until they broke into laughter, fell upon each other's shoulders, and decided to call it a draw.

Sirs Allyn, Morgan, and James, each seeking to impress Lady Beatrice, got into a three-way on foot. They clanked their swords above their heads. Sir William stumbled backward, fell, and dropped his sword. Sir Morgan picked it up and returned it to him as Sir Allyn helped him to his feet. Just as they reorganized themselves to fight another round, the trumpets sounded ending the tournament.

Filthy, sweaty, and in high spirits, the survivors returned to the reviewing stand to receive their tributes from the earl. Each winner was paid a modest sum, the losers slightly less. No one left empty-handed. The spectators cheered. The earl congratulated himself that he had collected the rents and grain owed him and made the donors feel good about it.

The visitors and the contestants with their entourages began to disperse. Not so, the Four Knights. The young suitors, riding alone, wandered across the field away from the others, seeming to be in deep conversation. Their voices rose, attracting the attention of the marshals a hundred yards away. Their camaraderie disintegrated into hostility.

Sir William the Courageous wilted under the assault as Sir James the Restrained beat him mercilessly with his sword. Sir Morgan the Just joined in the fray. Sir Allyn the Wise attempted to intervene and promptly fell under the sword of Sir James. The marshals galloped at full speed toward them, but they arrived too late. Sir James finished off Sir William. In an outburst of mutual destruction, the two men still standing set upon each other, flailing away. The marshals arrived just in time to watch James and Morgan expire. Four once-happy young knights lay dead in the dirt.

~~~

What form of madness has led to this?" asked the earl.

Lady Beatrice, her face wet with tears, lied to her father for the first time in her life. "I do not know," she said.

Chapter Fifteen

Alice Amores

The Earl of Warwick doubled the rents on his manors and since had been facing an armed insurrection of farmers and peasants led by his own vassals. Six months of conflict had depleted his resources, and he needed outside help. Kenilworth Castle was abandoned and had fallen to ruin. It was a neighbor from which Warwick would have sought aid in earlier times. His best option now was his brother, the Duke of Normandy, recently routed from the duchy by the king of France. The duke and his sizeable armed force had taken refuge in the Scilly Islands, located on the trade route between Normandy and Ireland.

Upon receiving the plea for help from his brother, the duke replied that he would send his son Sir Thomas de Beauchamp and ten of his knights to quell the uprising. Sir Thomas bade farewell to his wife, promising he would return to her in six months just as he had left, in complete devotion to her and only to her. Cogs arrived from Plymouth to transport Sir Thomas's force to Bristol, where they would begin their march northward to Warwick Castle, a two-day ride of seventy miles.

The lake, moat, and River Avon that surrounded Warwick Castle worked to the earl's disadvantage in defending himself against adversaries intent on starving him out. Under cover of darkness, the earl sent a scout to meet his nephew. He wove his way through the various vassal knights' encampments that formed a large perimeter around the castle.

"They have cut off our supplies, your lordship," said the scout. "We have plenty of water, of course, but our foodstuffs are dwindling."

"What do you estimate the size of their force to be?" said Sir Thomas.

"We know there are ten vassals, each with his own knights. The earl believes there must be a hundred or more of them. Each of the vassal's knights also has a following of yeoman farmers and their sons."

"Who is their leader?" said Sir Thomas.

"Sir Malcolm Scoville of Milverton Manor, my lord. They are protesting the earl's rent increase. They are trying to get him to back down."

"My uncle is a stubborn man. He is not likely to let a band of disgruntled tenants get the better of him. Go back and tell him we are here. I have five hundred men-at-arms. No point in my making some kind of grand entrance into the castle. Scoville will discover our presence soon, if he has not already. He will feel the sting of our military might before he figures out how to maintain two fronts. Tell my uncle that we do not want to engage in a wholesale bloodletting. I prefer the decapitation strategy. Take out their leadership and the followers will fold."

"Yes, my lord. I'll give him your message."

~~~

The earl's ward, Lady Alice de Toeni, arrived at Warwick just before the uprising after her long tour with the Monks of Arden.

"I shall defend the castle, my lord," she said in a moment of bravado.

"Dear Alice, I know your heart is in the right place, and that you have become an accomplished warrior, but you would be no match for the hoard that surrounds us."

"I feel some sympathy for them, my lord," she said. "I know these people. I cannot believe they mean for serious harm to befall us. What they are imposing is a pressure tactic."

"I wish I felt as kindly toward them as you," said the earl, "but it is necessary that I raise more revenue."

"Can you not negotiate with them?"

"Negotiate with vassals?" said the earl. "To negotiate is to show weakness. How could I continue to be their lord if I let them get the upper hand?"

"But they seem to be winning, my lord. You and I still have enough to eat. The rest in the court are on short rations. God only knows what the servants and soldiers are eating. I heard a rumor that they ate one of the horses. The grain reserves are dwindling and soon we will have to give in to their demands or starve."

"I have one last option I have not told you about. My nephew Sir Thomas de Beauchamp is here with a force of five hundred armed men, and they have surrounded the castle outside the rebellion's perimeter. Sir Thomas is a canny strategist. I have every confidence he will quell the uprising in short order."

~~~

Sir Thomas sent out scouts to pinpoint the ten vassal's encampments beyond the castle walls. Their presence three miles away had not yet been detected. Sir Thomas decided to carry out lightning stealth attacks on the respective camps. One by one, under the cover of darkness, armed men disguised as peasants crept into the camps, overcame the vassal's bodyguards, and spirited the knights away. They disappeared into the wood before the protestors had a chance to marshal a defense.

Each of the leaderless camps chose a deputy to meet with the others to decide what to do. The speed and stealth of Sir Thomas's force shocked them into the realization that they either must withdraw or elect a leader with an effective counter plan. They chose to withdraw, tacitly admitting they would have to accede to the earl's proclamation, go back and tend to their manors, and give up more of their meager incomes in rents.

Casualties were few. The insurrection collapsed, and Sir Thomas and his men entered Warwick Castle unmolested. They had but ten captives, the rebellious vassal knights, whom they presented to the earl without a scratch on any of them.

~~~

The earl ordered that hostels be prepared for Sir Thomas's men inside the castle walls. Sir Thomas met daily with the earl's garrison commander, who had been unable to leave the castle during the insurrection. Their relations were cordial. Sir Thomas assured the captain he was there on a temporary assignment at the request of his father and uncle whom he could not deny. Since their expulsion from the duchy, his men had been idle. They needed a martial exercise and the earl's supply lines had to be reopened. It was an opportunity convenient to all but the insurrectionists.

Now that the abortive siege was over, Alice was becoming restless. She needed to return to Beaudesert and her fellow Monks. The earl pleaded with her to remain a little longer now that the local situation had stabilized.

"In honor of your homecoming and in honor of the lifting of the blockade, we shall have a feast," he said.

~~~

Guests arrived to the sounds of a musical ensemble ensconced in the loft above the dais. Tabor*, timbrel,* and tambourine* accompanied harp, lute, vielle,* and rebec.* Trumpeters stood at the ends of the head table on the dais, there to sound fanfares announcing the arrival of notables as well as the serving of the many courses of the feast.

The Greenwood Men, a group of touring mummers, provided acrobats and jugglers for the entertainment of guests before the dining began. The man known as Arkwright headed the troupe. Upon hearing that name, Lady Alice sent a maidservant to make an inquiry of him. "My lady wishes to know if the man Kallias is still with you." she said. "She wishes to have a word with him."

"That will not be possible, miss," said Arkwright. "Two or three years ago we were set upon by the king's men in London. Most of us got away. Kallias did not. They took him away. We never heard from him again."

~~~

Against the wall perpendicular to the head table was a buffet bearing an assortment of ewers, wine pitchers, tankards, plates and saltcellars from which servitors provided arriving guests with pewter goblets filled with water, wine, or ale according to the guests' wishes.

The walls of the great hall were festooned with banners, ribbons, and pennons. The underlying tapestries provided a degree of insulation from the cold in winter as well as softening the sounds of activities within. Servants arranged trestle tables in a U-formation with the open end toward the dais. The steward ordered carts of comestibles to be rolled into the U from which servitors would provide for the guests seated on benches on the outside.

The trumpeters announced the arrival of the nobles and guests of honor with a noisy fanfare. The earl and his wife Lady Maud entered the hall through a doorway to the left of the head table. They stood waiting as Lady Alice de Toeni made her entrance to approving murmurs from the audience.

As everyone was about to sit, the earl raised his hand. The guests grew silent. "But for the able military assistance of my nephew Sir Thomas Beauchamp, we would not be gathered in such felicity this day." He pointed to the handsome young knight seated below. "Please join us at the head table, Sir Thomas."

The self-effacing young knight strode forward, glancing about the hall for approval. He mounted the dais. The earl directed him to take a seat. "Sit here beside Alice. I do not believe you have been properly introduced. Sir Thomas, this is my ward Alice de Toeni." The knight bowed slightly. He and Alice inspected each other, as he sat down.

The nobles and other notable guests at the head table took their seats, followed by the guests in the hall. Fanfares introduced the successive courses.

"Sir Thomas," she said. "The earl holds you in high esteem. He is in debt to you for your service."

"I considered it to be my duty to my family, Lady Alice."

"And you will be returning to . . . to the Scilly Islands? Is that correct?"

"You are correct, and, yes, I shall return. The earl has requested that I remain for a year, well beyond the six months I had planned."

"You will be feted and rewarded if you stay, Sir Thomas. It could turn out to be quite profitable for you."

"And you, Lady Alice? What are your plans?"

"I must soon return to Beaudesert Castle. I have been a ward of Princess Gwenllian ap Llewellyn through whom I was tutored."

"I have heard that you are extraordinarily accomplished," said Sir Thomas. "A beautiful and most worthy woman. I have heard also that you are one of the mysterious Monks of Arden."

"You have heard correctly," said Alice.

"Tell me about the Monks."

"We are five women," said Alice, "who have cultivated certain special talents not often attributed to women."

"Tell me about them," he continued.

"Perhaps another time, Sir Thomas."

Alice knew that soon she would have to leave Warwick and return to Beaudesert to rejoin the Monks. About that she had not had a moment's doubt, until now.

The feast concluded with the young women and men dancing the carol* and the round dance to the accompaniment of the musicians. It was an opportunity for the young people to meet each other in a socially acceptable public setting. Of all the possible combinations of young men and women present in the hall, Alice and Thomas seemed to be the most constant.

"I would be pleased for you to visit me in my chambers, Sir Thomas. There we can have a more private conversation away from the distractions of a noisy social gathering."

Sir Thomas hesitated before answering. An image of his wife immediately popped into his imagination. His lovely and devoted spouse waited patiently for his return, for him to come back to her unblemished by the exigencies and temptations of the wider world.

"I shall be honored," he said.

~~~

Alice blushed upon seeing the young knight enter her chambers.

"I am glad that you accepted my invitation, sir knight," she said. "That we did not seek each other's company sooner is to have done an injustice to Fate."

"I agree, my lady, that Fate has placed us together through no agency of our own."

"Fate indeed has guided us," said Alice, "but Isis certainly guided Fate."

"I fear it may be so," he said. "She has led me into Cupid's snare."

"Fear?" said Alice. "Do you fear love?"

"Fear toys with reason, my lady. I fear that love could be turned to offense."

"Fear and love do not belong in the same sentence, sir knight."

"They do, when they both reside in the bosom of one so wretched as I."

"I see before me a noble young knight of courtly manners and pleasant mien," said Alice. "What hides behind your mummer's mask?"

"Like most men, I cannot deliver one part in ten of what I wear. Though I speak with the voice of Dionysus, I walk with the limp of Epictetus."

"What so afflicts you, sir knight, that casts you into the pit of self-loathing?"

"You are the most worthy of women, Lady Alice. That you look kindly upon me sends me both to soaring heights and to miserable depths. I am torn. I do not eat. Neither do I sleep."

"I too have succumbed to the malady," said Alice. "Move closer and touch my hand, so for a moment we are joined in that least measure."

Sir Thomas complied. Looking into her eyes, he said, "I am not worthy of one so noble as you. That which you perceive to be hidden seeks to tear me apart. Show me how a man can be better than his word."

"Hmm," she said. "A challenge worthy of a casuist."

"You speak lightly to my dilemma. You know not how near the truth you have wandered."

"I speak only to lighten the burden that so hobbles your sensibilities. Speak freely. Love commands you."

~~~

"Your nephew is a married man," said Lady Maud to her husband.

"So I have been told," he replied. "I have never met the young woman, but I assume my brother has seen to it that she is up to the family standard. He would not knowingly allow a betrayal our noble heritage. I am indebted to my brother and his son and must spare no expense in rewarding Sir Thomas for his service. But for him we would not be exchanging pleasantries today."

"What do you propose to do above and beyond what you have done already?"

"If he accepts the charge, I intend to make him steward over all my lands. He is both talented and humble. I cannot imagine a better representative to the people."

"Such a move would give him strong encouragement to become a permanent resident of Warwick," said Lady Maud.

"It would indeed. I hope the rewards coming from the appointment are sufficient inducement for him to make Warwick his home. He would gain wealth and power, and I would gain peace of mind."

"Does he know of your intentions?"

"I shall make the offer tomorrow."

~~~

Lady Alice summoned Sir Thomas to her chamber. "You have news, I believe. The court is rife with talk."

"Yes," he said. "The earl has offered me the stewardship of all his lands. I hardly know what to say."

How foolish I am, she thought, *to be taken unawares by this stranger. If I let myself slip further into Love's embrace, I shall fit myself for mourning weeds.*

"You shall be leaving soon," she said.

"And so shall you," he replied.

She handed him a golden ring on a leather necklace. "I beg you to wear this token of my esteem."

"Take this amulet, the Eye of Horus," he said in return, handing her the lazuline engraving. "It will sweep away the clouds that blur your sight to all that is about you."

~~~

The earl convened a court leet,* a turning point in Sir Thomas's career. The court would be charged with dispensing justice to the ten rebellious knights who tried and failed to blockade Warwick Castle into submission. The earl had a duty to appoint his steward to take charge of the legal proceedings. The offer of the stewardship was now in Sir Thomas's lap. His choice was between accepting the assignment and thus committing himself to the position, and rejecting it, by which he would not only disgrace himself, but also fall in esteem in the eyes of his beloved Lady Alice.

Memories of his patient wife, the grip of Lady Alice on his emotions, his sense of duty to his lord and to his family, all converged on Sir Thomas at once. The earl requested his decision on the stewardship within the week. Lady Alice held her breath pending his decision. His wife remained in the dark.

~~~

My dear Katharine, he wrote to his wife. *I pray that you and our sons remain well. I was successful in stopping the insurrection against the earl, and I am unharmed. As you might expect, the earl is eager to reward me for the service. He has already presented me with gifts and money. He now proposes to appoint me steward over all his lands. To decline the offer would be to bring shame on both Father and me. To accept would mean to prolong my residence here in Warwick. I am torn between my love for you and a sense of duty to my father's family. Fate often plays a crooked game, taking from one to reward another. The promise of my gain is balanced against the burden of a husband's absence that weighs upon you. I am beset with indecision but must take a stand, lest I prove to be unworthy of the earl's expectations. I have, therefore, decided to accept the earl's offer. If the new arrangement works out to everyone's satisfaction, perhaps, after a year or two, I can send for you and the children to join me. Yours i'faith, Thomas.*

~~~

Until his appointment as steward, Sir Thomas and his men had been housed in the garrison's barracks. With his promotion came a move to the keep* to apartments on the same floor as Lady Alice's private chambers.

The earl assigned Sir Thomas a personal chamberlain, Edwin Markey, Esquire, who was a clerk under the Lord Chancellor in Westminster before accepting an assignment to Warwick. Though no words on the subject passed between the earl and his nephew, both were confident that the new chamberlain should be an effective advisor to a young knight with no judicial experience.

~~~

Two weeks passed before Sir Thomas and Lady Alice were to meet again. The proximity of their living quarters made it inevitable that from now one their meetings would be more frequent. Passions between them were building.

"Your decision has made me a very happy woman," said Alice. "When we are apart, I am overwhelmed by a feeling of uselessness. I think only of the next time we are to meet. But you are conflicted. I can see it in your eyes. Am I not fair enough for you?"

"Fair enough, dear Alice? My esteem for you grows by the day. You are the fairest of the fair."

"Perhaps it is the gravity of your mission," she said. "The fate of ten once highly regarded members of your noble knights' league is in your hands. It is a heavy responsibility."

"Yes. Yes. Perhaps that is it. I am in the midst of jury selection," he said, thankful for the fortuitous diversion. "The challenge vexes me. Under ordinary circumstances the ten defendants are the very men I would choose to be the jurymen. But they shall be in the dock, so I must find ten freeholders to represent your guardian, the earl."

"The Arden has never been a King's Forest. It is dotted with villages of freeholders who might be pressed into service. I know of one, the mayor of Leamington Robert Giveney. His daughter Charlotte is one of my sister Monks of Arden."

Sir Thomas's worried expression lightened. "I shall take up the matter with Mr. Markey," he said. "This is a Warwickshire matter," he said, "and I prefer to confine the selection to that area."

Alice had contacts, and, with her help, Sir Thomas was able to recruit ten disinterested jurors from the various neighboring manors as well as from Stonele Abbey. Markey advised him that the usual punishment for rebellion was hanging, but that records of the King's Bench at Westminster showed that lesser punishments, such as heavy fines, could be imposed.

Sir Thomas convened the Lord's Court one month after he had suppressed the rebellion and the leaders had been imprisoned. He placed his men under the temporary authority of the captain of the castle garrison. Interest in the trial was high, and several hundred people had converged on the surrounding villages, hoping to gain admission to the proceedings.

Security was high. The captain deployed his men around the castle and posted a special guard at the entrance. Everyone seeking admittance was searched for weapons. The spectators were limited in number to one hundred. Among the commoners was the swarm of provincial lawyers hoping to collect fees by representing the defendants. The captain selected ten of them at random, one for each defendant.

The great hall was the only room in the castle large enough to accommodate the crowd attending the trial. The march to their judgment was short for the defendants. The dungeon lay beneath the great hall.

Sir Thomas and Mr. Markey sat at the head table on the dais. The defendants stood in shackles in front of the audience facing Sir Thomas. The lawyers were permitted to wander the area between the defendants and the head table, arguing their cases and offering up points of English criminal law.

At issue was the justice of the lord's tithe, an old institution established to provide funds for the church that were lately being redirected into the manor's general revenue stream. The arguments went on for two days, but boiled down to the fact that the idea for the revolt originated with Sir Malcolm Scoville, and he had recruited the others to join him. On the morning of the third day, Sir Thomas dismissed the lawyers and proceeded to render his verdict.

"Rebellion is punishable by death," he began. "Social order cannot withstand an assault such as this without a strong and principled response. Sending these rebellious knights to the gallows has two kinds of consequences. The first is that felonious behavior is punished. We cannot expect to survive as a civilized people without strict adherence to the law. On the other hand, to deprive their estates of their leadership is to weaken the bonds of the community that allows our system to thrive.

"Punishments for the kind of behavior exhibited by the defendants was codified in the Dictum of Kenilworth of 1266. Whereas formerly the defendants would have had been hanged and their lands seized, conditional pardons could be granted, depending on their degree of involvement in the transgression.

"Sir Malcolm Scoville, as leader of the rebellion, I sentence you to hang. I grant to you nine others pardons and restoration of your lands, contingent on the payment of one-half the value of your lands calculated as five times their annual yield, and binding you in an oath of allegiance to the king and his representative the Earl of Warwick. Bailiff, return the men to their cells."

~~~

A letter arrived from Sir Thomas's father the duke, requesting his son's immediate return to the Scilly Islands. Seafaring Breton marauders were besieging his stronghold, threatening to overwhelm them by the number and fierceness of their warriors.

Sir Thomas immediately dispatched a courier to the shipyards in Plymouth with orders for ten cogs displacing one hundred tons each to be built as soon as possible. They were to be constructed as war machines with castles fore and aft.

Though he had not yet completed the full term he promised the earl, he begged to be allowed leave to go to his father's aid. The earl was distraught, having placed such high hopes in his nephew, but he finally agreed, in the name of his brother the duke. Sir Thomas agreed to return as soon as possible, within sixth months to a year, depending on how the operation went. The earl was pleased with the knight's promise to return, having no knowledge that there might be another motive hidden behind his expression of family solidarity.

For Thomas, the most difficult part was yet to come.

~~~

The young knight was determined to be open and candid with Lady Alice. His love for her, his love for his wife, and his sense of duty to his father and uncle, had tied him in emotional knots.

"I have news, Alice," he began, "news that is not altogether felicitous."

"Please tell me nothing that will break my heart, Thomas."

"I have been called back to the Scilly Islands. My father is under attack from the sea and requires my assistance, much as did the earl so recently."

Alice went pale. "When will you go? How long will you be gone? Will you return?" Her voice trailed off, and she grew unsteady on her feet. She fell into a swoon, but before Thomas could catch her, she slipped to the floor. She tumbled onto her back and her robe fell open. Before him lay a body he had only imagined before. Whether by accident or design did not matter. He took her head in his hands and smothered her face with kisses. Without stopping, he moved down to her breasts. Alice revived just as Thomas, on the edge of losing control, prepared to mount her. She grabbed his buttocks and drew him onto her, but at the final moment his flesh failed him. Unable to consummate the carnal union that had so inflamed his imagination, he rolled over and covered his eyes in shame.

~~~

Sir Thomas summoned his captains and Edwin Markey in preparation for their departure. Notice had arrived that the ships were nearing completion. They would begin their march south in three days.

Alice feared this would be their farewell meeting. Her cheeks were streaked with tears. She had always prided herself in her fortitude, honed through her training in the martial arts, but on this day, emotion overcame her.

"Thomas, my brave and noble knight, I shall not live, but only exist, until your return. My love for you can only grow until you are back in my arms."

"I shall do anything you wish, my beloved. Say when I must return, and it will be done."

"If it were my choice, I would beg you not to go at all, but you are a man of the world, and that world beckons to you. Conclude your task expeditiously, my love. Come back to me so that we can marry."

Thomas's blood turned to ice. *To marry Alice*, he thought, *would be to consign my soul to hell. In God's eyes no man can marry one, then marry another. Such a deception would be a mockery of the sacrament of holy matrimony. Besides, the earl knows I have a wife and he would never permit it.* Thomas grappled with the urge to turn his back on his sense of personal morality, to yield to his instinct to flee to another land with this woman. He finally steeled himself and said, "I shall return to you, beloved, as soon as my work is finished."

~~~

Sir Thomas and his men marched to Bristol and thence to Plymouth. They boarded their vessels, and five days later sailed into a fleet of galleys from Brittany preparing an assault on Tavistock Abbey from one of the small, nameless outer Scilly islands.

The raiders towed several barges equipped with trebuchets to be used as artillery platforms. The invading force was designed to besiege fixed fortifications on land. Their galleys were heavily laden with soldiers and assault gear, dangerous on land, but unwieldy and cumbersome at sea. It was because of this vulnerability that Sir Thomas was able to bring to bear his most formidable weapon, the English longbowman.

The Bretons should have anticipated the possibility that archers would be brought to the Scilly Islander's defense, but their leader was the brother of John of Normandy who had been steeped in the French tradition, a fact that doomed them to failure.

The duke spotted his son's fleet and immediately deployed his archers along the crest of the main defensive wall surrounding the abbey. Sir Thomas maneuvered his ships into a line behind the attacking galleys. The Breton commander ordered his men to load the trebuchets and prepare for a landing. As his would-be assault force swarmed on deck, English archers on land and on sea cut them down. Realizing that his men would never make it to the shore, the Breton commander ordered everyone below decks to man the oars. They began their slow retreat in the midst of a hail of arrows that soon littered the decks like a deadly game of pick-up-sticks.

Sir Thomas elected not to pursue his hapless enemy, choosing instead to follow just long enough to make sure they were heading back to their home port. The battle had continued for three days, and Sir Thomas's men had suffered just one casualty, an archer who slipped and fell on deck, hitting his head with enough force to render him unconscious for several hours. He awoke after the fighting had ceased and complained that he had missed the best part of the fray.

In port, Sir Thomas was greeted by his father the duke, who hailed the victory and praised his son's abilities as a military commander. To one side, standing in the shadows, was a young woman cradling an infant in her arm as she led a small boy by the hand. Her name was Katharine, and she was Sir Thomas's wife.

~~~

With familiar ease, Thomas and Katharine slipped into each other's arms. "I sense that you are troubled," she said.

"I am being pulled in two directions," he replied. "Here, I have my obligation to my father the duke and to you and our sons. Elsewhere awaits my stewardship of Warwick, which obligates me to the earl. I have returned to you as promised, earlier than I had originally planned because of the invasion from Brittany, but in the eyes of the earl I am on a temporary mission to aid his brother. He expects me to return as I promised. I have promised too much to too many."

"You are a good man, Thomas," said Katharine. "You must decide where you can do the most good for the greatest number of people. Follow your heart, my dear."

Katharine knew not what she had just said. Thomas set his jaw in order to hold back tears.

~~~

Two letters arrived at Warwick Castle, one addressed to the earl and one addressed to Lady Alice.

The earl read his with great pleasure. Sir Thomas would be returning for an indefinite stay. The stewardship over his lands was to be in good hands.

My beloved Alice, began the other. *In our moment of passion prior to my departure, I failed you. The flesh was not weak, but rather, it was serving notice on me. St. Matthew tells us we cannot serve two masters. Either we must love the one and hate the other, or hold to the one and despise the other. As an imperfect man, I withheld from you the knowledge that I have a wife and sons. I love my wife and I love you, Alice. I cannot hate or despise either of you. I must beg your forgiveness for this deception. I will understand if you are unable to grant me this wish. The less than noble part of me was in control. I shall be returning to Warwick Castle with my family. I intend to make it our new home. You are now free to follow your original plan unencumbered, returning to Beaudesert and the Monks of Arden. Godspeed, and I shall never forget you. Yours i'Faith, Thomas.*

Chapter Sixteen

The Arden Academy

Of the three legs of the *trivium*, logic, or dialectic as he preferred to call it, was Albertus Pidgeon's favorite. He viewed himself as a true peripatetic philosopher, traveling from place to place to wherever a sufficient number of pupils could be gathered. The day the number of students at Malmesbury shrank to unsustainable levels he moved on.

Lord Thurstan de Montfort had sent letters to both Lincoln and London in search of a tutor for his children. When Albertus heard about it, he immediately contacted de Montfort, citing his credentials and requesting an interview.

~~~

By way of his own introduction he explained to Lord Thurstan that his father had taken great care to see to his education. His father, a knight, was dismayed at his son's decision to eschew the military life in favor of the life of the mind, but recognizing his son's exceptional talent for letters, he acquiesced. With his father's support, Albertus mastered Latin and Greek, and went on to study under William of Ockham at the Franciscan School.

"What is your view on the education of girls?" Lord Thurstan inquired.

Albertus paused only briefly. "Many scoff at the idea, my lord. I prefer to take a neutral position."

"I have five daughters, sir, as well as two young female wards who have come under my protection, all of whom, save one, will become your pupils. Permit me to introduce my eldest, Lady Caroline, who will not be your pupil but will serve as my representative on behalf of your endeavor."

Albertus bowed before the comely young woman. "Your ladyship," he said.

~~~

The new tutor found lodgings in the village. His landlady Mrs. Dinwiddie made it clear to him that he would not be entertaining women on her premises, and that if he came home after a bout of drinking, he would be locked out of the house. She did not countenance any form of drunken or licentious behavior among her tenants. Albertus assured her that he was a sober and devout scholar, a teacher of young people who would never stoop to such vulgar behavior. He was a handsome young man with an engaging way with women. Mrs. Dinwiddie was far from invulnerable to his charms, and, after having had her say, welcomed him as a lodger.

The first task for Albertus at the castle was to introduce himself to his pupils in a way that would not send them fleeing to their governess for refuge. He arrived at the castle, and a servant conducted him to a room dubbed The Academy. Seated before him were six young women. Standing beside them was Lady Caroline.

"Greetings," he said. "I am professor Albertus Pidgeon. I will examine the competence of each of you in Latin and Greek, and if you have been sufficiently schooled, I shall direct you to the art of disputation and Aristotelian philosophy."

The six girls' faces went blank.

"Tell me your names," he said. One by one the girls stood and identified themselves.

"I am Maude."

"I am Antoinette."

"I am Helen."

"I am Juliet."

"I am Mary."

"I am Anne."

"Professor," said Lady Caroline. "May I have a word?" She dismissed the girls and sat down with the new tutor. "There is a reason my father has put me in charge of the girls' education. I myself am quite prepared to engage in a philosophical colloquy with you. These girls are not. You might as well have been addressing them in Urdu. You have never taught young girls before, have you? You must take them by the hand, metaphorically speaking of course, and lead them to knowledge."

~~~

Albertus was less indifferent to women than inexperienced. As a lad in Brittany, there were the local dairymaids and willing servant girls who lent themselves to the kind of instinctual behavior that would guide them throughout their lives, but he was never exposed to purposeful young women who had their eyes set on being more than brood sows who weep, sow, and spin. He was never invited to soirees held in honor the local baron's daughters. The only times he ever tried to make eye contact with any of them was during mass on Sunday morning, an unrewarding undertaking at best. Albertus's mind, rarely troubled by carnal thoughts, carried him above the quotidian fray that determined the course of all but the saints' lives. Or so he thought.

In truth, just beneath the surface, he struggled to keep the beast at bay. By sheer force of will, he had managed to channel the normal energy building below the girdle to the higher realm that lay between his ears. Believing he had effectively subdued the demon, he was unaware that, although it slept soundly, it could be aroused with sufficient provocation. The intrusion of Lady Caroline's sister Maude into his well-ordered life was the rooster that crowed at dawn.

~~~

"Brother Clement has served you well," said Albertus to his class. "I am pleased with your progress in Latin and Greek. We shall delve into more texts in order to improve your skills."

Lady Caroline sat nearby. Albertus focused his attention on his pupils without deviation, with the idea in mind that Caroline would report to her father in his favor. The routine was the same as the days went by. Albertus would arrive soon after dawn to hold his class. After three hours, the girls were dismissed for a period of leisure. For two hours in the afternoon, they would spend time at the stables, learning how to be around and to handle horses. Lady Caroline saw no need to seek outside help for their equestrian and martial arts training. She had trained with the best, and when the Monks returned, they would join the faculty.

The girls' education and the normal rhythms of castle life proceeded in an orderly fashion up to a point. Albertus, whether through boredom with his charges, or from some unseen other factor, was becoming distracted. He spent more time in discussion with Caroline's nubile sister Maude than with the other girls. When Antoinette was reciting, he stared at Maude. On the days Lady Caroline attended his classroom, he glanced nervously at her. The Septuagint in Greek and Virgil in Latin were difficult enough when given undivided attention, but when the tutor lost interest, everyone lost interest. When Maude complained to her sister that the tutor seemed to be more interested in her than in his books, her ladyship decided it was time to conduct a tutoring session of her own.

~~~

"I must ask you to refrain from appearing in my classroom," said Albertus in a heroic effort to seize control of the exchange from the start. "Your presence distracts my pupils."

"According to my sister, your observation that the girls are being distracted is off the mark. Perhaps it is you, instead, who is distracted."

"I assure you, my lady, that my energies are devoted exclusively to matters of the intellect and that affairs of the heart . . . what I meant to say was, in my heart I have the proper education of your sisters and wards foremost in my mind at all times."

"How then do you account for their perceptions? Be a man, Albertus. If you have something to say to me, why do you not just come out and say it?"

"I must confess," he said, "that my life in a world of women is filled with experiences new to me. The world of men is one of sharp elbows. The world of women is softer."

"Softer, perhaps," said Caroline, "but not weaker. Be aware that a velvet glove can conceal an iron hand. Do yourself a favor and give a rest to the hope of romance with the women of this house. Save your dreams for a someone you have yet to meet."

~~~

Charlotte and Lady Alice arrived at Beaudesert together. Lady Elizabeth appeared a week later. The four Monks gathered around the inert Princess Gwenllian.

"Recently, she returned briefly claiming to be a prophet," said Caroline, "but soon lapsed into her usual dreamy state. She spoke of sibyls and warned me about the new tutor, whom you will soon meet."

"What was the warning all about?" said Alice.

"According to my sister, Albertus was distracted by a growing infatuation with her, something of an exaggeration as it turned out. One time I observed Maude glancing coyly at him. She clearly enjoyed the attention. However, inattention to his proper duties was taking its toll on the others, and so I had a little talk with him. He is quite inoffensive and he is an effective teacher. How the princess had any sense of this, I cannot say."

Lady Elizabeth's engagement with two of the four knights left her with child, though she had not yet begun to show. She broke the news to her sisters, prepared to be admonished for her indiscretion but instead, they showered her with affection.

"We shall welcome your little newcomer with open arms," said Caroline.

"It is ironic," said Elizabeth, "that the same urges that drove those fine young men to impregnate me, also drove them to self-destruction."

"Thus it is," said Charlotte. "I have seen mighty stags in the forest, antlers locked in a death embrace, unable to disengage, so to die for want of food. The earth's sun bleaches their bones even as their sons burgeon to repeat the errors that brought their fathers down."

"They do indeed make more copies of themselves," said Alice, "but willy-nilly, they also make more copies of us."

~~~

A chastened Albertus Pidgeon tried to hide his dismay at the entrance into his classroom of not just Lady Caroline, but also three additional young women who quite resembled her.

"If I may have a moment, Professor," said Caroline. "We are the Monks of Arden, reunited here at Beaudesert Castle with our sisters and wards. One speaks for all, Professor. All speak for one."

"I am Lady Elizabeth Marmion,"

"I am Charlotte Giveney."

"I am Lady Alice de Toeni."

Albertus bowed slightly, "Your ladyships. It is my pleasure." His pupils could not suppress their smiles.

"One day, Professor," said Caroline, "these young women will be inducted into the sisterhood of the Monks of Arden."

~~~

Lady Caroline requested that the Monks join her in Princess Gwenllian's apartments.

"The princess is away, today," said Mrs. Bradford. "When I am able to reach her, she seems to be in the company of her late husband, where she spends most of her waking hours."

The Monks stared reverentially at the dozing woman, present in body even as her spirit wandered in another land.

~~~

The first year of instruction at the new Arden Academy was a success. Word had spread to regional barons, the more progressive of whom had begun making inquiries about enrolling their own daughters. The Monks decided that the anniversary deserved special recognition and decided to host a celebration to which would be invited the nobles who had expressed interest in the school and who might become patrons. Lord Thurstan was pleased with his daughters' tradition-breaking success and readily agreed to host the party.

Lady Caroline sent out the invitations, and one by one couriers arrived at Beaudesert with replies. The invitations included a statement that she was actively seeking new pupils for the women's academy. No one declined. In keeping with his wish to spread goodwill among his tenants, de Montfort added two dozen villagers to the guest list aimed especially at their more educable daughters. This experiment in education had become his challenge, as well as that of his daughters and wards.

Mrs. Bradford's tender ministrations had resulted in Gwenllian's occasional return to periods of lucidity, though she still drifted between the universe of the Monks at Beaudesert and other places in her imagination. Mrs. Bradford informed Lady Caroline that the princess had requested their presence. The Monks, pleased with the chance to speak to her, dropped everything and hurried to her side.

"I congratulate you," the princess began, "on the success of your efforts with the academy. Mrs. Bradford informs me that you are to stage a celebration in honor of your first year."

"That is correct, your ladyship," said Caroline. "It is through your inspiration and foresight that this has come to pass."

"But I sense a certain sadness among you," said Gwen. "You have so much to be proud of. What distresses you?"

"Lady Fortune has extended her hand to each of us," said Charlotte. "She seemed to offer me a chance at connubial bliss in the form of a handsome young knight, but at the last minute snatched him from my arms, placing in my hands instead, a sword with which I smote the instrument of her perverse nature."

The floodgate was open, and Alice's story spilled out. "Princess, I was so taken with you when you were a man I thought I could not live without you. But the fickle Lady Fortune soon had her way with me and denied me the object of my affection when you revealed yourself to be one of us. As if my torment were not enough, Fortune then sent me a worthy young noble, the nephew of my protector. He wooed me with such gallantry and restraint that I immediately fell deeply in love. He seemed to be holding back something, but I ascribed it to the nobility of his character, entirely misplaced as it turned out, when he informed me that he had a wife and sons residing on one of the Scilly islands."

"My sisters' grief is all their own," said Elizabeth, "but mine is also laden with overwhelming guilt."

"Elizabeth," said Caroline. "You must not do this to yourself. You are one of us and we are part of you. If there is guilt to be borne, then we all share it, but I, for one, reject that. You have committed no sin in our eyes."

Gwenllian witnessed this confessional and sharing of tales of misfortune with sympathy. Her own experience with the loss of a beloved husband who died protecting her reinforced the growing sense of solidarity she felt with them.

"Being the cause of the death of four fine young knights," Elizabeth continued, "is almost more than I can bear."

"Like all men," said Caroline, "the instinct that drove them to seek your love is the same instinct that caused them to erupt in a moment of lethal violence toward each other. Had their minds not been poisoned by unreason, they would still be alive and best of friends with each other. But nature and fortune being what they are, they fell prey to fleshly desires and, like hungry carnivores, devoured each other. You did not destroy them. They destroyed themselves in their quest for animal superiority. Like rutting stags, they locked themselves in a dance of death, leaving you, my dear sister, as their sole survivor."

Elizabeth wept. "But I am not their sole survivor. I am carrying the child of one of them. I know not whom."

"And so their deaths were not in vain," said Caroline. "Perhaps their mission has been accomplished."

"To what end have we left so many dead men in our wake?" Elizabeth asked.

Caroline explained. "There is no end in itself. It is the way of the beast. In the wake of death, some create a universe peopled with phantasms, insubstantial images at once suffused with imaginary substance that will merge with objects of flesh and blood. Others retreat forever into private unseen worlds. The princess seeks solace in the belief that in death one day she will be reunited for all eternity with Sir Guy. The assurance that the love is not lost, but rather momentarily beyond reach, permits us to survive. As goes the princess, so go all of us."

~~~

In the days leading up to the celebration, guests began arriving, seeking lodging in the village inns. Some of the lucky ones even found rooms within the castle walls. Knights, barons, and lords, along with their retinues, converged on the area creating a festive atmosphere and a minor economic boom for the local innkeepers and merchants.

Young knights, seeking to impress the ladies, engaged in impromptu jousts. Men and boys from up and down the social ladder, as well as a few of the high-born ladies participated in archery contests. Lord Thurstan's gamekeeper arranged a stag hunt for the older men and whichever knights cared to join in. The festivities wound up with a horse race, three laps around the castle wall.

On the day of the main celebration, a large feast was held in the great hall. The overflow according to rank was accommodated outdoors under large canopies decorated with hunting scenes. Pennons bearing the family crest flew everywhere.

Indoors, the noble guests were treated to roasted haunch of stag, boiled potatoes, and a constant flow of wine. Outside, the knights' servants, the invited tenants and the lower ranking courtiers dined on roasted pig washed down with good ale.

The de Montfort family and the Monks sat on the dais. Seated with them on a litter, covered in a robe, was Princess Gwenllian. The other pupils sat just below them along with their professor, and the new candidates seeking admission to the academy. Seated in front on the ground level were the young knights seeking favor with the women seated above them.

Lord Thurstan welcomed everyone with a toast to the king followed by a toast to their special guest Princess Gwenllian. "The princess has not been well of late, but has found the strength to join us today in a celebration of the first year of operation of the Arden Academy for Women, a school inspired by her and whose work is being carried on by her acolytes the Monks of Arden."

~~~

At the conclusion of the banquet, servants cleared the floor of the great hall. Musicians took their places, and the young knights, the Monks, the pupils, and assorted others danced the round while singing and holding hands.

Even Albertus joined in, doing his best in his unpracticed way to keep up with the others. Paired with him was Miss Agnes Magill, sister of the knight Sir Thomas Magill. They were both in their twenties, contemporaries of the Monks and slightly older than the pupils and wards. When the ungainly tutor stumbled during a lively circling of the dancers, he moved out of the group to find a place to sit. Miss Magill followed him, the circle closed, and the dance went on without them.

"I am Albertus Pidgeon, madam," he said somewhat breathlessly. "My young charges are not easy to keep up with."

"I am Agnes Magill, Mr. Pidgeon," she said. "You are quite right. I do not mind sitting out this one myself. Your charges, sir? Would you be the tutor?"

"I am indeed," he said. "This has been a rewarding first year."

"Tell me, Mr. Pidgeon, how did you secure your position?"

"Lord Thurstan sent out a notice he was looking for a tutor for his daughters to replace Brother Clement and I responded. I studied under William of Ockham at the Franciscan School. My father wanted me to pursue a military career, but I preferred a life of letters."

"So, you have been teaching girls," said Miss Magill.

"I have. I was skeptical at first, but after a year I find them to be quite apt pupils. Tell me about yourself. Are you here looking for a husband?"

"You are being presumptuous, sir. I could take offense, but choose not to. I should think your experience during the recent year ought to have disabused you of such a notion."

"Please accept my sincere apology, Miss Magill. I meant no offense. It's just that . . ."

"It's just that you automatically assume that women are your intellectual inferiors and best suited to the bedroom and kitchen. You should know that I received instruction under Thomas de Pizan in the Court of Charles V and that during my tenure at court publically reproached Jean de Meun for the disgraceful misogyny he expressed in *The Romance of the Rose*."

"I see," said Albertus. "Now I understand how my innocent remark might have raised your hackles. May we start over? If you will forgive my inquiry, what brings you to Beaudesert, Miss Magill?"

"I have been corresponding with Lady Caroline de Montfort regarding a teaching post at her academy."

Albertus's face went pale. "A teaching post?" he inquired timidly.

"Do not worry, Professor. The academy is growing. I am informed that six new girls will be admitted from among the candidates presented here today. More pupils require more teachers."

~~~

During the second academic year, three new courtships were set in motion as a result of the first anniversary celebration. Albertus paid court to Miss Magill, Sir Malcolm Mallory proposed to Charlotte, and Agnes's brother Sir Thomas Magill asked Caroline for her hand. In due course, Lady Elizabeth returned to Tamworth Castle for her period of confinement. She gave birth to a healthy daughter, and several months later they both returned to Beaudesert.

Chapter Seventeen

Darkness

Dr. Kareena Falkener clicked though her e-mail messages. Among them were responses to the threads she maintained with her colleagues around the world. They had to be answered. What did not were the unsolicited queries from people who claimed to have unearthed ancient treasure in their back yards or found lost documents proving that Abraham Lincoln was only five feet tall and walked around on stilts to fool the people.

She almost dismissed the one with *Llewellyn ap Gwynedd* in the subject line. Out of curiosity she opened it. *Good day, Dr. Falkener. I am Owen Griffith, a descendant of the last prince of Wales, Llewellyn ap Gwynedd. I am a student of your colleague Dr. Thomas Spenser in the Department of History and Archaeology at Cardiff University. I am in possession of some family letters dating back to the early nineteenth century that might be of interest to you. Dr. Spenser suggested I contact you because of your interest in the origins of schools in the Medieval period.*

Reply: *Thank you for contacting me about the letters. I am interested. If you would scan them and send me the images I might be able to give you a more informed reply.*

~~~

Letter 1, dated 1798: *Dear Roger. I am saddened to inform you of the death of your aunt Amelia de Coucy, a descendant of Lady Caroline de Montfort. She was eighty-two years old. She was fond of reminiscing, often harking back to the age of her grandparents and before. Her grandest recollection concerned Lady Caroline and her participation in an experimental school for girls. There are no known records of such an institution and its supposed existence was so long ago that it has become more of a local legend than historical fact. Very truly yours, Cousin Emily.*

Letter 2, dated 1818: *My Dear Florence. We enjoyed our trip to the Normandy coast. The wind was brisk, the air chilly, altogether lovely weather. You asked me if I had any knowledge of a school for girls that may have existed near Henley-in-Arden a long time ago. All I can say is that what is left of the old Beaudesert Castle lies half a mile to the north of us. As far as I know there's nothing much left of it, perhaps a stone or two, but mostly just a big mound of earth. The story about a school has been circulating for as long as I can remember, but no one I know has any proof that it ever actually existed. With affection, your sister Emily.*

* * *

With help from the National Science Foundation and Cardiff University, Dr. Falkener was able to take a crew to Henley-in-Arden to study the site. She, her graduate student Cora Lynn Simmons, and two interns, Allison Gregg and Shelley Moncrieff, flew to Birmingham and took a cab from the airport to the Arden Hotel, located about half a mile from the site. There they met Owen Griffith and Professor Thomas Spenser, who had arrived by car. Besides the usual shovels and trowels they would need for the dig, Griffith and Spenser had brought the department's ground-penetrating radar to be used in conducting the initial survey.

The next morning, the two professors, the interns, a photo documentarian, and the two graduate students gathered over coffee to discuss the project.

"First," said Dr. Spenser, "I wish to welcome our colleagues from America. This project promises to be very interesting. Dr. Kareena Falkener will take the lead and so I'll turn the meeting over to her."

"Thank you, Dr. Spenser, for the warm welcome, and I wish to extend a special thank-you to Owen Griffith for bringing his old family letters to my attention. We wouldn't have put this thing together, if I didn't think we were really on to something. We only have two weeks, but thanks to modern technology, we will be able to work better and faster than ever before. With luck, it should be enough time. Owen, you are the geophysics technician. Tell us a little about ground-penetrating radar."

"Thank you, Dr. Falkener. GPR allows us to scan the surface down to a depth of a few meters. What we get is a radar scan of what is buried under the surface. We will have to rely on digging trenches as always, but GPR can tell us the best places to start looking without disturbing the site. It's a great asset for site conservation."

~~~

"There isn't much to see on the surface," said Dr. Falkener at the site the next morning. "Most of the stone from the old ruins was hauled away centuries ago for use in other construction. We do have the large mound, though, as you can see. That will give us an idea of the general boundaries. While Owen sets up the radar, I want Allison and Shelley to flag the corners. Don't waste any time, people. The preliminary scans will take the rest of the day."

"Where do you want me to start?" said Owen.

"We're standing on the southwest corner. We have some evidence that the chapel was located about here and the keep along the north wall (if we can locate it). So, Owen, build your grid beginning at this point. Cora Lynn, you'll want to go with Owen to learn more about the radar."

~~~

At the completion of the first day's work, the crew returned to the hotel and gathered around a conference table. Owen began printing out the GPR scans.

"Excellent work, Owen," said Dr. Falkener. "Look at this. I'm sure this large oval represents the foundation of the curtain wall. It appears to be under about six feet of earth and rubble, wouldn't you say?"

"That would be the average," he said. "The GPR can easily fix the depth to within a few inches. I don't see anything here that would identify the keep."

"Probably made of wood," said Dr. Falkener. "How about this rectangle near the southeast corner?"

"That would definitely be the outline of a major building," said Owen.

"Can you zoom that part of the scan?"

"Sure," he said, as he watched a small screen and fiddled with some buttons. In a few minutes, he had printed out the part of the scan that contained what they hoped would be a building. "There appear to be two rectangular objects inside the perimeter."

"The one on the north end could be a stone altar," said Dr. Falkener. "This could be the chapel."

"What about the other rectangle?" said Owen.

"I can't say," she said. "I guess we'll just have to start digging."

~~~

Back at the site the next morning, with the aid of coordinates from the GPR scans, they staked out the corners of what they hoped would turn out to be the chapel. Owen and Cora Lynn ran a line crosswise between the two objects and began their careful excavation of the soil. This was the slow and tedious part. The students provided the labor while the two professors looked on.

By noon of the following day, they had opened a trench five feet deep and three feet wide that extended across the width of the foundation. Dr. Falkener divided the team into two groups. One would dig a new trench in the direction of what she supposed could be the altar and the other would dig in the opposite direction toward the unknown block. By the end of the third day, each team had reached its goal. They brushed the dirt from around each of the stone objects. As Dr. Falkener had suspected, one indeed appeared to be an altar. The other object, however, appeared to be a sarcophagus. By this time it was dark, and they decided to call it a day and return to the hotel.

The next morning, they excitedly returned to the site in order to take a closer look at their find. The team spent about two hours cleaning up the top of the sarcophagus as the cameraman took hundreds of photos to document the project.

"There's an effigy carved in the cover," said Dr. Falkener. She dropped down into the trench for a closer look. Using a brush, she cleared away the last traces of debris to reveal three initials carved at the foot of the effigy: GaL. "I wonder what they stand for," she mused.

"I think I know," said Owen. "Gwenllian ap Llewellyn, the last of the royal Welsh bloodline."

The discovery was of such significance that Dr. Spenser called a conservator at the National Trust in London, who told them to finish up with their documentation. He would send in a team to lift the sarcophagus out of the trench and transport it to a laboratory in Birmingham, where they would open it.

~~~

With the help of the students, workmen ran three straps under the sarcophagus to make a sling. Raising it out of the trench, they moved it onto the bed of a covered lorry and headed out to Birmingham fourteen miles away.

"We need to follow the truck," said Dr. Falkener. "Tomorrow we'll come back and restore the site."

~~~

The laboratory was a small, converted warehouse. The driver backed the lorry up to the loading dock, and, using a forklift, a workman transferred the sarcophagus to a heavy-duty platform for further processing.

"The effigy appears to be that of a woman," said Dr. Falkener. "She seems to be represented as wearing clerical garb."

"There weren't any female clerics in the Medieval era," said Dr. Spenser, "nuns of course, but no priests or bishops. Are you ready?"

"Ready," said Dr. Falkener.

Owen, Allison, and Shelley began working to free the lid. They used their trowels and brushes to clear the seal that had secured their treasure for centuries. When it was loose enough, they slid the lid sideways to allow the forklift to raise it. The spectators drew a collective breath at what they saw. A skull lay face up inside the cowl of a monk's habit. Lying across the where the legs would be at the foot of the sarcophagus was a box. The cameraman took several pictures before Dr. Falkener attempted to remove the box. She was barely able to nudge it.

"Very heavy," she said. She motioned to a burly-looking workman who stepped up to the sarcophagus and lifted the box out with ease.

"I can open this for you, doc," said the man.

"Yes, please. Take it over to that table so we can all gather round," she said.

The box had no obvious top or bottom, no lid. It turned out to be made of lead, or at least sheathed in lead, and sealed all around. The man carefully made a hole in one corner and, using a pair of diagonal cutters, worked his way around, opening the box like a tin of herring. Inside was a well-preserved codex. On the front board were inscribed the words, *Historie of the Arden Academie for Women.*

~~~

After restoring the site and completing the onsite documentation, the team delivered the codex to the British museum. The conservator's men shipped the sarcophagus and its remaining contents to their London facility, where they would all meet to begin a close study of their discovery. There, the first order of business was to digitize the pages of the codex so they could be studied and distributed without actually handling the fragile original document.

A week later, after examining the body in the sarcophagus, Dr. Falkener and the rest of the team gathered around a table in a conference room at the museum. Images of the codex were distributed and the reading began.

"The author of the history identifies herself as Aurelia de Coucy, daughter of Lady Caroline de Montfort," said Dr. Spenser. "According to de Coucy, her mother was one of the original five Monks of Arden, as they called themselves."

"It's becoming clear," said Dr. Falkener as they read through the early chapters, "why Princess Gwenllian's middle years have been unaccounted for in the historical record. She was known as someone else. For a time, even she didn't know who she was."

"It's fascinating," said Cora Lynn, "how she was able to gather young women around her who were so amenable to her training methods."

"She was familiar with the legend of Robin Hood," said Owen. "De Coucy tells us so in her narrative. Five young women, armed to the teeth, wandering through the forest, taking from the rich and giving to the poor . . . you don't suppose . . ."

"If Robin Hood was an actual historical figure," said Dr. Falkener, "he came long before. The women may have taken their idea from him. Certainly not the other way around."

"Princess Gwenllian, Caroline de Montfort, Charlotte Giveney, Alice de Toeni, Elizabeth Marmion," Owen enthused. "What a find. We'll be writing papers on them for the rest of our careers."

The bulk of the narrative was devoted to the adventures of the five young women. It was not until the final chapter that they were able to answer the question of why the academy had disappeared from the historical record.

~~~

This year we celebrate the thirty-fifth anniversary of our founding. I fear it will be our last. A great mortality is spreading across the land. A blanket of death creeps ever westward, snuffing the breath out of all who get in its way. Terror in the cities drives the inhabitants to the countryside, but there is no escape. The unseen lethal force that overtakes them leaves in its wake a silent army of putrid, rotting corpses. Many lie unburied. Many do not receive the Last Rites. The lucky ones die immediately; the unlucky ones linger on their journey to the grave in the grip of unspeakable torment. There is no escape.

We have sealed off the castle. No one is allowed in or out. Pitiable cries of the dying ring in our ears day and night. The ones who make it to the gate die in their tracks. By the end of the first month, the Pestilence has seeped inside, and now we are dying. I have left instructions for this document to be placed inside the sarcophagus with the body of our revered Princess Gwenllian.

I have little time left. This morning I developed a cough. It seems to be getting worse. I must hurry before . . .

Glossary

Albion – Britain

Baldric – Leather belt worn over shoulder from which hung dagger and sword

Banneret – knight entitled to carry banner into battle

Bailey – Castle grounds surrounding castle keep and inner buildings; enclosed by curtain wall

Braies – Medieval undergarment

Brutus – Brutus of Britain, great grandson of Aeneas

Cambria – Wales

Carol – A old round dance often accompanied by singing

Castellan – Senior officer in a castle garrison

Churl – Freeman with property who owed his allegiance to the king

Cog – A coastal transport ship widely used in the medieval era

Court leet – A court convened by the Lord of the Manor, here, the Earl of Warwick

Destrier – Large warhorse

Donjon – Castle keep

Estampie – An early medieval dance

Florin – Coin worth six shillings

Gambeson – A quilted cloth jacket

Girdle -- Belt

Godsib – Medieval term for godparents in the plural

Greek fire – Incendiary artillery

Gwynedd – Pron. gwinneth

Halberd – Short lance with sharpened metal point and ax-like blade

Hastilude – Martial games

Hauberk – Mail shirt

Jongleur – Minstrel, musician

Justiciar – King's viceroy or vice-regent

(Castle) Keep – A round or rectangular fortified main tower

Kirtle – Knee-length coat

Knight – Each knight needed a war horse (destrier), a riding horse (palfrey), pack animals, and servants

Lance -- One heavy cavalryman (could be a squire or gentleman), an armed servant, a page, three to six armed infantrymen

Marches – Region between England and Wales

Melee – A tourney with few rules; a free-for-all

Motte – Hill or mound on which was built a castle, i.e., motte and bailey construction

Pallanteum – Rome

Pantler – The servant or officer, in a great family, who has charge of the bread and the pantry

Psaltery – Plucked instrument

Rebec – Bowed, stringed instrument

Seneschal – Castle steward

Schiltron – A tight formation of pike men used to repel mounted cavalry

Shawm – Double reed instrument

Sour wine -- Vinegar

Tabor, timbrel, tambourine – Percussion instruments

Tabor-pipe – Three-holed flute

Trencher – A plate of hard dried bread

Trivium – A curriculum composed of grammar, rhetoric, and logic (dialectic)

Van – Covered wagon

Varlet – Page who assists his knight at the tourney

Vielle – Bowed, stringed instrument

Warmblood charger – Medium-sized horse smaller than a destrier used in jousting matches

Woad – Blue dye obtained from *Isatis tinctoria*